SHADOW

BOOK 1 OF THE ILMAEN QUARTET

HELEN BELL

First published in Great Britain in 2015 by Light-Carillon
Publishing

A CIP catalogue record for this book is available from the
British Library

Version 1.0 printed edition ISBN 978-0-9932599-1-3

For Karen: thank you for being such an inspiration.

To everyone out there who knows her, note the word 'inspiration'.

Karen is not Jez; Jez is not Karen.

They just look (and occasionally think and act) uncannily alike.

Praise for *SHADOWLESS*

'Has an epic feel to it with richly painted characters and settings.'

M.L. Hamilton, World of Samar Series

'A mix of Celia Rees and Mary Webb.'

Jane Alexander, Walker

'I was pulled in right away. There's so much energy in the story. It really comes alive.'

Alecia Stone, Talisman of El

To find out more about the Ilmaen Quartet, go to
<u>helenbellauthor.com</u>

THINK HOW IT WOULD BE,

IF YOU COULD SEE THE FUTURE...

NOW THINK AGAIN.

Chapter 1 – The Vision

The sound of gulls squabbling woke Renia. She lay and listened, picturing the ill-tempered dispute outside, recognizing some of the more distinctive cries. Whatever it was they were squabbling over, it sounded like Notch-wing was winning. No change there, then.

She yawned and fidgeted till the covers settled closer round her, savouring the warmth. Spring had arrived, but the mornings were still chilly. She could hear Melor was up and about, and judging by the light coming round the curtain that screened off her sleeping space, the shutters were back already. Breakfast was needed; and breakfast was her job. Reluctantly she reached out and pulled her clothes under the covers to warm them up a bit.

'Morning, Melor,' she called.

'Morning, *cariad*.'

'What's it like out?'

'Cold, but bright. Vel thinks it'll turn into a nice day. He's lit the range and gone already. Did you get that? The range is lit, the kettle's on the hob. Does that make getting up any easier?'

'Yes, all right, I'm coming.' She smiled, thankful he made his point by teasing. Most farm children in the district would have got a clout if they weren't up with the dawn. That had never been Melor's way, he had never once lifted a hand either to her or to Vel. A confirmed bachelor until he adopted them, he'd always pleaded ignorance of the accepted wisdoms of raising children and had just worked it out as he went along.

As his adopted daughter, she felt he'd done well; and by using a light hand he probably got more work out of them, not less.

She dressed under the covers, turned the sheets back to air and headed out into the parlour to the welcoming heat of the range.

It looked like Vel had taken some cold cuts off the joint in the larder before he set out; he had left his dirty plate and knife beside the sink. Since Melor liked a hot breakfast (and today's chilly start justified it), she put a skillet on the range, cut a few more slices off the joint, and tossed them in the pan. As she pushed the slices round to stop them sticking, Melor came over to check on their progress, ruffled her tousled hair and headed out to the well with a bucket.

She and Vel had always known they were not Melor's own children. He'd adopted them when they were very young – in Renia's case, too young to remember. The early years must have been hard going, but he had promised their dying mother he would bring them up himself, and keep them off the Charity list. He could never quite explain why he had made such a promise; the woman had, after all, been a stranger to him. But then again, as he often reminded them both, he had never had reason to regret that promise.

A moment of madness, the rest of the village had thought it. Not that Melor cared: the village could think what it liked. He was somewhere between accepted and tolerated by them; they already considered him a little crazy, their godless clansman who lived alone in his strange cave-house up on the sea cliffs. Adopting a stranger's children was just another example of his oddness, though in their opinion a particularly ill-considered one. After all, the children would bear the brunt if it went wrong, as surely it must.

He'd proved them wrong though, settling into the sudden and unfamiliar role of fatherhood with much less trouble than everyone expected. Inevitably eyebrows were still raised and tongues were still wagged, when for instance he strapped baby Renia to a hurdle he hauled behind him whenever he worked outdoors. It had made her cross when she'd heard about the gossip, years later. The village seemed to forget that he'd had a farm to run: she was a toddler and, if he'd left her on the loose, it wouldn't have been long before she went straight over the cliff edge. Vel had been five, a self-reliant and sensible child, so he'd been no trouble. To hear Melor tell it they were both easy children – right up until she started having fits.

Melor padded back in, topped up the kitchen water barrel, and sniffed appreciatively: 'That's cooked enough for me, jewel. You serve up, I'll make tea.'

They ate and drank in silence, comfortable enough together not to have to fill the quiet with talk. He had his lambing list on the kitchen table this morning and looked through it as he sipped his tea, working out which fields he needed to check. She let her thoughts run on.

Renia had started to forget about the fits, it had been so long since she'd had one, but something had roused her during the night and though it might just have been a bad dream she couldn't quite remember, chances were it was a fit. She had been six when they started, and it had been common knowledge around the village; it wasn't something Melor had ever tried to keep secret. Sometimes it was just a minute or two of disconnection from the world, as if she was awake and daydreaming. She'd frequently talk to people during such fits, but a prod or a pinch couldn't wake her from it, not like normal sleep. Others were full-blown seizures, frightening to her and to those who didn't understand what was happening; she would fall down and go into convulsions. While the sight scared some people, mainly it roused pity in them. If as a child she had a falling fit in the village, folk would sit her up and smile at her when she woke, and tell her she'd 'seen the fairies again'. That had been her own description for the strange, sparkling haze she saw before a seizure. At six, she hadn't realized how her words were going to come back and haunt her later.

One day as they got ready to go to market she'd had a waking fit and told Melor in a dreamy voice about all the things that were going to happen in town, from the innkeeper returning some money he'd borrowed so long ago Melor had forgotten about it, through to Old Ifan the butcher dropping a side of mutton and tripping headlong over it. Melor had listened and smiled at her imagination and once she was fully restored from the fit they'd gone off to town. At the market she stayed with the other children, playing tag round the village carts or knucklebones underneath them; Melor went off to sell his meat and make small talk with the stallholders and shopkeepers.

When he came back he was a different man; unsmiling, unnerved. He'd been silent all the way home. That night he took Renia aside and explained to her that the returned money, the dropped meat – everything had happened exactly as she'd described. He didn't know how she had done it but she had seen the future… and no one else must ever hear of it, he'd warned her.

Then she'd understood the change in him. Six was old enough to know how it would be seen. The Catastrophe was long centuries past, but it still tormented the sleep of many and spilled over into waking memory. Not everyone had the dreams; but she did, and Vel, and many others, all the same dream.

There was a city on the horizon, unfathomably huge. It could be any one of hundreds all across the known world, but all were similar, as was their fate. The city towered over the landscape and burrowed as far beneath it, its citizens beyond numbering, invisible from that distance but imagined, like ants busy about their lives. Then the blinding light from the heart of the city, followed by the absolute dark of the nothingness that replaced it; and finally the implosion that sucked the air from the dreamer's lungs and woke them, gasping with relief, knowing they were safe in their own bed and not on the edge of oblivion. The belief that witchcraft had done this, wiped every city and its people from the face of the earth and nearly eradicated mankind, wasn't simply based on a story; the memory was innate in the descendants of those who had witnessed it.

Renia had been frightened by what Melor said because *he* was frightened; she was scared that he was frightened of her. She'd never seen him so serious. She'd asked him outright then, 'Am I one of *them*?' and it was like his heart broke and then mended, right in front of her, and he hugged her for what felt like an age. It was the old Melor who'd looked her in the eye when he was done with hugging, the way he always looked at her when he was saying something important. 'No, Renia. You're not. You're not bad or evil. But what you can do – it *looks* like witchcraft, and that would be frightening to some. People make bad decisions when they're scared, even sensible people.'

So they had hidden it from everyone but Vel (who was too close and too smart to miss it), and for years Renia had bitten her tongue and let any events she foresaw unfold as they must.

By the age of eleven when she was apprenticed to the seamstress Ceri Ty'r Llyn in the village, Renia was less wary and more open-hearted. The passing of several untroubled years made her naïve enough to think she might use her power to do good. It seemed the right thing to do, telling Ceri when she future-saw her little girl Rhyanna becoming seriously ill, but no sooner had the child fallen into a raging fever than Ceri blurted out the warning she had been given, by the girl who saw fairies. From that moment the village was divided into two camps: those who believed Renia truly saw the future and were scared of her powers, and those who accused her of causing the events that she had 'predicted' by poisoning the child.

The little girl had recovered, but fears had been awakened, and they ran too deep to be ignored. Folk would catch sight of Renia and cast a glance east: that was where the Hampton Citywild lay, though no one from the village had ever been there. A forsaken crater miles across, they said, like a bite out of the south coast, where once there had been one of those unfathomably huge cities so many of them dreamt of – gone in the instant of the Catastrophe, along with all its citizens. The crater lay like a scar on the landscape, a constant reminder of the city's fate, and was not somewhere folk willingly set foot. After all, if you believed in witchcraft you'd like as not believe in ghosts; and if the stories were true, Hampton Citywild had fifty million of them.

So it was that a frightened eleven-year-old found herself called before the Hendynion, the village council of elders, to see if there was a case to answer. If there was, then eleven or not she would be tried; either for poisoning Rhyanna or, worse, for being a *gwrach* – a witch.

She remembered little of it now, five years later, except for certain faces which stayed sharp in her memory. Those of the seven old men who were to pass judgment on her, and Melor's, and Ceri's.

Most of the old men wore unreadable expressions. Two did not, and it was to those faces that Renia's eyes were drawn repeatedly throughout the hearing. One man's face spoke a simple message: loathing and distrust. Clearly he had not a shred of doubt that she was guilty. The other face took her a while to read, until the man smiled briefly at her. To her relief she realized he would have been amused by the whole ridiculous business, only he looked at her and saw a frightened child and was angry on her behalf.

Melor's face she recalled too. He was always at her side or in her sight, so she knew he was watching over her. Much was made in the Hendynion of her unknown parentage, the fact that she was Melor's adopted and not his true daughter, but no one would have thought them anything other than blood kin if they had not been told. He was with her unfailingly that day and it was only now, years later, that she realized how much she owed him for that.

But the face she recalled best was Ceri's. Her employer did not look Renia's way at all while she gave her statement to the Hendynion, but she spoke quietly and steadily, and her words were in support of Renia. Ceri told them how perceptive a child her apprentice was, and that she must have seen some sign of Rhyanna's fever coming that Ceri herself had missed, for she knew that Renia would never harm a child. She confessed now that her reaction to Renia's prediction had been a hasty judgement, born of fear for her child when she fell ill so suddenly. The signs had been there, Renia had seen them and Ceri had not; she had been thoughtless and wrong to say otherwise.

Ceri saved her that day, beyond question; there were others in the village who would have pursued the matter, but Ceri was the one who had started the outcry and with her retraction there was no case to answer. So the Hendynion pronounced, and Renia was free to go. Ceri had looked as relieved as Renia at the verdict, and filed out of the hall with everyone else.

Outside, Ceri's sister was waiting. Her son Dailo scowled at them from behind her and little Rhyanna squirmed in her arms, eager to get back to her mother. Ceri gathered up her daughter and turned just as Renia and Melor passed by. That was when she finally glanced at Renia.

There had been no signs of fever on the day Renia had warned her about Rhyanna's illness. The look said Ceri knew that; and whatever reason she'd had for helping Renia out of trouble, she still believed that when she warned her, Renia had seen into the future.

After that Renia had kept away from the village. It was the only way Vel and Melor could carry on anything resembling normal life. She lived like a recluse now, avoiding people where she could and rarely venturing far from Melor's house. She had abandoned training to be a seamstress, much to Ceri's relief; she was not a bad woman, but like much of the village Ceri believed in evil spirits and would never again be comfortable in Renia's presence, thinking her a *gwrach*. And while most who thought like Ceri wanted only to be left alone by Renia, there were others who felt she needed 'attending to'. The majority contented themselves with remarks and sly comments, but a few hinted they were prepared to go further.

Eventually the remarks ended Vel's apprenticeship too; someone repeated them once too often at the blacksmith's, and the smith reluctantly decided that, talented though Vel was, an angry forge hand with a white-hot piece of metal and a hammer in his hands would not be good for business. Melor's response was to say nothing, increase the size of his flock of sheep and start a herd of goats. Vel was promptly taken on on full-time as his assistant.

There was more than enough work to be done on the farm so Renia threw herself into those jobs that Melor and Vel left her. She also studied herbs and healing; Melor bought her old books – she had learnt to read and write early, at his insistence – and she absorbed from them and experimented. More talk from the village over that, of course, but she was beyond caring, so long as they left her alone.

oOo

Melor came back early from the fields, bringing only two ewes ready to drop their lambs. Renia had done her tasks around the house by then, thinking he would need help; now she had some unexpected freedom. She decided to venture as far as the woods to collect herbs – mostly for cooking, but some for her medicinal experiments. The wood was a treasure trove; but it was also the main haunt of the older village boys in their free hours. Still, it was the middle of the day and she could take a route that would help her avoid them.

Much of what she wanted was to be found in the dappled shade, where the trees sloped down into a flat stretch near the stream, and that was where she headed. Wild ramsons covered the approach to the water, their pungent garlic smell calling to the hungry. She filled most of her basket with them; she also broke off a few strips of bark from the willows beside the stream and tucked those in too – a pain-relief staple for many healers, but one of her books contained a method of concentrating the tincture to make it more effective, and Renia wanted to try it out.

The low, early-morning sunlight glanced off the stream as she waded through it, looking for early herbs in the ground beyond. She had taken several steps further when she noticed that sparkling lights still remained, dancing in the corners of her eyes. It was not the sunlight on the stream she was seeing but 'the fairies', the glittering that denoted the onset of a fit. She sat down quickly and waited nervously for it to arrive, remembering how when she was little, she had truly believed there were fairies who danced there, at the edge of her vision, about to take her somewhere no one else could go…

oOo

When Renia's mind emerged from the fog that possessed it, hearing was the first sense that returned to her.

'Do you think she's dead?'

'No. Though it could be arranged...'

Her heart sank. The nightmare her wandering mind had taken her to had been bad enough; now she was waking to another. The last voice was that of Dailo, Ceri's nephew. The Hendynion might have decreed that Renia was guiltless and should be left alone, but the only thing that exceeded Dailo's hatred for her was his contempt for the old men.

There was nothing she could do, not for a minute or two until the rest of her senses and the power to move came back. Nothing but build terrifying pictures of what Dailo could do to her in that time. But it sounded as though he was moving away.

'Dailo... no, not when she's like this...'

'What do you take me for, Ianto?' There was a thudding sound as Dailo returned and dropped whatever he was carrying. 'I'm just preparing for when she wakes up. I want her good and scared before I'm done with her.' *Well, that's a certainty*, thought Renia. Mind and body were in connection now and the fearful images her thoughts had conjured up were making her heart race. *Come on*, she willed her body, *be mine again.*

'We're with you there. We don't even have to hurt her. Mind you – ' an unpleasant laugh from a third voice was echoed by others around him ' – if that's what it takes to make her see she's not wanted round here, I'd not be averse.'

Sight was back. They were starting to surround her. Renia could see light and dark through her eyelids when they passed between her and the sunlight. Her mind raced to think of a way out of this, and she was aware of feeling returning to her body.

'What's she been collecting in that basket, d'you think? Poisons?'

'Something to help her with her hexing, I'll be bound.'

Now she felt furious. These idiots spent more time in the woods than she did, and they didn't recognize a basket full of ramsons? She pitied the village girls, if they ever had to endure any meal their menfolk had cooked. That bolstered her up a little, and she decided to try opening her eyes.

She saw legs. She looked down towards her own feet, as best she could from that angle, and saw Dailo standing there, hefting a stone the size of an egg in his palm. Bigger stones still lay in a pile beside him.

'So, the "demons" that possessed you have departed, have they?' he enquired in mock concern. 'Good, because my business is with you, Charity bastard.' He dropped the stone on her leg, hard enough to hurt but not to harm. 'Get up.'

Renia did as he said, unsteadily. She swayed a little but caught herself from actually falling – sure enough that none of the boys would. The stones they held were softer than the expressions on their faces. She knew that most of them saw anyone who received Charity as less than human. She stared back at Dailo, but took in the people to either side of her from the corners of her eyes. Find the weak spot in the circle; that was her aim. Damn, Ianto wasn't in view, the boy who had at least shown some principles. She'd thought to go past him, but he must be behind her and there was no telling who was to either side of him – it could be the biggest bully boys in the village, barring Dailo of course.

Dailo had moved to pick up her basket and what was left of its contents. He held it away from him as though it was full of sewage, the handle balanced on one finger.

'They're ramsons.' He turned his look of disgust on her. 'Wild garlic; you cook with them,' Renia persisted doggedly.

He tossed the basket contemptuously at her feet. 'As if any of us would be stupid enough to eat anything you'd made, child poisoner.'

She drew a breath to defend herself, let it out again knowing it would be wasted effort. He stared at her a moment longer and bent to pick up his remaining stones; then a click of his fingers and the circle of boys started to walk slowly round her.

'See our faces, Charity bastard? You can't walk into the village without one of us seeing you, and you know that wouldn't be a good idea.' The faces passed before her, eight in total, all set in a way that confirmed Dailo's threat. Even Ianto's. 'We'd really have to do something about it if you did.' A stone lofted from behind caught her on the arm, again not hard but the unexpectedness of it made Renia cry out. A moment later a second stone hit her; she had clamped her mouth shut, but couldn't help flinching still. 'And I can't say how far—'

She'd manoeuvred her foot under the basket and picked that moment to flick it up into her hands and swing it by main force into the faces of Ianto and his neighbour. It cleared a gap between them momentarily as she had hoped, and she was through it and on to the path out of the glade before they could gather themselves. She took the blows of the few stones that hit her while she ran with a feeling of perverse satisfaction. That was time wasted on aiming them that her persecutors could have used to catch her. Now she had a lead, as she had hoped; she just had to do something with it.

The temptation to veer off the path was great but she stuck to it, knowing how easy it would be for her pursuers to catch her if she wasted her lead on beating a track through the undergrowth. In a short while the true path curved, branched then branched again, giving her a good chance of losing them.

She turned the bend and her stomach lurched as she saw the figures at the fork in the path rise from a crouching position. More of the gang; they must have had time to plan while she was out of her senses, and sent these two to delay any passers by while the rest of them dealt with her. Instantly she went left, trying to recall where she would end up as she steered a course through the trees and undergrowth.

Further into the wood, this way. There was a big glade somewhere up ahead, with three paths leading from it; damned if she could get her bearings for it though. Every turn the trees forced her into seemed to take her through brambles that snatched at her skirts or tore at her ankles. She could hear her breath catching, more like a sob than a gasp, as she reached the end of her sprinting strength; she could hear too the sounds of others in the wood, pursuing her. Even if she made the glade, she wasn't optimistic about the outcome.

The trees thinned and she was surprised to find herself there, more by luck than judgment. A fast scan of the paths out of it, and hope died. She could hear her pursuers on all of the routes, could see them on one. Though she was neither God follower nor star worshipper she looked heavenwards in her despair, and found herself staring up into the branches of two tall trees that leant together like conspirators…

oOo

The next stone bit hard. It got her right on the anklebone and really hurt, way past screaming point. But Renia was too high for them to throw anything harder than that. She peered through the branches to the neighbouring tree, the only one nearby that could be climbed; Dailo clung to the branch that

extended towards the tree where she sheltered, and Renia
knew he'd never have the courage to scramble over to this one
as she had done, however much hatred there was in his eyes.

'Stone the *gwrach*! Stone the *gwrach*!'

She settled her back to the trunk behind her,
exhausted, clutched a nearby branch and let the gang's
chanting wash over her.

She had three alternatives. Wait, and hope they'd go
away eventually; wait, until she fell asleep and out of the tree;
or go down and face them. She hadn't the courage for the last;
that had been drained by the jump from the first tree when she
had nearly lost her hold with a thirty-foot drop below her.
Instead she sat and felt tears run down her face.

A sudden roar of unbridled rage came from below,
followed by yells of alarm and fear. The group of persecutors
scattered from her sight, to be replaced by a lone figure who
stood there, panting and furious, then turned in a full circle
with a branch held aloft in his hand like a cudgel, looking for
anyone foolish enough to stay. She could only see the top of
his dark blond head but knew him well enough: her brother
Vel. He was six feet four compared to the slighter village folk;
big enough to scare her eight attackers who, when it came
down to it, were nothing more than bully boys. He peered up
and spotted her, his expression still furious, when a movement
from Dailo caught his eye and the look went another league
beyond fury as he threw the branch down and walked over to
Dailo's tree. Vel was out of Renia's sight now, but Dailo's
reaction confirmed what her brother was doing. Dailo tried to
come further out on the branch towards her, then thought
better of it and just hung on as Vel's furious face appeared
beside the trunk, barring his safe retreat. Vel stared at him for
over a minute – Renia would lay odds it felt longer to Dailo.

'Vel, don't hurt him,' she called across. Her brother

didn't react, just carried on staring at the bully. Then he thrust out one finger.

'You. If you want to get down from here alive, do it now,' he told Dailo, glowering still. Any hesitation on the boy's part was brief; a short scramble, a squeeze past Vel to cling to the trunk, a rapid descent, and he was scampering on his way after the rest of the gang.

With Dailo gone, Vel studied his sister from his vantage point. 'How in a believer's Hell did you get up there, Ren?'

'Jumped from where you are.'

He whistled. 'Well, don't even try it back again. Climb down as far as you can, I'll find stuff to break your fall.' He disappeared; she gathered her strength and began her own descent.

By the time she reached the lowest branch and clung there, arms and legs shaking with exhaustion, Vel had built up quite a pile of dead leaves and dried bracken. The drop was about twelve feet, not something she'd even dream of trying on her own, but she trusted his judgment. He'd had more than his fair share of rescuing her from situations she'd got herself into, failed tomboy that she'd been as a child – and then, more recently, from things like this…

'Oh, *cach*, look! This was one of my best shirts, too.' He was inspecting a tear he had found in the sleeve, far more bothered by that than he was by the deep scratch on his arm beneath it. He gave up on the shirt as a lost cause. 'Right, I'm ready for you. Come out a bit further and try to drop about here.'

She wiped her eyes with the back of her hand and wriggled out, keeping chest and stomach close to the branch.

Then she hooked her hands around and willed them to hold on as she slid herself off the branch, dangled for a moment, and let go. Vel didn't try to catch her, rather directed her roll into the thickest layers of leaves, then scrambled over to help her up.

'Thank you, Vel.'

'Well, I could hardly leave you up there, could I? Though how you were daft enough to get caught in the first place, I don't know.'

Now they came to it. A sick feeling washed over her, and it had nothing to do with what had just happened. 'They were already there when I came round. I ran but I didn't have a chance to get away.'

'Another falling fit? You're all right?' She nodded. A long pause, then he asked, 'Did you see anything?'

She couldn't muster a response; the terrible sense of loss from the vision had returned and overwhelmed her.

Vel sat down and patted the ground beside him.

'Come on then, out with it,' he urged her. 'We're going nowhere till I hear it.'

It was such a simple vision, but the range of emotions it brought scared and confused her. Still, she managed to describe how she'd found herself on a journey that seemed endless, and the further she went, the more isolated and trapped she felt. After what seemed an eternity of travelling, she'd entered a place that she knew was crowded with many people but everyone was a blur and insubstantial, compared to something in the midst of them that seemed to pull her ever closer. She worked her way nearer and nearer, until finally it could be seen clearly. Or rather she should say they; she had been drawn towards three hangman's nooses. But there was something within each noose, and again she felt herself drawn forwards until she came close enough to see.

The first of the nooses surrounded a silver sun, blazing brightly. The second held a golden eagle, frozen in flight as though about to seize hold of something. The third... the third had her puzzled for some time. It held a circular grey metal band. Try as she might, her numbed mind could not make sense of it. Then, just as she was about to give up, she realized what it was.

She halted, having reached the crux of her story, and found she was shredding what she had left of her nails. Vel was looking at her in consternation but she couldn't seem to stop herself. He put his hand gently over hers; that stopped it.

'And?' he prompted gently. 'What was the grey band?'

'It was a ring. A ring I knew.' Her gaze travelled to his hand and he looked down too at the battered pewter ring he had worn since his coming of age, two years before.

oOo

It took some doing to calm her, because she had shocked him; Vel had never been part of her visions before. But he put up some good arguments about how unlikely it was he would ever do anything he could be hung for, and how many people must have pewter rings, and how she had worked herself up into much this same state over Rhyanna, who had soon recovered from her fever. His arguments settled Renia enough to get her started for home. At his suggestion they took the route along the beach rather than the cliff path. That would put them further out of reach of Dailo's gang, should that bunch of bullies regain their courage.

Once they were on the beach Vel relaxed a little, dawdling and skimming stones. After all these years he still marvelled at the way the sea could change its nature. Now, it was as calm as a millpond; when he had walked along the cliff top just after dawn, delivering mutton to the village, the water had been choppy. He stood a while longer gazing out to sea, the waves breaking at his feet; he could feel the beach pebbles shifting under the thin soles of his boots.

A sudden cry from Renia broke his contemplation, and his hand went for his knife. He'd just about had enough of Dailo's gang.

'Look, Vel, look!' It was not Dailo; Renia was pointing ahead at the surf's edge, not back to land, to a bundle being washed by the waves. A body. It was a body!

They both broke into a run, Vel arriving first and kneeling down beside it. Whoever it was lay almost face down, jacket half off, one boot missing, one arm flung protectively round his head. Vel turned him over – a young man, well dressed in foreign clothes and with what would have been a handsome face, were it not grey from drowning.

Vel whistled. 'No one in town this morning mentioned a shipwreck. They must have got caught on the cape, not knowing the waters. In these fine clothes this poor soul will soon be pickings for the shore scavengers. We should bury him.'

'But he's not dead,' Renia said. As if on cue, the young man groaned weakly and coughed out a mouthful of seawater, and turned a faintly better colour.

'Hmm,' conceded Vel, 'but he's not far off. We're nearly home… Melor will know what to do. You run on ahead and ask him to bring a hurdle back. Meanwhile I'll see what I can do here.'

Renia needed no second bidding and scudded off over the stones. Vel meanwhile tried to use the method Melor had once taught him to get the air back into a drowned man's lungs. As he did so the young man's jacket collar fell back into place and revealed a heavy gold brooch. A moment more and Vel registered its shape, a bird in flight; and then, what kind of bird it was.

He sat back on his heels. For a moment it felt like he'd been punched in the chest; he was winded and couldn't get his breath. Finally he recovered, and glanced up the beach at his sister. She was a long way off now. She wasn't going to look back.

Carefully Vel unfastened the brooch, fished out his handkerchief, wrapped the brooch in it and thrust it deep into his pocket.

Chapter 2 – Jetsam

Even deep in delirium, Kerin was vaguely aware that
something was wrong with him. He knew he had an important
task to accomplish, but before he could remember it, his mind
gadded off, reliving a scene from his past. Drained of his usual
self-discipline, he was powerless to stop it.

He was in some sort of limbo. Perhaps he slept and
was dreaming, or perhaps he was dead and on his way to the
next life. He could hear plates clattering, not far away; such a
mundane sound suggested that this must be the real world. Old
life or new, he should make more of an effort to get there–

And suddenly his father was before him and Kerin
had to talk to him, to ask him why he had acted as he had.
Kerin had been fourteen at the time, his beloved sister newly
dead; it was the moment when he had stopped thinking of this
man as his father. After all, what sort of parent would send
away a child so badly in need of comfort?

'Why Federin? Why must it be so far away?' Kerin
had demanded, angry in his grief.

And his father had looked at him, sad but stern-faced.
'Because there is fever in all the neighbouring countries as
well as here. I *will* not lose you too. Remember why else you
are going; you will be companion and support to the Crown
Heir. Jastur will have need of you there; and even more need
when it is his time to return and become Crown. You will
journey with him to Federin, far from the fever. There you will
learn and you will grow into the man I know you can be.
Sarol, the Crown, commands it.'

Of course, Kerin knew that. This had all happened
years ago. And Jastur had indeed gone from Crown Heir to

Crown Designate on Sarol's death. Kerin was fast losing track of what was dream, and what reality.

So, was the cave-like room he saw when he opened his eyes real? What of the elusive people he saw, or thought he saw? He would shut his eyes but a moment and the white-haired man who had been standing over him would be transformed into a tall blond youth, or a brown-haired girl with such sad eyes. And they would speak to him, but their words came to his ears as though he was under water still, muffled beyond his understanding.

Then another scene intruded; he knew this for a memory, and a recent one. It was so vivid that he could still feel the sea spray and hear the ship's ropes creaking above him as he stood on deck. He could see Lemno Tekai very clearly, although it was night; the moon was high and full, lighting their course across the expanse of sea between Federin and Ilmaen. It lit Lemno's face, catching the grey just starting to streak his black hair and making his pale skin ghostly. Everything about his face was sharp; the salt-and-pepper grey beard trimmed to a neat point, the angular cheekbones; the lean frame was the same, its leanness masking his strength. It was too dark to see his eyes, but memory registered their appearance – a pale blue-grey, like new-forged iron. Deceptively innocent-seeming until they looked directly at you, when Lemno seemed to be looking inside, so people said. Kerin had never had that experience, but he didn't like the man.

It was four years since they had last met; four years in which Lemno had gained the trust of Maregh – and since Maregh was both LandMaster of Karn and brother of Sarol, four years in which Lemno's influence had grown. When they had last met, Lemno had been a lowly weapons master. As one of the best swordsmen on the continent, he had been selected to teach Kerin, whose talents hinted that he could be one of the best in the future. And Lemno had always demanded Kerin's best, always stretched him to his very limit; a risky business when it would have cost Lemno his head if a killing blow had got past Kerin's talented but youthful guard. Kerin couldn't tell if it was professional pride or personal resentment that drove Lemno's approach to his training; it certainly wasn't love of his talented protégé. Now, for the first time as they journeyed back to Ilmaen, Lemno had actively sought out his pupil and started a conversation. Kerin had been surprised; Lemno was not usually one to bother with those he disliked. Perhaps he was tempering his attitude because Kerin was so close to the new Crown; but no, that was out of character too. If Lemno didn't like you, he didn't trouble to disguise the fact.

It had always galled Lemno that he couldn't put the fear of hell into Kerin. That pleased Kerin – but mystified him too. How did Lemno create fear so easily in others? Granted he was a dangerous opponent in a fight, but Kerin had seen many a gallant man show visible fear just at Lemno's approach, or even the mention of his name. Kerin derived unrighteous pleasure from remaining calm or even provoking the other man when everyone else was as tense as a bowstring around him. He knew he shouldn't. If things had turned out differently, Lemno would have been his equal, not his weapons master. He had lost his high position through no action of his own, but by his father's treason. Even his name, Lemno Tekai, had been stripped of any family honour. No honorific 'Hed' for him, when even the poorest citizen used it; and he was forced to use his grandfather's name, Tekai, rather than permitting his traitorous father's name to be spoken. Yet Kerin was immune to sympathy where Lemno was involved; and given what had happened next, with every justification.

A sensible man always watches his back, even if he pretends otherwise. It was a rule Kerin had failed to follow that night. Lemno started a conversation, on a subject he had every reason to raise. He relaxed against the gunwale as they spoke and soon Kerin had found himself doing the same. So as he hit the water after Lemno had deftly up-ended him over the rail, he could only think, *Fool!* He should have expected as much.

His right side had smacked into the gunwale, his arm too when he snatched vainly for a handhold as he went over. He came up for air with both of them hurting like hell, despite the painful shock of the icy water coursing through him. He worried lest his arm was broken, then cursed himself for a fool once more. Lemno wanted him dead, and he was worried about a broken arm? On the surface again, he flexed it experimentally and found it wasn't broken. Treading water, he turned round to sight the ship – and just in time. He was still alongside it and Lemno was heaving a barrel at him. He surface dived, but the barrel caught him under the ribs, knocking most of the breath and half the sense from him.

He did not know where he was for about thirty seconds, until he rolled over and felt air on his face. He breathed in and nearly choked himself – his mouth had still been underwater. Once he had finished coughing and spluttering, he looked around. The ship was a fair way away now, but he could just make out the helmsman leaning over the stern and shouting something. Then Lemno barked a command and the man, after a moment's hesitation, turned away and went back to the helm. Kerin had nursed no illusions that the ship would turn back; Lemno would ensure that. But it was a desperate feeling, to watch it sail away while the freezing cold sapped him of strength.

He trod water again, turning slowly. The barrel was the nearest thing to him and that was a surprising distance away already, which must mean that either he or it was in a current. It rode high out of the water. If he could reach it, he could use it to keep himself afloat. Strangely neither his arm nor his side hurt now, probably numb from the cold, but he was sure he was a strong enough swimmer to reach the barrel. He struck out, his arms making watery arcs of silver in the moonlight, but found it an incredible struggle after a very short while. He stopped briefly to tread water – and found he could not stay up. Now he started to panic until he felt the pulling round his neck and realized it was his sodden cloak that was drowning him. He struggled with the clasp at his collar, fingers clumsy with cold and fright. He remembered that his boots would have filled with water too, and tried to kick them off, but only succeeded in getting rid of one. At last he got the cloak off, and the weight literally fell from his shoulders. He paddled for a moment, summoning what strength he had left, then fixed his eyes on the barrel and swam unsteadily towards it.

It was a hollow relief when his fingers finally touched the rough wood. He could have cried but had already had enough of saltwater to last him a lifetime. He wrestled some kind of a hold on the barrel and clung there shivering, not certain how long he would be able to hold on. He could feel the tow; thankfully it seemed to be pushing him against the barrel rather than trying to pull him away. However he didn't know if the current he was in would take him to the nearest land or further out to sea. He was far too tired to work it out; fate would decide now if he lived or died.

As he clung on with the last of his strength the badge of office on his jacket reminded him of its presence, weighing his collar down and jabbing into his neck, and he named himself fool for a third time. He should have dropped it with his cloak! All the gold and symbols of rank in the world couldn't help him now, and he knew his frozen fingers wouldn't manage the fastening to rid himself of its weight. All he could do was hang on, beyond even shivering and knowing what that meant. His time was nearly over. He didn't want to die, but he knew he might not have a choice any longer. He was so tired, and the cold was overpowering everything, mind as well as body...

oOo

…He dreamt of seagulls, their cries cutting through the air like plaintive ghosts.

The more he listened, the more he knew they were real birds. He forced his eyes open and focused them in the dim light. He was lying on his back, slightly propped up and looking to his left; he found himself staring at a sandstone wall with a niche cut into it, in which stood a water jug, bowl and cloth. It was the room from his dreams.

Well, he thought, unless they make you wash in the Afterlife, I am either reincarnated or else I survived. He decided on the latter, and felt the same rush of tempered joy that getting off a battlefield alive gave him.

The feeling invigorated him, and he tried to sit up. He found he couldn't.

A long sigh made him look down, and he saw why. Someone sitting on the floor beside the bed had fallen asleep, and was using his stomach as a pillow, one arm flung across his chest. His attempt to sit up had roused the person – the brown-haired girl from his dreams. She sat up, another sigh for her stiffness turning into a yawn; she rubbed her face and had a stretch before she noticed him watching her and gave a little cry of surprise. Then she smiled nervously at him, turned and yelled as though calling someone, but no one came. She sighed. Turning back to him, she laid her hand on his forehead, made a noise that suggested she was satisfied with what she found, and began talking to him. It was a foreign language, but one that he knew. His brain got up to speed and he caught the last few words she said.

'...I can get you something against the pain if you need it, with all those bruises. Nothing's broken, thank goodness. Why am I telling you all this, it's not going in, is it? I hope you're good at learning languages; I've never tried. I'm no good at miming either.'

'Mhrydaineg… I'm in Mhrydain,' he said to himself, and the girl's mouth dropped open at the realization that he did understand her language.

'Where in Mhrydain?' he asked her. The girl's mouth snapped shut and she pulled herself together.

'The Southlands. The nearest town is Dorster?' She made it a question, unsure how well known the place might be to an outsider. He knew of it, nodded recognition.

Speaking made him realize that his mouth was very dry. He asked her, 'Could I have something to drink?' and the girl jumped up and disappeared beyond a curtain. A minute later she returned with a cup of water and helped him to sit up and drink it.

'Sip it slowly,' she advised him. 'It's nearly three days since you had anything, so more than a sip'll be a shock to your system.' It was a few sips and several seconds before that sank in.

'Three days?' He thrust the cup back into her hands and pushed the bedclothes back, making apologies as she protested.

'I have to go…' His head suddenly spun and his legs buckled as he put his weight on them. He had the foresight to snatch at the bedclothes as he folded into an untidy heap by the side of the bed, realizing too late that he did not have a stitch on.

'I did try to warn you.'

Through the buzz of dizziness, he was sure he heard suppressed laughter in her voice as she helped him back into the bed and under the covers.

oOo

The episode left him light-headed and sick, as if the embarrassment was not bad enough; it took some time for the nausea to fade after she left. If he needed a slow recovery... well, nothing to be done about it, but he cursed the thought inwardly, and despair mounted within him.

His ship would have made the coast of Ilmaen two days since. To a backwoods place like this, foreign news might be weeks in arriving, if anyone bothered with it at all. He tried to remember the name of the town the girl had mentioned, but it escaped him. Normally a thing like that entered his mind and was fixed solid. Damn! He would have to ask her again. In the meantime, he worked out the likely progress of events. A week more, he thought, and recent news would spread the length of Ilmaen. Quicker still, with Lemno's network of spies, in the places he and Maregh wanted it spread.

That had been another mistake: to dismiss rumours of Maregh's ambitions for the Crown. But then, would such ambitions have even existed, let alone come to anything, without Lemno's influence? And how fast were they planning to move? Heaven, let there be time still for Jastur! It would rouse too much suspicion, surely, to put an end to them both on one short journey. Surely Lemno at least was too clever, too patient after all these years on the margins of power, to let Maregh's greed threaten his own plans. Please Heaven, let it be so!

When Kerin left here, he must be careful; while he was here also. One mention of him from these people in the nearest village or town could easily reach the ears of a spy. He knew now, from Lemno's murderous actions on the ship, how far his reach extended, and what Maregh's money could buy him. Kerin had thought their Federinese helmsman beyond corruption.

That galled him; to be wrong, and wrong again. He dared no longer trust his instinct, which was to be open with these folk who had taken him in: instead he found himself questioning their motives, judging their words, though all their faces spoke of was humanity, openness and genuine concern. The switch from trust to doubt was all too easy to make, these days. But it was what they had trained him for, and at some point he had learnt the lesson.

He dozed a while, woke to find a drink being set down beside him.

'Oh! I'm sorry. I didn't mean to wake you.' It was the girl again – the men must be out working, he surmised. 'But it's for the best anyway. If you can drink plenty, it will help you. A fever's bad for the body like that.' She gingerly offered him her arm to help him sit up; strange reticence considering she had fallen asleep across him, and had hauled him naked back into the bed earlier. Shy because she'd done and seen more than was proper for such a slip of a girl, perhaps. He took the help she offered, and then the drink. It was tea of some kind, but with a strange taste to it. It was the milk that seemed to be different.

'You don't like it?' she asked, dismayed.

'No, no, it's good. It just tastes strange. The milk?'

'Goat's milk. We've that or sheep's. We can get you cow's milk, if you like.' She spoke as though giving him goat's milk was the worst crime anyone could commit, and getting him cow's milk might be her redemption.

'No. Goat's milk is fine. Thank you.'

She nodded, but watched him sip it anxiously with her brow furrowed.

'The dizziness has gone?' she asked after a while longer. He nodded, finished the tea.

'I've put you to much trouble. My apologies. I was anxious not to impose, but instead I've given you more work – and made a fool of myself too. I'm not used to feeling so weak... How long, do you judge, before I'm fit to leave?'

'Some days, at the very best,' she said with a frown. 'There's something you want done, isn't there? Is it something we can help with? A message to someone?'

'Thank you, but no. It's something only I can do. It will have to wait.'

'Is it why you were travelling?' Innocent curiosity, in all likelihood, but how to answer her without telling her too much?

Tell her that you cannot tell her; it was the simplest answer. In the absence of anything more inventive, that was what he did.

oOo

Shy though she might be, she was a firm nurse still, and all in all Kerin thought it best to lie back and take orders. They seemed good people; but he knew he should trust no one. He had their names now; she was Renia, her brother was Velohim – Vel for short – and their guardian was Melor. In addition Kerin now knew that there were just the three of them on this sheep farm, that it was away from the main village, and the beach where he had washed up was on an isolated part of the coast. It was reasonable to assume that only these three knew he still lived. Again, an advantage; and he got this information without revealing anything about himself. She had looked worried that he would not give his name, but not offended, which for some reason he felt would have mattered more. She had let it go, thankfully; he could only hope the others would too.

Before she went to get some sleep, she brought him some food. Not much, just enough to get his fever-starved system used to it again. It was mutton stew; she warned him apologetically that he would see a lot of that in the next few days. He didn't care; it tasted wonderful to him. He had not felt hungry until he took his first mouthful. Then it seemed the amount on his plate would never be enough; he would have to ask for some more. But in his weakened state, even the simple act of chasing it round the plate with his spoon was very tiring...

oOo

Renia woke up after a few hours, and the first thing she did was go to check on her charge. His covers were pushed down around his waist, one arm draped over the edge of the bed where his plate had weighed it down before it slipped from his grasp. Since it had landed on the matting and he had scraped it clean first, no damage was done. She bent and picked it up, and took in the sound of his breathing as she did so. It was slow and even now, not laboured as it had been during his fever.

She looked at him, rested and not fever-racked as before, and wondered at the contradictions his body posed. He was around Vel's age, clearly looked after himself and took plenty of exercise. But something had happened to him recently; the right side of his torso was one massive bruise, his right arm a series of smaller ones. In addition he bore many old scars, especially on his left arm, long-since healed. He must have done some living, to be so battered; yet his face bore no mark that she could see.

And what a face. He was as beautiful as the angels painted on the wall of the village chapel. Sleep had chased away the frown from features that managed to look both youthful and worldly-wise. His eyebrows were very dark, which didn't quite seem to match the light brown of his hair and his fair skin, and he had a quirky little cleft in his chin, but put them together and the end result was the most beautiful man she'd ever seen.

She heard barking: Happa their sheep-dog. A sign that Melor and Vel were nearly home, and supper would be needed, and she hadn't put the stew back over the range yet. She was neglecting her duties standing here looking at this man just because he was so beautiful; an indulgence that couldn't be afforded.

She stole one last glance at him before hurrying off to quieten Happa.

Chapter 3 – Shadows

Once it was clear he wasn't fit to leave, Kerin surprised himself by tolerating three days lying quietly in bed. It was something he had rarely experienced before. Other than meals and drinks and help to reach the necessary, they left him pretty much to his own devices. This was despite knowing nothing about him, not even his name. Vel had asked him directly, once, but hadn't pushed him when he saw Kerin was reluctant to say. But as his strength returned, so did his impatience. By the third day he was starting to fret.

It was a huge relief when, that afternoon, Vel's long, honest face appeared round the curtain, his dark blond hair loosened from the band that tied it back by the incessant wind, and he said: 'You all right? I won't come over…' he held up his hands '…I've got the grime of the fields on me. Melor and Ren say you can get up today for dinner, if you feel up to sitting out in the parlour.'

'That's good news. I know these four walls much too well,' Kerin said, but from Vel's expression it seemed his impatience to be out of his sickbed was already obvious. Earlier he'd tried staggering the length of the room on his own and, despite feeling light-headed, he'd managed it. The thought of Jastur's plight lent urgency to his efforts. He must be up and gone soon!

'I'll bring you some clothes later. You'll have to have a jacket of mine and a pair of my old boots, I'm afraid – yours were lost or ruined in the sea,' Vel told him. 'I'm back to work now, I only came in for a knife.'

'Till later then. Oh, Vel, did you find…' But the young man had already gone. No matter. If they'd seen his badge, they'd have said. Kerin was growing ever more confident of their honesty and there was no mistaking the badge's value.

oOo

A few hours later Vel was back, helping Kerin dress while the table was laid and, when he was ready, giving him an arm to lean on.

Kerin took his support as far as the curtain. When Vel pulled it back to reveal Melor and Renia seated at the table with expectant faces turned towards them, pride got the better of Kerin. Letting go of Vel, he tottered like a drunk towards the table and sat down heavily in his seat. He was touched when the others cheered and gave him a round of applause for his efforts.

'I barely walked five steps,' he said dismissively.

'Just days ago we thought we'd be taking you out of that room feet first. Those five steps are quite an achievement, especially when those boots are about three sizes too big for you,' Vel assured him as he slapped him on the back. Kerin beamed across the table at them all. He'd not realized how far removed from family ties he had become, nor how much he had missed them.

Dinner today, for a change, was rabbit. As he ate, he looked around. They were sitting in the main room of the house; parlour, kitchen, dining room and scullery combined. Small, considering all the purposes it served, but cosy. There were curtains across the entrances to two more bedrooms. All these rooms had been dug straight out of the rock, except for the front wall, which was built from sandstone blocks – presumably carved out when the cave-rooms were made. In one corner was a cooking range. On it a flat iron stood warming, and beside it some clothes hung drying. Beyond that was a wooden porch with a sturdy door that stood open to the daylight. From the sounds and the light, that door faced the sea. Everything about the place was simple but comfortable, and Kerin felt another pang at the realization. Stupid. He'd be leaving soon, no point in getting too comfortable.

He finished his stew. Melor took his bowl from him, tidied the dishes to one side and started the tea brewing. Then he settled himself and turned to Kerin, who had expected something like this; Renia and Vel were suddenly intent as they leant forward.

'Sir,' said Melor, 'now that you're rested and fed, perhaps you'd tell us a bit about yourself. We've kept your presence here from the village, as you asked, and please understand that you're welcome to both our food *and* your privacy, if you feel you must choose so; but we're all a little curious. Who has the sea has brought us, and in such strange circumstances? A body, yet no wreck.'

'No, no wreck.' Jastur sprang into his mind again. 'And no other bodies, you're quite sure?'

Melor put his mind at rest with a firm shake of his head. Kerin weighed up how much of the truth he dared tell them. They waited, not pressing him. At length he sighed and brushed his hair back off his forehead.

'Sorry. You must forgive me, but it's been as much for your benefit as mine that I've kept quiet. Once you know my story, I think you'll understand why.

'I'm going to keep back my name still, but some things I can tell you. Where I come from, for instance. I'm Ilmaenese.' They looked at each other. 'You know the country?'

'Before I was a farmer I was a sailor,' Melor replied, 'so I know the north coast. And these two are orphans, but their father was Ilmaenese. We'd assumed, from your clothes, that you came from the west, not the south.'

'I was sailing from the west with Jastur Hed Sarol, Ilmaen's Crown Heir. He was in Federin, finishing his education – and avoiding the fever on the continent – but then Crown Sarol died. That was about two months ago. As his eldest son, that made Jastur Crown-Designate. To take the title in full, he had to return and name himself Crown – traditionally that's done in the presence of the Council.'

'And this makes you…?'

'I'm in the service of Jastur – his bodyguard, if you will.'

Which was no lie. He pressed on with his story.

'When Sarol died, his brother Maregh sent for Jastur, and despatched a man called Lemno Tekai as escort. Neither of them ever intended Jastur to make it back to Ilmaen. I believe Maregh has usurped the Crown, and Lemno was sent to kill Jastur along with any supporters loyal to him.

'We travelled by sea despite the risk of storms because Lemno had taken over a month to make the journey by land, through Mhrydain. I've worked out now why it took him so long: he was setting up a network of spies. That's why I have kept my own counsel. Lemno is a very clever and very dangerous man. His father was an Ilmaenese LandMaster – the lord of a province. Lemno should have inherited that province, but it was forfeited through his father's treason, long before I was born. Lemno holds a grudge against the Crown and his family because of it. He may have remade his fortune in the service of Maregh, but he knows he'll never hold a province, not at least while Sarol's heirs hold the Crown.

'Lemno has put Maregh up to this. He doesn't have

the guts or the imagination to mastermind a coup on his own. The whole business stinks of Lemno's scheming.

'So, five – no, six – nights ago, when our ship passed near here, Lemno caught me unawares and dumped me overboard. Just to make sure of the job, he tried to brain me with a barrel. As it turned out, that barrel probably saved my life; I was able to hang on to it and must have floated ashore on a current. And that, presumably, is when you found me.'

'It seems that way,' Vel agreed, 'although there was no sign of the barrel. It must have floated out to sea again.'

'I'm just glad *you* found me. It could easily have been someone who would take what they could and leave me for dead – or if they were one of Lemno's spies, make sure I was dead. Ah, thank you.' This last was to Melor, who had brought mugs of freshly brewed tea to the table.

'I've told you all this because while up to now you were better off not knowing, things will change. If Lemno learns that I still live, he'll stop at nothing to kill me. He knows I won't rest until I find out what's happened to Jastur. I was keen to leave at first because I couldn't be sure how isolated this place was, and if it was safe – not just for me, but for all of you too, since you're harbouring me. When it was plain it was secure – and that I didn't have the strength to leave anyway – I kept quiet, because the less you knew, the more peace of mind you'd have. But now I have to ask if I can stay here a while longer, just until I'm stronger. I promise it won't be for long. I must get back to Ilmaen, and find out what's happened to Jastur. I can't rest easy till I know.'

They sat in thoughtful silence, interrupted only by the sipping of hot tea. Finally Melor broke it to ask, 'You said Jastur is the eldest son – that suggests there are others. Surely they stand in this Maregh's way too?'

'There's a brother, but he'd make a poor Crown. Besides, if they manage to get rid of Jastur, they'll remove any other claimants too.'

It must sound like a madman's story to them, but no doubts were voiced. Still, it would have made him feel better if he could prove his words. There were the clothes he had washed up in, of course, they must have noted the quality of them...

But wait – there was his badge. Solid gold and clearly not the possession of a madman or a teller of tall tales; that would prove his story was true. His hand went to his collar – and he let out a groan, remembering he had lost it.

'Damn!' he exclaimed angrily. 'The Golden Eagle would have been proof.'

Renia nearly spilt her tea in her lap, and he was on his guard immediately.

'The what?' she asked faintly. She had gone astonishingly pale. He chose his words carefully and delivered them nonchalantly, trust gone in an instant.

'The Lestar Eagle. It's the badge of office for the LandMaster of the Province of Lestar. It was in my safekeeping. It would have proved the truth of my tale – but too late now. The sea has it.' He spoke dismissively, but scanned their reactions carefully.

'No. Your Eagle's safe,' said Vel. 'I took it off you when we found you. It's stored with our valuables.'

'Well, I'm glad to hear that.' Kerin's relief was tempered by horrid suspicion over Vel's motive for taking it; he had seemed – what, guilty? – as he spoke.

'I had wondered,' Kerin added, 'why you didn't question my—'

'*You knew.*' Renia's accusation interrupted him – but it was aimed at Vel, who almost squirmed with guilt now.

'All along you knew! It's started, hasn't it? And you let me look after him and never said a thing!'

'We both knew, *cariad*. We decided not to say anything to you till we found out a bit more.' Melor had risen and gone to stand behind Vel.

Renia stood up herself, and shot a look at Kerin. 'We have to tell him. He has to know.' Then her face crumpled and she ran from the house.

Vel was on his feet by now, but Melor sat him back down again.

'No, let her go. She'll be all right. Sit, lad, sit.' But Kerin didn't move, husbanding the little strength he had and fearful of what he might now have to do with it.

'What did she…' he began. Melor signalled him to wait, brought a bottle of something stronger than tea out of a cupboard, and sat down opposite him at the table.

'Now we owe you an explanation. If it helps you to know it, our secret will put us in your hands just as much as you are in ours.'

Melor poured them all a drink. Vel took his glass as though it was a life preserver, knocking back a mouthful, and dropped his head into one hand. Kerin took his warily, with no plans to drink it. Why had Renia reacted as she did? What had he said to frighten her so? He thought back over his words.

It was the mention of the Eagle. As soon as he'd mentioned it she had known who he was, had known he was a man she should be afraid of – nothing else could have provoked such a response from her. His wariness was justified; these three were in Lemno's pay. Where did that leave him now?

But wait. *She* was scared of him; the others were not, even though they knew of the Eagle. They did not know what it meant, who it was they faced, or they would have done away with him while he was in his fever and defenceless.

So what was she scared of? What was this secret they were keeping?

Melor threw back his drink. Kerin put his down in front of him untouched.

'Sir, would you say you were open-minded?' Melor asked. Kerin spread his palm in a so-so gesture.

'Reasonably open-minded, yes.'

'Do you believe in witchcraft?'

It was just about the last question he had anticipated. He thought before he gave his answer, knowing his opinion was not the conventional one – but who knew what the right answer was in this situation?

'No, I don't. It's just a superstition put about by those who want to justify their abuse of others, fuelled by people who don't understand what they see. It's a tool used by evil men, and by believing in it, fools let them triumph.'

'Then how do you explain the Catastrophe?' Melor challenged him.

'The Catastrophe? That was some kind of human madness, but it wasn't witchcraft.'

'You don't have the dreams, do you?' Melor surmised.

'What… of the cities being destroyed? No, but I don't dispute it happened. I just maintain it wasn't by witchcraft.'

Melor gave a slow approving nod. Vel raised his head. They glanced briefly at each other, Kerin noticed, before Melor asked his next question.

'Then what would you say, if I told you that the people of the nearby village think that Renia's a *gwrach* – a witch?'

Kerin responded with stifled laughter.

'If she's a witch, I'll eat my boots… I'm sorry, Vel, I'll eat *your* boots. What the hell is this about? Does she think me a witch hunter or some such?'

'She thinks,' Vel told him, 'that you're a danger to my life.'

'How so?'

Vel looked at Melor.

'Go on. You had the story first hand,' Melor prompted, pouring himself another glass.

And so Vel related Renia's history, down to her vision a few days earlier. Kerin, sceptical at first, found himself struck dumb as the latest vision unfolded.

Into the long silence that followed his account, Vel added: 'Mind you, we don't see where the sun fits in – maybe it's some clue to a place, or a date…'

'No, to another person. Jastur, the Light of Ilmaen,' Kerin replied. They looked at him. 'It's a title given to the Crown.' But while everyone used the title, only the very highest in Council used the symbol of the sun, a secret code known only to them. Suspicion rose briefly in him again. Could the information have been passed on by Lemno, to help these people win his trust? But no. He recalled Jastur saying that Sarol had not thought his brother Maregh trustworthy enough to give him the code, and Lemno would not have learnt of it from anyone else in Council. There was no way these people could have known what the sun symbolized to him.

He glanced down at his drink, thinking he was ready for it now, to find he had nearly finished it. He drained what was left.

'You seem to take your sister's prediction seriously,' he observed, and Vel nodded.

'I do. She made it that morning, just hours before we found you. I suggested we come back along the beach. She couldn't have known you'd be there.' Vel paused and gave the grain on the tabletop an unnecessary amount of attention. 'Besides, I've never known her to be wrong.'

Vel had known all this, then hidden the Eagle from her. Little wonder Renia had looked so betrayed.

'But why did you take me in, if you took these portents seriously?' asked Kerin.

'You were in need of care. I wouldn't have left a sick dog to die like that, let alone another person. Besides, you may be part of this vision, but that doesn't mean you're its cause. We couldn't judge you until we'd heard your story. And you were so weak, Ren could've knocked you over without trying. You weren't any threat to us, not as ill as you were.'

'But now I could be.' Kerin assessed the situation coldly. 'She'll have no peace while I am here. None of you will. I must move on.'

Melor raised an eyebrow at this assertion.

'The door is there, sir. The nearest village, the one you have been so keen to avoid up till now, is a mile and a half away. If you wish us to have wasted our time caring for you this last week, you can try and make it there. I'd prefer it if you went back to bed again.'

'But…'

'You need another week to recover, sir, then you can think about it. We two have reached that conclusion, regardless of your story. Renia is the only one who needs convincing now. It's scared her, that's all. A little more thought and she'll see you intend no harm to us. She was quite taken with you before today. I'm sure you can charm her again.'

As Kerin walked outside, the light of the setting sun struck at his eyes like a dagger. It flared off the whitewashed walls of the house, and glittered fiercely on the sea that stretched out endlessly before it. As Kerin's eyes adjusted, he saw Renia standing nearby and made his way unsteadily towards her. She offered no help; too wrapped in her own misery, he realized, to notice his fatigue. He sat down where a rocky outcrop made a convenient seat, and gestured to her to join him. She did, reluctantly, and sat staring at the ground in front of her.

'Melor and Vel have explained to me.' Her head jerked up, but still she did not meet his eyes.

'Everything?' she asked.

'I think so. I'm not psychic so I can't be… sorry. That was crass. And I'm sorry to repay your care of me in such a fashion. None of it need signify. Soon I'll be fit enough to leave and you can all forget I ever existed. This situation wasn't of my making; please don't resent me for it. I'll leave, and when I do, the danger passes.'

'I wish it were so simple, sir.' She looked directly at him now; he had not thought those sad eyes could look any sadder. He tried to think of a suitable response, because having no way to ease such misery felt intolerable to him.

'You find it hard to live with this talent of yours,' he surmised.

'Talent?' The concept surprised her. 'It's always seemed more of a curse to me.'

'But isn't it a force for good – warning you of events to come so that you can prepare for them?'

'Once I thought so. What a wonderful thing it would be, if only I could use it for good! But it uses me. It forces on me visions I can't avoid, and can't do anything about, because they won't let me.' From the jerk of her head, he took 'they' to mean the people of the nearby village.

'I hate the way they fear it… fear me. On the other hand – would I really behave any differently if I were in their shoes? You haven't seen what one of my fits looks like.' That thought agitated Renia so much that she sprang up and walked away, towards the sun; he had to shield his eyes against the glare again. When she turned and realized this, she came back so that her long evening shadow fell across his face and let him see properly.

She wasn't looking at him, he realized, but at her own shadow. The smile on her face was wry.

'A beautiful sunny evening, and still I'm reminded of it. See that? The villagers say that isn't really my shadow; *gwrachod* don't have shadows. I've just conjured it up.'

He shrugged. 'They say much the same in Ilmaen: there the word is *Eivarjoa*, Shadowless. It doesn't make you one.'

'Ah, but once the name's been given you *must* be one, or that's how most people think. Shall I prove it? I'll make it go away.' She made a gesture towards her shadow, as though casting a charm – and like a fool he looked to see if it had any result. 'Oh, it's still there? That must mean I've used up my power for today,' she said bitterly.

It was too much. Kerin jumped up and grabbed her arm; saw stars again and had to sit back down. Renia's self-destructive mood was gone in an instant; she was back to being the girl he'd known for the last few days, full of anxious concern for him.

'Are you all right?'

He had to shake his head, not wanting to heap guilt on her but unable to say anything else. 'Not really.' He tried to make a joke of it, but she was contrite and wouldn't forgive herself.

As she helped him up and inside, he knew he'd been right. This girl needed him to be on his way as much as Jastur did. He must leave as soon as possible.

Chapter 4 – Decisions

'Ren! The washing!'

Vel's sharp yell startled her out of her daydream. Three of the goats were nibbling at the clothes on the line as the fitful wind let them drop within reach. She jumped up – and knocked over the pail of milk at her feet.

She snatched up the pail, saving a little of the milk, and waited for an angry outburst from Vel. There was none; his look was eloquent enough. Dumping the pile of logs he was carrying, he strode over to shoo the goats back into their pen.

She stood the pail on the stone seat before hurrying to the line to survey the damage. When Vel returned from latching the pen, she apologetically handed him a pair of trousers with the waistband half pulled off.

'That's another bit of clothing I owe you. Sorry.'

'Is there a problem?' They both turned in surprise; their guest, as they'd taken to calling him, had come to the doorway and was standing watching them.

'We'll sort it out,' she told him. 'You can go back to minding the meal.' He nodded and went back in. 'And hope that you've still got some clothes to go home in, the rate I'm going,' she added under her breath as she took the rest of the damaged stuff off the line.

Vel was still inspecting his trousers, turning them this way and that. 'No good for me now, but our guest's a bit shorter in the waist and leg than me. Can they can be remade for him?'

She sighed and made an effort to look more closely. 'I expect so, if I get the time.'

'By the way, how much longer is this going to go on?'

'I'm sorry?'

'The sleepless nights, the fretting, putting off the decision…'

She gave him a look meant to plead ignorance, but it ended up as one of her intense stares, trying to fathom how he read her so well.

'All right. I think we have to go with him. But there again, I don't want you anywhere near him. But then, I know what I've seen is going to happen anyway, so…'

Her voice trailed off, miserably. Vel folded his arms.

'Would it help to know what I think?'

'I don't know. What *do* you think?'

'That you're right. What will happen, will happen. It makes no difference if we stay here, or go to Ilmaen with him, or run screaming to the Northlands for that matter. What you've seen is going to come about, and you'll be there to see it, and it looks scary, but *we don't actually know how it will turn out*. Agreed?' She nodded reluctantly.

'Fine. Now, let's look at our choices: stay or go. What's likely to come of staying? Mmm. That'd be you facing Dailo's gang every day, and – supposing we all get through whatever it is you've future-seen – you becoming an old maid that all the women are afraid to employ and all the men are afraid to marry. Me: I'd be stuck with sheep farming when I'd rather do almost anything else – no disrespect to Melor – and if I were to get married, I'd be stuck here with my old maid of a sister and my wife at each other's throats all day. Ah, no, don't you tell me you wouldn't resent someone else in your kitchen,' he declared, drowning out her protest before she'd made it.

'On the other hand, what if we go? No guarantee of anything – but Ren, this man's a friend of the future ruler of Ilmaen. The possibilities are almost limitless. Perhaps I'll be no use at all to him – but if I am, we'll be set for life!

'But there's one last thing about going and it's this. Even if the worst comes to the worst, you'll have made a fresh start. In Ilmaen, no one but he and I will know about your future-sight. You're a clever, able girl, Ren; you could get by on your own over there, if you had to.' Vel sighed heavily. 'I don't know how long it is since you got a decent night's sleep, worrying over all this – but, believe me, I've spent far more sleepless nights these last few years, worrying about what's going to happen to you, and I don't need future-sight to predict the worst if you stay here. Please, can we just make the decision, and go?'

She stared at him. She'd had her knuckles pressed to her mouth to hold back a retort, since his comment about having a feuding wife and sister. Now she was chewing on them absently while she thought. Finally she dropped her hand.

'You're right. But there is still one problem.'

'What?' he snapped in exasperation.

'Our guest. How do you know he'll agree to take us?' The look on her brother's face gave her some satisfaction, since it told her that her he hadn't even considered that possibility.

'And I'll want Melor's blessing as well,' she added as a parting shot. She took the trousers back from Vel, added them to the pile of repairs she had to do, and went inside.

oOo

'Foolish children. Of course you have my blessing. Now kindly knock this pole in to celebrate.' Melor was amused, not displeased, to Vel's relief.

The pole was soundly in with three strikes. Vel dropped the mallet and mopped his brow with the back of his hand.

'I thought maybe you'd be offended.'

'Ah, that accounts for it. And I thought you'd move on a lot sooner than this.'

'I'm sorry. I really tried to fit in, but I never felt I did. I don't think it's just the way they are with Ren. I don't think I ever could fit in when I don't know who I am. This way, I might get a chance to find out. But I feel very ungrateful, after all you've done for us,' Vel said awkwardly.

'I raised you, boy. I don't own you. Oh, I grant you, I held hopes of being looked after in my dotage by Renia, but the villagers killed off those hopes long since. It was even longer ago that I gave up hope you'd stay on. But you did; and you've worked hard and well into the bargain. This farm hasn't made me a rich man, but it brings in enough for me to hire another lad when you go. There's a bit put aside for you and Renia too; you can take that with you. Heaven knows, I shall miss you, but you're right. You need a challenge, and there's nothing like that here for you. There's worse than nothing for Renia. Whatever the village bullies might or might not be capable of, they're scaring her into taking terrible risks. From what you said, it's a miracle she didn't kill herself up that tree the other day. Here, let's get the crosspieces in.'

Out came his hammer and some fencing nails while Vel offered up one of the beams, steadying it in its slot as Melor secured it. The second beam went in too, and he stood back to check it. Vel had already judged the frame sound, and was bringing branches of gorse to infill it. Melor let him finish the section off then voiced his thoughts.

'This vision's a worry, though. Mind you, our guest ought to be a worry, even without it; he's a long way beyond cautious, nearer paranoid, and he still hasn't given us his name. But somehow he makes me trust him. There's no standing on ceremony with him, which isn't usual with the sort who wear clothes of that quality; and he's downright badgered me to give him some of the easier tasks to do, to try and pay us back. I suppose I ought to worry that he's trying to buy our favour, or that he's not the man he claims to be; but I can't make myself see anything other than an honest, adaptable young man who's experienced enough of life to know when to change to suit the circumstances. Above all, he doesn't judge you two, and he's not scared of what Renia can do. If things go right, you might have a career in Ilmaen, and Renia could have the chance of a proper life. If only the vision passes off for the best, eh?'

Melor said no more. They both knew better than to hope the vision was wrong.

oOo

That afternoon, Melor and Renia stayed discreetly indoors while Vel spoke to their guest as he filled the animals' trough. He took the suggestion calmly and thoughtfully, clearly not surprised by it.

'I knew you had something planned.' He rested one boot on the edge of the trough and leant his forearms on his raised knee as he poured, his way of sparing the bruised muscles in his side. He put the bucket down, and leant forward again. 'I had thought I would be taking you only, and Renia was trying to talk you out of it.'

'You don't want her along,' Vel suddenly surmised, his voice flat. 'You think she'll be a problem.'

'On the contrary. It would be safer to travel with a girl in the party. Men alone – people can be suspicious. But if you seem fit company for a girl to travel with, people think of family men, breadwinners, salt-of-the earth folk. It does not matter what you are in truth.'

'But all the same, you aren't sure about taking Ren.'

'No. After all, she's barely more than a child; and while she would make it safer for us, there are limits… If Lemno thinks I am alive, there will be people out there trying to kill me. And when we reach Ilmaen there will be an entire army with that as their task. I won't lie to you, Vel. What she has seen is one very possible outcome to events.'

The animals, no respecters of person, were pushing round the trough now. Their guest swung his foot out of their way, retrieved the bucket, and they started back to the house.

He asked Vel, 'What Renia said to you, about both wanting and not wanting to go. You can understand that, I take it?' Vel nodded. 'And you still want to go?'

'Yes.'

Kerin paused for a moment, a thoughtful frown on his face.

'I need to speak to Melor and Renia before I make a decision. But not straight away. She's worried and confused,

so she is trying too hard to find arguments to justify one
choice or the other. If I push her now I don't think she'll make
the right choice. We can still plan, and make that decision
later. A few more days. Can you give me that?'

oOo

With the decision put off, Renia settled into resigned
acceptance. She had already replaced friendly shyness around
their guest with quiet efficiency. The others seemed to
consider things were back to normal, but he seemed more
aware than they of the times her mood would swing to
something darker. She tried to hide it, but often it took her by
surprise – even the most innocent of things he said or did
could set her off.

But then he needed efficiency more than friendliness
right now. Information on the nearest ports and trade routes
was essential. Without it, he couldn't work out how best to
reach Ilmaen undetected. Melor's sailing days had been from a
port further west, and twenty years ago. Kerin needed current
knowledge, and Renia got it for him. From the second week of
Kerin's recovery she took Melor's tiny sailboat on regular
fishing trips along the coast, checking ports large and small for
regular shipping routes to the continent. When the men came
in from work in the evenings they would be met with the smell
of yet more cooking fish and a table spread with notes on ships
posted for travel and ships seen. For the first time ever they
found themselves wishing for a bit of mutton to relieve the
monotony of fish baked, grilled, stewed and steamed.

Kerin's thoughts were settling in favour of
Greatharbour. It was further away than he would have liked
and frankly much bigger, but it gave more chance of
anonymity and less time spent waiting for a suitable vessel,
and that would make up for the extra days of travel to get
there. In addition he was obsessed by the idea that his pursuers
might spot him. While he was confident he could shake them

off again, he feared that they would trace his route back in the hope of finding someone who could be 'persuaded' to reveal his destination. For that reason, he decided to go well inland and east and then follow one of the rivers that fed into the estuary at Greatharbour, and hope their trail would be too hard to follow.

He worked hard at his plans, and at getting fit – too hard, to Renia's thinking, and she limited him strictly to light work in the house. She took on jobs any man would have run to aid a woman with, sitting him down with a stare if he chafed at it, and managed well enough by herself. Most of the time. The day inevitably came when she tried to set a heavy pitcher on a high shelf and struggled. As she did he appeared beside her, not taking it off her but merely helping her to lift and set it in its place. Tall as she was, he had a few inches on her so she knew he was taking all the weight, and with no effort or pain on his part. Having made his point he went back to the table and studied his notes for the rest of the morning.

Renia found she could not settle to any work for the rest of that day. Granted there were no urgent jobs but still, it bothered her to do nothing. She brewed a pot of tea and poured herself a mug, settling into the bench seat beside the fire. That left her with nothing to do but drink it and brood.

Kerin returned from the woodpile, clumping to the fire in Vel's over-large boots and noisily dropping his pile of logs by it. He banked the fire and stacked the rest of the wood neatly beside it.

She had not realized she was staring at him until he asked if the brew in the teapot was fresh, and she saw him frown. She broke the stare and looked down at the floor, angry with herself; but out of the corner of her eye she still watched him. Kerin poured his tea, but did not take the seat on the other side of the fire, where he normally went; he came to join her on her bench, mug on his knee.

'I think Vel will do well in Ilmaen,' he said, out of nowhere. 'He has the makings of a good swordsman; fast reactions, adaptability, stamina. Some training and practice, and he'll be ready for this trip.' A turn of the head and he gave her a long, hard look. 'Unlike you.'

'You're refusing to take me?'

'That's not what I said. I said you are not ready for it. Now tell me I'm wrong.'

Since she said nothing he leant so far forward she could not avoid looking at him.

'We have to talk, Renia. I have to understand why you want to come to Ilmaen, and it's not enough to say that you must. And truth be told, the looks you've been giving me – no sane man would trust his back to you. And if I cannot trust you, I cannot take you. Too much is at stake.'

'I'd never betray you, if that's what you're thinking,' she protested, and then admitted, 'you do scare me though.'

'I do?'

She shrugged awkwardly.

'Well, you're so single-minded. About rescuing Jastur, and about that man Lemno. I know one's love and one's hate but there's the same kind of... obsession there when you talk of them both. It feels like you'd push me or Vel aside if we stood between you and either of them.' It resembled what she'd seen in the eyes of those who tormented her, though she didn't say that.

Kerin looked astonished, as though he had never thought about this. She hurried to get past this, before he attached too much importance to it.

'It's not really you. When I look at you, I can't help but think about the vision. I know we have to go with you– I know in his heart Vel is longing to! – but I remember how the vision made me feel, how desperately I want that moment to come, but at the same time feeling it's going to bring some terrible loss...

'Look, you aren't going to get a sensible answer from me. I don't know why I want to go; I only know that I must. Whatever happens, I will be there. I've seen that. That's the future. It doesn't matter what I do, I can't prevent that. But I do know that when it comes, I'm going to lose something – I'm scared that it's Vel...'

She tailed off, angry that she couldn't explain her fears more clearly. How could you explain a gut feeling? She felt as frustrated and foolish as a child trying to make an adult understand why she was afraid of the dark. She must sound so stupid; but a glance told her nothing, other than that Kerin was looking thoughtful.

After a while he said, 'I appreciate some things are hard to explain. I couldn't give you a sensible reason why I believe in reincarnation, or why I choose to fight – though maybe I'm prepared to risk myself in battle because I believe in reincarnation. It's not because I'm not scared, I can tell you that. It's years now since my first battle, in Federin, but the memory is still vivid. They have clans there, and some long-standing, complicated disputes with their neighbours; and they like to settle them as a clan. Sometimes it's just a skirmish; sometimes it ends up bigger, and my first battle was much bigger. Intelligence was coming back one piece after another and it all confirmed the odds were against our side. I can recall the constant wavering of my courage, terrified by the prospect of battle at one moment but at the next half dreading that the fight would be abandoned. I was barely fifteen, and hadn't the remotest idea whether I would live to see the next day; I just knew, unshakably, that if it came to it, I would fight in that battle because it mattered to the clan.'

'So that's where you learned to fight?'

'No, but it was the perfect opportunity to improve. Or die. Ironically, in sending us there to avoid the fever, Father sent us to the most dangerous country in the world to be a fighter. The rules of challenge don't apply so rigidly there, a dispute is as likely to be resolved by a battle as a duel.'

'How can they work the land to feed themselves if so many are fighting?'

'They're a populous nation. Theirs was one of the last cities to be destroyed in The Catastrophe, so some were able to flee. With fewer lost, their numbers have grown faster than other nations so they value the holding of land and livestock over life. Father believed that within a few generations Ilmaen could face the same challenges and wanted Jastur and myself to understand and be prepared.'

'So the Federinese are very different people then?'

'They are an experience not to be missed, for sure. I enjoyed their company, they are live-in-the-moment people like me: but their obsession with possessions and their willingness to take lives so lightly was very alien to me.'

She was quiet for a while.

'You've killed people, then?'

'I have. I first took a life there: but it was in the heat of battle and I'd had to take another three to survive before I had a chance to dwell on it. In those circumstances, it's frighteningly easy to do.

'I haven't had to take a life in a duel yet. A duel's

much easier to control: there you focus the fight to a single point, and unless you get it very wrong it's a point outside yourself. It doesn't matter if a huge crowd watches you both, or no one; everything is concentrated on that point.

'At first a battle feels like it has no focus. It is all around you. Then, as you try to follow it, you realize it is inside you. You feel and see and hear and smell everything that happens to those around you; you are them, and they are you. You may walk off a battlefield without a mark on you, but you carry all the damage it did around you for the rest of your life. Despite that, you'll do it again if you have to; something compels you to fight despite the fear, and you don't know if you rush into it in order to get it over, or to get better at fighting, or for darker reasons. Is that how you feel about your visions?' he asked her suddenly.

It was close enough. She gave him the smallest of nods.

'Look,' he continued, 'I'm not going to lie and say it's not dangerous; we are taking a great risk. We are challenging dangerous people. Know also that I will do what I think is the right thing for Jastur, whether it fits with your vision or not. But if you can live with that, well, I for one would be very glad of the company. And I promise…' he caught her by the chin now, looking her in the eyes so she would see he was being truthful '…*faithfully*, I will take no unnecessary risks. Not with your life, not with my life, and most certainly not with Vel's life. Can you handle that?'

She managed another tiny nod.

'Then you are coming with us.' He freed her chin and went to leave, then turned back. 'But no more of those looks, agreed? They *really* bother me.'

oOo

That same evening, Melor pronounced Kerin well enough to travel. He also produced a small wooden trunk from which he took a considerable number of gold coins, packed into four small leather pouches. He emptied them out on the table; Renia and Vel were open-mouthed with wonder. They hadn't realized there was that much money in the house.

'I thought it might be wise to buy horses. I'm told if you look after them they make a good investment; when you don't need to travel, they are easily sold again.'

'Where will you buy them?' their guest asked.

'Spetswll, day after tomorrow. It's not the biggest horse market around here, but it means we don't have to pass the village, so there's less chance of someone there seeing me with horses than if we went east to the proper horse fairs like Dorster or Waymes. We'll have a choice of second-hand or brand new tack, whichever you think best. But I should warn you, I've never ridden. I barely know the back end from the front on a horse. I'm relying on your advice when it comes to buying them, and you'll have to teach these two to ride...'

So two days later, Melor and Vel set off well before dawn on the long walk to Spetswll.

Chapter 5 – Unwelcome News

When they entered Spetswll, Melor had given Vel a surprise.
The younger man had turned right, ready to go to the horse
market, but Melor had tapped him on the shoulder and
indicated that they were turning left instead. Vel followed,
confused until they entered the street where the fine
metalworkers had their shops. He stopped and turned to Vel.

'Well, young man, which shop shall we try first? I've
seen you gaze eagerly into the windows. Who does the best
selection of swords?'

'We're to have swords?' Vel could not hide the
excitement in his voice.

'I wouldn't let you go without them. I know it's a lot
of money but it's a lot of steel too, and you know how little of
that there is since the Catastrophe. In fact I'd prefer that you
had guns, but they're well out of my price range, not to
mention illegal for private citizens in Ilmaen. Seriously illegal,
boy. Our guest says don't even try it unless you want to prove
your sister right. And I want Renia to have a knife. I don't
suppose she would care to use it, but she'd have it if she
needed to. Our guest says he will train you up. It seems he has
some reputation as a swordsman.'

'You talked to him about this?' Vel was a little put
out. Melor laid hold of Vel's arm, to draw attention to the
importance of his next words.

'Yes, I talked to him. We have spoken about a
number of things, including his background. Remember, he
may be younger than you, but he has spent his life being
trained to fight, trained to lead. He must be in command; your
lives may depend on reacting quickly to an order from him –

not just his life and yours, but Renia's too.' He relaxed his
stern attitude a little as Vel's belligerent expression turned to
one of concern for his sister.

'Lesson one for a prospective general, boy: before
you can give orders, you must learn how to take them! Now,
which shop should we look in?'

Vel virtually dragged Melor to his chosen shop. He
knew precisely the sword he wanted. It was at the back of a
display in the window, not given the prominence of some
more eye-catching weapons, but it had simple, solid lines and
Vel had admired it on their last trip to Spetswll, months ago.

Yes, it was still there! He was in the shop and had it
down off the rack, giving it a few practice swings, before
Melor had a chance to explain to the owner what they had
come for; but the man's pique quickly faded on discovering
that, despite appearances, they were serious buyers. There was
space in his shop for his discerning customers to establish the
weight and balance of a blade. Vel knew nothing of weights
and balances; he only knew as he flourished it that it felt
heavier than he had expected, but otherwise it felt entirely
right.

Getting a sword for their guest took a little longer.
They did not know his tastes, only what he had asked Melor to
tell the swordsmith, but they eventually picked one out of
three shown to them. It was a little more ornate than Vel's, but
then, that seemed only proper. Vel quickly picked a pretty yet
sturdy knife for Renia; they paid and were out of the shop
again. Melor let Vel gaze at his new possession briefly before
urging him to put it out of sight in his pack, and they went
back over their steps towards the cobblers' street.

They had brought their guest's remaining sea-ruined
boot with them to match against a new pair. They hadn't
hoped to match the fit, let alone the quality, of the original –

but it turned out near-perfect ones were just coming off the last. With a price agreed and a time set to return for the finished boots, they went on to the horse market. Here they would make no snap decisions. They looked around for some time. Again their guest had told Melor what to look out for, and there seemed a good choice for such a small town.

In the end they opted for two bays, a mare and a gelding, and for Renia a smaller blue roan gelding with a sweet temperament. Vel spent some time talking to the mare they had decided should be his mount, trying to accustom himself to being close to such a fine animal and getting her used to him. However, Melor wanted to haggle with the seller, which inevitably involved some colourful language on both sides, and he still disliked doing that kind of thing in front of Vel even now he was full-grown. Melor solved the problem by pointing out the lateness of the hour, and that they still needed to pick up maps and saddles yet. The saddles he hoped to include in his price with the horse dealer, since the man sold both. So Melor dispatched Vel to the printers' enclave, four or five streets up.

This was an easy purchase to make, as he had very precise instructions. Three maps were needed: one that covered their area and the roads to the east, while the other two covered the south-west. He made more fuss about getting the latest editions of those, so if anyone did come snooping, it would seem they had gone south-west. He had found it a little unnerving, the way all these details aimed at covering their tracks had come pouring from their guest as if they were second nature to him. At first Vel had been inclined to think him paranoid. But then he saw Renia actually *relaxing* for the first time in weeks, and Melor noting the instructions down approvingly. It had made Vel rethink his decision to go; but in the end he had reached the same conclusion – if with more misgivings than before.

He was pondering all this when a bill-seller passed

him. He was crying the news as usual, but due to his busy thoughts Vel walked on some way before he registered what the man was saying.

'Read a bill! Read a bill! Crisis for Ilmaen. Crown-Designate and his brother dead in double tragedy. Read a bill!'

Vel waved the man over and tendered the money for a broadsheet, which was duly presented. He read it through as he walked.

Melor met him on the fringes of the horse market. Vel said nothing, just handed the bill over. Melor read it; they stared at each other wordlessly. Both of them knew what this would mean to their guest. Vel gazed bleakly at his bay mare, who returned the look with a sympathetic eye.

'Do you think he will still want to go, Melor?'

'I don't know. And you?'

Vel nodded firmly. 'If he still wants to. This was no accident, not the Crown-Designate *and* his brother. This is Lemno getting rid of the claimants on Maregh's behalf, like our guest said he would. Since he thought this might happen, I'm guessing he's got a backup plan.'

Melor heaved a sigh.

'Well, we'd best pick those boots up. Then we must get back and break the news.'

oOo

It was deep into the evening when the sound of horses' hooves rang down the cliffside path. Kerin heard them first and called Renia out; they had lamps to light the way, and blankets for the horses, and indoors a hot meal to welcome the travellers.

Kerin took the bridles; he used the chance to check out the horses and was satisfied with their choice. Renia had instantly gone to the roan horse, guessing it to be hers. He noticed how she caught its great head lightly despite having little experience with horses, rubbing its nose and showing no fear of it.

They stabled the horses and tidied away their tack; Melor and Renia had gone inside to serve up supper. But when they got in out of the chill, Melor did not seem to have got much done; he was poking at the fire, but Kerin knew Renia had banked it just a little while before. She meanwhile was swinging out the cooking pot and lifting it off its hook when Vel went to help her. He saw her look at her brother questioningly; he knew full well she could manage it on her own, so why was he helping her? He saw Vel glance at her briefly, then avoid her eyes. Something was wrong. Kerin hated the thought of questioning them after all they had done for him, and doubted he would like the answer anyway; a check of the swords they had bought seemed a good way to avoid any awkwardness.

First he drew the more ornate blade and hefted it, checking it for balance, then he took some practice swings, parrying and thrusting at an imaginary opponent. He did not put much force into it, there being little room in the parlour; even so, he hoped they were impressed. It took a long time to get a sword wrist as flexible and strong as his. This was what he was good at, and he was proud of his skill; it might help to allay some of their fears if they saw he was way ahead of any swordsman they were ever likely to have seen. He put down that weapon and took up the second, plainer one, repeating the practice strokes, but he was more intrigued by this one. Vel mentioned, as if in passing, 'I thought I'd have the plain one, and you the other.' Kerin looked at Vel, whose face reddened just a shade.

'What made you choose this one?' he enquired. Vel

shrugged in answer.

'I don't know. I just liked the look of it. I chose it on impulse, I suppose.' He seemed to be steeling himself for a lecture on his poor choice.

'Good impulse. It's a better sword by far than the other. You've paid for pure craftsmanship here, not ornamentation.'

'Oh! Then I suppose you'd better have it.' The reluctance in Vel's voice was not well disguised. Kerin smiled and held the pommel out to him.

'Such a choice augurs well for your swordsmanship. "The best sword ends up in the hands of the best swordsman," they say. I look forward to some rigorous practice sessions. Take it, look after it. I will show you how.'

Finally Kerin took up the knife, which was just a little too small for his hand; a glance at Melor confirmed that this was for Renia. It had come in its own sheath, the simple chased design on the handle repeated on its cover.

Resheathing it, Kerin handed it to her without comment.

Melor stepped forward now, and actually put a hand on his shoulder. The old man had never ventured to touch Kerin before, outside of tending him in his illness. Kerin looked at him, surprised but not offended by the gesture.

'A few words with you in private, sir?' Kerin glanced briefly at the other two, and acquiesced. Melor led him off towards a sleeping alcove.

'A cup of tea with supper, eh, Renia?' he suggested as he drew the curtain shut behind him.

Plans must have changed then, Kerin concluded; maybe they would not all be going. From the looks that had passed between them, Melor and Vel were in the know and Renia was not, so doubtless she was out of the trip. She would be upset, from what she had said earlier; and he would be the reason they changed the plan – her slowing him down or some such. He felt angry with them for leaving it so late to decide; it was not his fault, but she would resent it and he would be the obvious target for that resentment. Her good opinion had come to matter to him.

Melor was ready to speak now. 'I'd sit down if I were you, sir,' were his first words. How strange! This decision was late, but not entirely unexpected and not one he needed to sit down for. 'I would prefer to stand, thank you,' he replied.

Melor shrugged and continued, 'We'd bought all the gear and the horses before we came across this.' He drew a paper from his pocket, and Kerin saw now that this was something else entirely. Melor unfolded it, carefully flattened out the creases and held it out to him.

'It's news about the Crown. It's… not good.'

Kerin took the broadsheet and read it through, quickly the first time then more slowly. The first reading confirmed what had sprung so horribly to mind, the second was to get the details; but on seeing the news in print he felt as if a cord was tightening round his heart. The second reading was a struggle against the prick of tears behind his eyes.

He handed back the bill.

'Thank you for letting me know.'

'There's no right time with this kind of news. I'm sorry for your loss.'

Kerin nodded his thanks, still trying to compose himself. Too slow! He had been too slow. He managed to look at Melor, keeping his face expressionless, but the glistening in his eyes must surely give him away.

'Umm, I need some time to myself now. I can't say how long I'll be. Excuse me.'

oOo

He was gone a long time. They ate without him. After a couple more hours Vel became concerned and wanted to go out looking lest their guest had hurt himself, but Melor would not let him. One of the lamps was gone from the lobby; Melor reasoned that if the young man had had the presence of mind to take a lamp to light his way, he did not intend to stumble over the cliff edge. Instead Melor packed them off to bed, so that when their guest got back in he would not have to face any of them till morning.

But Renia could not settle. Melor had shown her the broadsheet after their guest rushed out, and myriad thoughts had flown round her head. Trying to work out how he had taken the news; judging the implications of this for them all; even picturing how she would feel if she were to receive this kind of news about Vel – a thought she had to shut down quickly. Lying in bed only set her head spinning until she felt dizzy and sick.

Jastur dead, already. Always her thoughts came back to that. The level of fear the vision had raised in her, tying Vel in with their guest and Jastur, could not be blanked out. She'd read it wrong somehow, they weren't all going to be in danger together. One of them was gone already, and she doubted that it was from a fever as the broadsheet had said. It must have been a violent death. If they went to Ilmaen now, what would they be going for? How long would it be before someone handed her such a broadsheet with Vel's name on it? If only she could convince herself that her vision was wrong, if only she could make her brother stay here, and let their guest go to his fate without them. But even wishing it, even knowing of Jastur's end, the path ahead of them was unavoidable: their guest and Vel would still go, and she would go with them, in dread.

There was no prospect of sleep for her. She rose quietly and went back into the parlour. The dying fire still gave a little light, though not enough heat now for a clear spring night. If she was cold indoors, it must be bitter chill outside. So she raked over the embers and added more wood, fanning it back into life. While it picked up she went to the larder to pour and spice a cup of wine for their guest's return, not watering it down as they normally did. She went to put the wine away; then she unstoppered the bottle again, and poured herself one too. Once the fire had retaken she made up a warming pan for their guest's bed, mulled her cup of wine, and settled down on the fireside bench to drink it.

It was perhaps quarter of an hour later that he came in, putting the lantern out while he was still in the lobby and shutting the doors as quietly as he could. He started in surprise when she rose from the bench and bent over the fire.

'What, are you not gone to bed yet?' he asked. She turned from the range towards him, a cup in her hands.

'I went, but I couldn't sleep. You're shaking with cold! Here, come sit by the fire and drink this, I've mulled it for you.'

He hesitated a moment, but the thought of the fire and wine was too tempting for him. He sank down into the seat. As the cup passed between them, they both spoke at once.

'You should've worn a jacket.'

'I should have worn a jacket.'

They smiled weakly at each other; he settled the cup on his knee. She sat to finish her own drink and watched him. He drank distractedly, great gulps broken by long minutes staring into the embers. She was intruding on his grief; she rose to leave.

'Stay,' he said abruptly. Then, 'Stay a while,' more gently. She sat again, curling her feet up under her. She was not sure what to do next; she wanted to talk more to him about her fears, but this wasn't the right time for that. 'What will you do now?' she finally asked. He sat up tall for a moment, then settled back again with a sigh.

'Something I should have done long ago: tell you the whole story. You're owed it, especially since I've been thinking very hard these last few hours as to whether to return to Ilmaen at all.' Renia made a barely perceptible movement, every muscle in her body tensing at his comment. He was unaware of this and carried on speaking.

'I'm sorely tempted not to go back. After so many years' absence, who will know me when I get there, let alone believe my story, even assuming I can keep one step ahead of Lemno? As to the Crown... well, that's the heart of it all.' He paused, preoccupied by his thoughts.

'With Jastur and his brother gone, who else but Maregh can be Crown?' Renia could have bitten her tongue as soon as she had said this, so keen to encourage him into staying she had spoken without thinking. He stared at her intently for long silent moments until a wry smile touched his mouth.

'Don't be fooled by that broadsheet. Jastur's brother is not dead.'

'You mean to go back and make him Crown then? But you said he wasn't up to it… and you can't be sure he's alive,' Renia protested.

'Oh, I can be sure, on both counts,' he said, his smile even more wry. 'Because I'm Jastur's brother.'

'You…' was all she could manage. Her voice had deserted her.

'I am Kerin Hedsarol.' He paused momentarily, took a deep breath. 'Kerin *Hed* Sarol now. Heir to the Crown.' That change, putting more emphasis on the 'Hed' must have been significant but it barely registered with her, compared to his revelation.

'And I don't want it, Renia. When people look at the Crown they see power and wealth and prestige, and they think it an enviable position. That is what Maregh has done. He forgets that with all that comes responsibility – crushing responsibility. Tens of thousands of lives are governed by your decisions. And when you are Crown you are Crown for the rest of your life, twenty-four hours a day. Every action is watched and judged; what you wear, who you do or don't talk to – whose range you sit by, drinking mulled wine in the middle of the night!

'I've far preferred life as a second son. It's not too demanding. All I have to do is keep from getting my head knocked off in combat, and fortunately I have a talent for that. It's let me keep body and soul together a bit longer.' He laughed a little, but it was a hollow sound. Yet his words had stirred up a desperate hope in Renia.

'The truth is, the thought of being Crown terrifies me,' he continued. 'I can't do what Jastur did. I can force people to do what I want them to, but that's only ever a temporary measure. Disarming or even killing a man is easy compared to what Jastur could do; he could create lasting change, because he could change people's minds. No one should be responsible for a whole nation without the ability to do that. What if I'm tempted to use force because it's what I know best? Ilmaen would be better off if I stayed here and took up the sheep farming Vel is so disillusioned with.

'The trouble is, there's one thing I fear more than this burden, than having power I *might* misuse, and that's leaving it in the hands of those I know *will.*

'I'm a selfish man in many ways, but my upbringing taught me one simple notion: that what I want will, *must,* always come second to the well-being of Ilmaen and its people. If I don't return then I'm no better than my uncle.

'So,' he said with a sigh, 'that makes two reluctant travellers on this journey. I only hope Vel has enough enthusiasm to sustain us both.' His empty wine cup came down heavily on the edge of the range. Renia stared at it, drained of hope herself. He had been so near to giving it up! Yet more evidence that this thing was inevitable, that it was a waste of time even trying to fight it. She might as well give in and follow the tide of events. Her turn to sigh as she got up from the bench.

'Vel's enthusiasm would get us twice round the world without stopping, sir,' she remarked, 'but starting out without enough sleep would not be wise. Do try to get some. I've put a warming pan in your bed, don't burn yourself on it.' She picked up her cup.

'A warming pan! Is there anything you don't think of?'

She shrugged. 'Don't you fall asleep on this seat, sir, or you'll be as stiff as a board come morning.' She reached across Kerin to take his empty cup. As she did so he caught her hand in his, an earnest expression on his face.

'Renia, can we drop the "sir"? That would be a bad habit to get into, out in the world. I'll take a false name at some stage, but till then it's Kerin.' His face softened. 'Thank you. For tonight, for listening. You have a good heart, Renia. Sleep well.' He kissed her hand lightly; it would have seemed gallantly romantic, only he released it at once and was back in his thoughts, staring into the fading glow from the embers in the range. Even though Renia was right in front of him, she might have become invisible. She hesitated in bewilderment before taking up his cup and starting uncertainly away, only to stop halfway to the scullery and look back at him. He didn't notice, not even when she stopped to stare a second time at the curtain to her room.

Sleep well? There was more chance the village would make her their May Queen.

Chapter 6 – Far-seeing

She managed a few, snatched moments of sleep that night, rising before first light and bringing her candle with her. Kerin was still sitting in the parlour, but looking less preoccupied this morning.

'You didn't go to bed, did you?' said Renia, making it a gentle accusation.

'No. But your orders were not to *fall asleep* here.'

'You must be exhausted.'

'A little tired. Very hungry.'

'You should go to bed when you've had something to eat,' she advised. He shook his head.

'There's too much to do. The others need to know who I am, and we must start the riding and sword practice today, as well as the farm tasks. I will go to bed early tonight, you have my word.'

He had managed to keep the fire in all night, which was good; it took her less time to get breakfast ready. In the meantime, she rummaged in the store cupboard and picked out two of the best of the winter-stored apples, and some cheese. He ate them neatly but quickly, then jumped up and grabbed the wood basket. 'I'll fetch some more...'

Kerin paused as Melor's curtain went back and he stepped out with his candle. If he was up, Vel wouldn't be far behind; with Kerin in his room, Vel was sleeping on a straw mattress on Melor's floor, and there was barely room for the old man to get out of bed without stepping on his ward. Sure enough, Vel followed, rubbing his eyes.

Renia touched Kerin's shoulder, took the basket from him. He turned back to the others.

'I have something to tell you both. Shall we sit down?'

'I'll fetch the wood,' said Renia, and left them to it.

Kerin ate a good breakfast on top of what he had already had, gave them two hours of riding practice, and between them they finished all the farm tasks by lunchtime. Renia helped Melor with the afternoon check on the sheep in the farthest fields, leaving the other two free for sword practice.

When they got back, Vel was already making progress. Kerin had set up a stack of straw bales and marked limewash targets on them. Vel's task was to stab the target named for him by Kerin and spin through three hundred and sixty degrees in time to stab the next one called. Being tall, Vel had always had a tendency to slouch, but there was little evidence of it now. Renia had never thought of her brother as an elegant man, but the technique this exercise needed lent him a new gracefulness.

Kerin stopped him and changed the exercise. He explained the basic stance and the workings of wrist, arm and upper body leading to an effective downward cut, and demonstrated how to make the attack from either left or right. Vel gave a reasonable approximation of the movement; Kerin made a small correction to his stance and Vel tried again. There was little of the bales left by the end of the practice session.

Soon evening was upon them. They ate their supper; it was a much quieter, more solemn meal than those they had shared of late. Kerin excused himself, literally nodding in his dish by halfway through the meal, and went to bed.

oOo

This pattern was repeated, with small variations, for the next six days. Time was also spent preparing what they needed for the journey, fetching up provisions from the deep stores, checking the oilcloths they would use for ground sheets and tents, and other details advised by Kerin.

But the heart had gone out of him. The quiet fire that had burnt in his eyes was quenched, and everything he did, he did mechanically. He spoke very little, smiled not at all. The charming youth had been replaced overnight by a taciturn man. The others were careful around him, trying to judge his needs as he asked for almost nothing now. How much of the change was due to the loss of his brother, and how much to the burden placed on him by that loss, they could only guess.

He insisted that they take at least one longer ride out during these days, to get used to being in the saddle. They chose a cove some hours away as their destination, rose in the early hours well before dawn, packed a cold breakfast and set out.

oOo

The coastline near the cove was sheer cliffs, the few beaches below them all inaccessible except for this one, where a stream had over the millennia cut a valley down through the cliff leading to the sea. If you tried to follow the stream from the top, its course was too steep; the path they needed seemingly meandered away from the cove along the sheer drop but eventually led down a sloping shelf to meet the stream again, where it turned from being a series of little waterfalls on to its course for the sea. They tied the horses up at the top, where there was both water and grazing for them, while they stretched their legs and braved the path.

Dawn had turned an hour since, and the sun was well over the horizon. It was cold in the valley, but bright. Everything about the place felt as alive as could be. The water babbled across the stones and a single bird, long-legged and skittish, pierced the air with its gentle but insistent piping. Vel was imitating it as he took the winding path down to the beach.

Renia stood at the top of the path, staring into the cove. The stream looked as if it was feeding into a sea of molten gold. Kerin came up behind her, pack in hand, and took in the same view.

'Isn't it lovely?' she asked him.

'Very lovely,' he agreed. 'You are still sure you want to go with us, Renia?'

She looked over her shoulder at him: there was nothing to be read in his expression.

'Don't ask me that. Otherwise I might ask you the same thing.'

This provoked a wry smile from him.

'You know I am going.' He looked down the path, and saw that Vel was already far along it. 'Come on.'

He started off, but realized she was not following him. When he turned back, Renia seemed to have grown tense, turned pale. She blinked at him slowly, swayed a little.

'Renia?' She was looking in his direction, but seemed unable to focus on him.

'The fairies are here,' she said, which made no sense at all, and started to sit down but instead pitched forward with a little cry and fell on to the grass. Kerin ran back and found her shaking all over, twisted up in muscle spasm with her eyes wide and staring. Her breathing came in little strangled gasps.

'Vel!' he bellowed, panicked by the look of her. 'Velohim!'

Vel scrambled back up the path, but stopped and took his time when he saw what was happening.

'It's all right,' he assured Kerin as he joined him. 'It's only one of her falling fits.'

'She looks to be in pain,' Kerin observed anxiously.

'No, she's told us she doesn't feel a thing, and it doesn't seem to do her any harm. Stay clear, though. Sometimes she jerks about, and if she catches you a blow you'll surely know it. Melor has read old books about it. He says something is happening in her brain that makes the messages it sends go awry – hence all the twitching and seeing things that aren't there. She'll be right as rain when she wakes up; we just have to make sure she doesn't hurt herself on anything.' Vel moved a stone Renia's leg was in danger of catching then sat down nearby. Kerin sat too, watching her in awful fascination.

'So this is when she has her visions?' he asked.

'It doesn't happen in every fit, but they do seem to make her more, I don't know – receptive. Sometimes she sees stuff without all this thrashing about, and you can talk to her then. We call them waking fits. They're harder to spot; unless she says something out of place or we notice her looking a bit daydreamy, it's hard to tell. Melor's books say that with either kind of fit, people often grow out of them. I was hoping she already had. It'd been months since she had one... at least until these last few weeks. At least they're getting shorter now than when she was young. The first one I saw, I thought she was dying; she was in it so long. Yes, look, her breathing's going back to normal. This is a short one. She'll wake up in a minute.'

Sure enough, the shaking was stopping and Renia's eyes closed. The tension slowly worked out of her, clawed hands relaxing into their normal shape. She looked now as though she really had gone to sleep. Vel moved across to brush the hair out of her face and spoke softly to her, letting her know someone was there. After a minute she gave a long heavy sigh, opened her eyes again, and started to get up. Both men moved to help her; she wanted to stand, but Vel made her sit on a grassy knoll in case she was dizzy. She let herself be seated, rubbing her arm and dusting the dirt from her face.

'How are you?'

'Fine,' she reassured him. 'I just caught my elbow when I fell.' She turned at once towards Kerin, a smile of pure radiance on her face.

'Kerin – it's all right. Jastur's alive!'

'What?' the two men chorused.

'Yes! It's true...' Her voice faltered as she looked hard at Kerin, and he could not guess what she was reading in his face. With an effort he mastered his shock, knelt down by her and held her by both shoulders, not daring to believe this. For a terrible thought had darkened his mind: that this was a lie, told to relieve his misery.

'Renia, are you sure?' Her look was steady, defiant even. She had seen what he was thinking. 'Positive.' He hated to continue this, but...

'Then you can describe him to me?'

'Dark hair, fair-skinned with a stern face, and bearded. Above the beard there's a little scar, just here.' She indicated on her own cheek, below and to one side of her right eye. 'I think it reminds him of you,' she added hesitantly.

Kerin's hands dropped from her shoulders and he stood up. 'That's Jastur,' he confirmed. 'I put that cut there myself in sword practice, the day before we left Federin.' He felt dazed; whether from shock or relief, he was not sure.

'Ren, do you know where he is?' Vel put in. She frowned in thought.

'Somewhere deep? It's really dark in there, dark and cramped. He doesn't want to be there. Maybe a ship's cabin?'

'Or a prison cell.' Kerin was coming out of his daze. He could think of many places that qualified as dark, cramped and unpleasant. But at least he was alive!

'If we eat quickly, we can go straight back. We must start out tomorrow now, knowing this.' He began to unpack their meal there on the sward, giving the job far more attention than it needed, using the distraction to calm himself.

'I'll eat in a moment,' he heard Renia say. 'I'm dirty, I must wash, and I want to check on Bluey.' She must have flicked her eyes towards the horses or something; Kerin didn't see what exactly but, whatever hint she gave him, her brother took it.

'Show me what you're checking for. I'll see if I can help.'

Vel followed her over to where she was making a show of fixing Bluey's bridle. 'What is it?' he asked. She tilted her chin towards Kerin.

'How did he react? Did I scare him too?'

Vel shrugged. 'Same as usual.' Her face fell; he tried to make light of things. 'He was mostly bothered because he thought you were in pain.'

Renia smiled slightly at his attempts to make her feel better. 'It must look that way.' She used the back of her hand to feel her face. 'At least I didn't drool in front of him.' But Vel's expression had turned apologetic.

'Sorry. I did clean you up a bit while you were waking.'

Renia sighed. 'Go and have your meal, I'm not hungry. I'll take Bluey along the cliffs. I want to see if he does what I tell him or if he's just been copying the other horses. Tell Kerin I'll be ten minutes, no more.' She stooped to drink from the stream and wash her face before walking Bluey up the slope.

oOo

Kerin handed Vel a mug of milk as he sat down. Breaking up the sweetloaf, he handed Vel a piece and took a wedge for himself but did not eat it, turning it around in his hand. Vel gestured at it.

'Something wrong?'

Kerin looked down at the bread, realized what he had been doing.

'No, no. I was only thinking.' He broke off a small piece and put it in his mouth, chewed and swallowed.

'Vel, is your sister seeing the future? She talked as though it was happening in the present.'

'I'd say this is the present.'

'I thought she had visions of the future?'

Vel smiled. 'She just has visions. It's no good asking either of us how it works; we simply don't know. Last time something was coming, and she knew that. This time she spoke in terms of here and now. The here and now ones make a bit more sense to her; she's spoken of feeling drawn out of herself, of looking in on things somewhere else, even of communicating with people there. The future ones are vaguer, she says, sort of out of reach; that's how she can tell the difference between them. Hell, ask her about it. All a mere mortal like I can do is give you second-hand information.'

Vel blanched as he realized what he had said, looking warily at Kerin.

'I didn't mean that the way it sounded. And, for Heaven's sake, don't tell Ren! It's the kind of thing that really upsets her. She's just an ordinary girl. Sometimes she can do this extraordinary thing, that's all.'

Kerin nodded. 'Mark you, she says extraordinary things too. Before she passed out, she said, "The fairies are here." I did not realize she believed in spirits.'

'She doesn't, though she did believe in fairies as a child. What she said was her way of telling you a falling fit was coming. She gets these lights, like sparks at the edge of her vision; when she was little she thought they were fairies flying up to her. She's got into the habit of using the phrase, though I wish she wouldn't. The trouble is, by the time she sees the lights she's most of the way into a fit and really is away with the fairies. Aagh – don't tell her I said that either!'

oOo

On the way back Renia and Vel spoke together now and then
while Kerin trailed a little way behind. It had given his shaken
nerves a degree of relief when Vel had made those slips,
though he doubted he could follow the advice to take Renia
for an 'ordinary girl', even though on the face of things that
was what she was. Renia had that sort of anonymous
ordinariness that was so rare, it ought to stand out more. Not
beautiful, not homely either, but somewhere in between; he
could not even recall what colour those sad eyes of hers were,
despite having known her for weeks. Known her? He had
known nothing till an hour ago. He had assumed much, taken
more for granted, even after what he had been told about her
first vision. Witnessing one for himself was very different. He
could not describe the emotion he felt now; it seemed to fall
somewhere between fear and excitement, and he was unable to
say which it was closer to.

Up ahead, he heard Renia say, 'Go on, then,' to her
brother, as Vel urged his mount into a gallop. She held Bluey
back, under control, maintaining a trot; she learnt fast.

Kerin steeled himself and rode up to join her. He got
ready to smile if need be, to answer any awkward question that
was posed. Her face wore a serious expression when she
turned it to him. Hazel eyes, he noticed, mind fixing on
anything rather than what he'd recently seen…

'Do you think I need more practice at a gallop?'
Renia asked with a frown.

'It couldn't hurt. You held Bluey back well there.
Make sure you can get him started on your own.'

'If I can, would you race me? The head start should
make it fair.'

So he raced her. He let her win; she knew and scolded him for it. Little had changed between them after all.

Chapter 7 – Bad Beginnings

They rose early again the next day. It was bright and clear, but a strong sea breeze was blowing up sand and dust in the yard, making the air hazy. Packs were quickly stowed on saddled horses. All that remained was to say their goodbyes. The wind eddied dust around Melor, but it was not dust in her eyes that blurred Renia's vision.

First Vel shook hands with Melor – something he had never done before. He was the kind of young man who usually slapped people on the back or else hugged them. But she could see Melor's face, and reflected from it was all the affection Vel had left unspoken but conveyed in that handshake. This was the last change Melor was ever likely to see in her brother, his taking on serious ways before facing a serious task.

Next Melor's hand was taken by Kerin.

'I will look after them, sir. They have been Ty'r Athre these many years, and are proud to bear your name. Though that will not change, from now on they are as brother and sister to me.' It might have been a traditional phrasing, for all Renia knew, but Melor clearly did not doubt that Kerin's words were spoken sincerely.

The young man turned away, and now Renia stepped up in front of Melor. He looked ready to deal with tears from her, but she smiled bravely and gave him the tightest embrace she could.

'Thank you for everything,' she whispered, her eyes prickling. 'You've been more than a father to us.'

She broke away and went straight to her horse. The

others waited until she was in the saddle before they too mounted up. Then with calls of goodbye on both sides they set off up the cliff path.

She knew Melor was watching them until they reached the bend that would take them out of sight. As she reached it, Renia gave him one last wave then turned to look ahead. Happa, quiet till then, ran up the path and barked at them in a frenzy until Melor's order silenced him. Renia ran the back of her fist across her eyes, and did not look back again.

The three riders cut north as directly as they could at a gentle trot, crossing Melor's fields first. Then they had to skirt a small wood as they kept to the edge of fields with summer crops in them – fields that would receive little attention at this time while spring crops were still being got in, so they could avoid being seen. In this way they covered five miles before they ever reached a public highway, and that was a northward-leading track from a group of villages some twenty miles south down the coast. If they were seen, it would appear that they had come from those villages. Kerin had been quite insistent on this part of the route; once again protecting Melor from people prepared to go to any lengths to track Kerin down.

The thought served to make Renia more nervous than she already was. Stealing a glance at Kerin, she saw him looking happier already now that he had started his journey, resumed his mission. He sat in his saddle in a manner quite unlike any other rider she had seen. Surely other people could not fail to see that too? She considered saying something, but it seemed equally likely that her nervousness would attract attention. She did not want that thrown back in her face if she ventured to criticize him. Best she keep her head down and her mouth shut.

'All right?' Kerin had noticed how anxious she was.

She nodded and was rewarded with a flash of a smile before a slight motion on the part of Vel, riding a few yards ahead, caught Kerin's attention. Travellers were coming their way. Before her eyes Kerin hunched his shoulders and rounded his back, completely transforming his appearance. She was caught between marvelling at his acting ability and trying to hide her own nerves, but the travellers who reached them minutes later were aware of neither, and passed by with the briefest of nods.

Half a mile later Kerin reverted to his normal posture. When they hit a stretch of open road he urged his horse forward to join Vel. Her brother passed some remark Renia could not hear, making Kerin roar with laughter. That was the first time he had laughed properly since they had known him. He was back in his element now, Renia decided; he might have planned and arranged endlessly, but *doing* was the thing that made him happy. She felt very alone, in spite of the company of the two men. To them it might be the start of a longed-for adventure; all she could envision was their exciting dream turning into a nightmare. She wished she was braver, desperately afraid she would be a handicap to them on this trip; but then she had already been braver than she ever thought she could be, by having got this far.

They carried on along the north road all that day and half the next before coming to a major crossroads. This was the furthest Renia and Vel had been on this road; usually they went west here, taking sheep to market at the fair town of Eppett. This time they were to carry on northwards and eastwards, down into the forest that they could see stretching before them, and on to the distant silvery ribbon of the river beyond. They would follow that down to Greatharbour.

By the evening of that second day they were deep in the forest when they found a glade, set up camp for the night, and rolled exhausted into their blankets.

oOo

Kerin woke suddenly. Instinct told him to keep absolutely still while he listened for whatever might have roused him. Not far off, perhaps ten feet away, he could hear movement. He risked opening his eyes carefully, and found the pre-dawn light so faint that his eyes were already adjusted to it, allowing him to make out two shadowy figures hunched over the packs. He moved his head slightly; now he could make out the shapes of both Renia and Vel still asleep on the far side of the burnt-out fire.

He watched and listened a little longer, to see if anyone else seemed to be with the two figures, but could detect nothing. Mentally he cursed himself for not thinking to keep any kind of guard; but two men should be manageable. Besides, they would all make so much noise that it would wake Vel, and then they would be evenly matched. All the time Kerin was thinking, he was cautiously freeing his hand from the blanket and reaching next to him for his sword. But the damned thing was evading his search.

Behind him he heard the *shnick!* of a blade being unsheathed; in a flash he was up and free from his bedding and facing his assailant. A dark figure loomed, the half-light glancing dully from the sword he held.

'I think this may be what you were looking for, friend. I recommend you keep quite still and make no noise.' The voice was no more than a whisper; Kerin could only stare wordlessly at his weapon in the other man's hand. More figures materialized out of the darkness beyond the armed man and passed Kerin to go into the camp. One of them stumbled and cursed quietly as he went; a cry and a scuffle proved that it had been sufficient to wake Vel.

Kerin took his chance to lunge at the man who had his sword while he was distracted in an effort to wrestle it off him. There was a brief struggle until someone yelled 'Stop!' and a lantern, previously dimmed, was flipped open. The man

bearing it held it so that it lit a swarthy-faced youth who held
Renia by shoulder and wrist, twisting until she dropped her
knife with a cry of pain. She continued to struggle until the
lamp-bearer stepped up to take the knife and held it against her
throat. She stiffened and shut her eyes as if she expected him
to cut her throat there and then, eyes popping open again in
surprise when she found he had not. Kerin had not feared that;
they would be dead already if that had been the robbers' plan.
He did start when the youth freed Renia's wrist and he saw the
dark glistening of blood on it; but the youth shook his hand
and sucked at his fingers, indicating that he was the one cut.
He followed that by rubbing at his shin; clearly Renia had
inflicted a painful kick there too. The grip he maintained on
her with his other arm was, understandably, none too gentle.

Having seen what was happening from the start,
Kerin knew that their lives were not in danger. These men
were robbers, not cut-throats. But that was quite bad enough.
They could do nothing but watch – Vel in particular glaring
with thinly veiled fury – as the half-dozen men packed and
removed everything but the clothes the three travellers stood
up in. With the mounts saddled and packed the men rode, two
to a horse, away up the north road. The forest quickly
swallowed them up.

It had grown lighter in the time it took for all this to
happen; by now they could make out each other's faces.
Brother and sister looked to Kerin who stood with a heavy
frown on his brow, thinking. He put his hand to his chest while
he did so; fortunately the robbers had been so excited by three
good horses and all the money they found in the packs, they
had not thought to search them personally. The Eagle was safe
in a pouch around his neck.

He came to a decision. 'Come on. We go north, to
one of the settlements we saw on the map last night.'

'What for?' Vel questioned. 'We can't do much

without money and transport. Shouldn't we try to catch them?'

Kerin shook his head resolutely. 'It would be a waste of time. We cannot match their pace if they've put the horses to a gallop. They are long gone, and our stuff will soon be sold on and scattered. No, we will have to risk it… risk selling the Eagle.'

'No!' Renia's forceful protest came as a surprise even to her. 'You mustn't sell it! You have to keep that with you. You can't sell it.'

'Then how do you propose we get to Ilmaen? Sprout wings and fly?' He rounded on her with such a show of temper that she flinched. Kerin was angry because he knew it was a huge risk; and if his planning had been better it would not be necessary. He knew at once that he had alarmed her, snapping at her like that, but compounding his error with anger only served to make him more obdurate. With an effort he regained his temper sufficiently to pass Vel his jacket, but as he looked around for anything else that had not been taken, he noticed Renia was barefoot.

'Damnation! I think they've taken your boots.'

'I know. I... I was going to try riding in my bare feet today.'

'What?'

'I couldn't feel the stirrups properly. I thought it might make Bluey quicker if he read my signals better. My boots were in my pack. Please don't shout at me again.' Her face crumpled and she hid it in her hands as she started to cry.

'Those men...' she managed to say. 'I thought they were Lemno's, come to kill us.'

Vel was still wrestling himself into his jacket. The look he gave Kerin as he did so made it clear that he had better do something, and quick, but his stubbornness had already crumbled.

'Renia, forgive me. I shouted at you because I was angry with myself. You did everything right; it was me that got it wrong.'

She nodded acceptance of the apology, but could not stop crying. He came to her and took her hands in his; tears streaked the road dust on her face. He pulled his shirt cuff into his palm and mopped up the worst of the mess. 'Since they have our water bottles, too, we will have to have a dew wash this morning. Come on. I will show you how.'

oOo

They set out the way the robbers had gone; north along the forest track. It was tough on Renia's feet, the track being composed largely of leaf litter, twigs and stones, so the pace was not fast. By midday they broke out of the forest to see the road continue down and across the plain. They could see smoke rising from some settlements, the ones they had seen on the map, about ten miles ahead. They could reach there by mid-afternoon – but what then? Tired and hungry from no breakfast and no lunch, they rested for a while in the shade at the edge of the forest before continuing.

The pace was at least faster over the plain. The road was a stone and dirt track here, bordered by stubbly grass in which Renia could walk more comfortably. The men walked there with her to keep her company, and because even with boots the potholed road was none too comfortable. To distract them all from their hunger and discomfort, Vel related a tale of rivalry between two fishing boats at their old village. The captains were so determined to beat each other into harbour with their catches and get the better price that they jammed each other into the narrow harbour entrance. They argued about whose fault it was, then about who was going to be towed out first (for neither vessel could go forward as they were). The dispute had continued for three days, and neither captain would let his men disembark lest the other ship's crew should be sent over to sabotage his vessel. Meanwhile the crews secretly developed a rota system for sneaking ashore to see their families, and men who had been hurling abuse at each other earlier in the day could be found having a sing-song together at the inn each evening.

Vel had reached the part where they finally docked and opened the holds and men passed out at the stench of the rotting cargoes, when there was a sudden metallic snap. Renia cried out and stumbled forward, giving a scream of pain as she fell awkwardly. When they hurried to help her up they realized she had stepped into a poacher's trap: the snap they had heard was it being sprung, slamming rusting teeth deep into the flesh of her ankle. Renia's momentum had carried her forward still until the stake holding the trap's chain took up the slack, yanking the trap back. Thus the teeth had torn her leg even more.

Vel found the stake and pulled it free; carefully they forced the jaws open and off her leg. It was clear to both men that her injury would need attention beyond their skills.

'It looks worse than it is,' Kerin lied reassuringly to Renia. 'If it hurts it is usually a good sign.' In fact it was bleeding steadily with no sign of letting up, and he feared for the tendon; the teeth had cut close to it at the back.

'Do you have a petticoat on?' he asked her. A slow shake of the head was her reply but Vel had followed Kerin's reasoning and stood up to wrestle off his jacket and remove his shirt. It was cotton while Kerin's was wool. Not ideal by any means, but they had nothing else. As Vel tore it into strips Kerin bound Renia's leg with it. When they had finished, they tried to get her to stand, but she could not bear any weight. It was probably the tendon, if not a broken bone. Sitting her down again, they moved off to discuss the problem.

'She cannot walk, and she cannot stay here. We need some way to carry her,' said Kerin in a low voice. The pair of them looked around; the plain of grass stretched in all directions, unbroken by trees or even a decent-sized bush. There was nothing they could use to make a hurdle.

'Nothing here,' Vel pointed out unnecessarily. 'Should I go back to the forest and get some stuff together?'

'No. By the time you returned and we had something built, it would be nightfall. That is not a wound that can wait a day and a half to be treated. Surely there will be a physician at the settlements ahead.' Kerin dearly hoped so; he began to doubt if anything would go right for them today.

'It wants cleaning up properly if nothing else.' agreed Vel. 'And a shirt with two days' travel grime on it is not the best bandage. If that wound should start to turn nasty...' Then he had an idea, picked up his discarded jacket and started yanking at the arms to check the stitching. He seemed dissatisfied, and motioned Kerin to take his own jacket off. Kerin did, and it received the same treatment; this time the jacket received Vel's approval.

'Look, if we take your jacket, and the rest of my shirt like this...'

Quarter of an hour later they had improvised a sling chair and were carrying Renia in it. It was tough going; she was slightly built but she was also tall. They had to change sides often to balance the strain, and interposed periods where Renia hopped along with their support. The settlements they had seen still felt a long way off.

Chapter 8 – The Three Villages

Late that afternoon, Jesral Ty'r Plethu reached the Low Plains crossroads, flung her basket down and scrambled up on to the great square marker stone, resting her bare feet gratefully on the coolness of its shady side. Then she examined her blisters and cuts.

'*Peli!*' she declared out loud. She should have cut across the lower downs; they were no worse to walk on in bare feet, probably better, and certainly quicker. But some corner of her mind had held her to the road in the hope of hailing a cart going her way.

Her family had always been poor, but this was the first winter she had been completely without shoes. Between December and April she had been out as little as possible, and then it had only been short distances she could manage with her feet wrapped in rags. Today she had been all round the Three Villages with her wares, but if she had known what the roads were like she would not have bothered. She must have found every sharp stone and foot-twisting rock on the Low Plains today, and what money she had taken would not even cover the week's food, so shoes were out of the question.

'Sod these roads!' Life was not currently being kind to her. Walking such a distance had been no trial at all in years gone by; she recalled the time she had spent living in Ilmaen, walking barefoot beside her wagon many a time with the travelling show. She had been happy in Ilmaen; it was hard to remember why she had ever come back. Well, for a while she had been happy. Perhaps she should have stuck it out after all. Time had dimmed the memories, but surely she had been better off over there than she was here. At least there she had not had to live on the charity of blackguards, which to be frank was the best she could call her cousins.

It had occurred to her that sitting down like this
would only make her feet feel ten times worse when she set
out again, but having sat down she intended to stay put for at
least ten minutes. If she was lucky, a cart *might* pass that was
going her way. With a pout on her lips she raised her gaze
from her suffering feet and surveyed the roads with dark
amber eyes. Her pout deepened. Nothing useful, damn it, just
some travellers on foot coming out of the High Plains to the
south. As she watched them she realized there was something
strange about their movements, but could not make out what it
might be. She felt for the knife at her belt in case they meant
trouble: once sure of it she settled back on the milestone to let
them get near enough for her to see them properly. She hooked
wayward strands of her long copper-coloured hair behind her
ears.

The reason they looked strange was because the party
of three consisted of two men helping a girl with a bandaged
leg, which she could barely put down as she walked. She
favoured it so much, the two men were almost carrying her
every other step. One of them was very tall, the other was very
good-looking. When they drew level with her, the handsome
one called out.

'By your leave, ma'am, we need help. My friend has
hurt her leg. Is there a physician or an apothecary at the village
ahead?'

An accent there she did not recognize, but it
definitely said 'foreign' to her. She shook her head. 'No, nor at
the other villages nearby. There's my mother… she knows
herb-lore and some doctoring. She will need paying, though.'
She eyed their condition suspiciously: no packs, the tall blond
man with no shirt under his jacket, and the handsome man's
jacket knocked completely out of shape. They looked like
beggars – but there again, they didn't. They didn't look
downtrodden, merely fit to drop – above all the girl. Forgetting
her own feet until she landed on them, Jesral jumped off the

milestone.

'She'd better sit down before she falls down.' The two men helped the girl over to the stone, and she sat down gratefully. She noticed Jesral's basket, saw an apple in it and eyed it hungrily. Jesral took the hint and offered it to her. The girl took two huge bites, saw the looks on the faces of the other two, and passed it to the tall one. He did not want to take it from her, but she made him; he took his share and passed it on to the other man, who finished it off. The whole process took about twelve seconds.

'Dear Lord! When did you last eat?'

'Last night,' the handsome one replied. 'We were robbed early this morning, and then this lady hurt her leg this afternoon – caught it in a poacher's trap.' Jesral winced, picturing what that would do.

'We'd pay for food and aid,' he continued, 'but right now we have no money. However, Renia must have attention to her leg, and soon. Can this be done?'

Well, thought Jesral, can it? Close to she could tell the quality of his trousers, even if they did look as though they had seen some wear and tear. Careful topstitching like that cost a lot in anyone's money. Federinese style, she was sure. And she knew now what was wrong about his accent; he spoke mostly town grammar, but with some local dialect mixed in. As if he'd learnt it as the former and now tried to imitate the latter. In all probability then, a well-off, well-educated Federinese who was down on his luck.

Being short, she was on eye level with his chin, and could see there was something round his neck, hidden under his clothes. That could mean he was lying through his teeth about their finances; but all three of them would have to be consummate liars for her not to read something, some signal between them, if deceit were planned.

'We can't give you something for nothing, friend,' she warned him, 'we're too poor for that. You'd have to contribute somehow. Can you labour? We have some summer planting left to do.'

'Of course.'

'Would five days apiece seem reasonable?' His willingness to compromise faltered. She wasn't surprised; it wasn't remotely reasonable. He looked to his tall companion, who looked at the girl who sat miserably before them. There were enough resemblances for Jesral to see the two of them were brother and sister. The look the tall man threw back at the handsome one was a plea.

The nod of agreement was curt and he was tight-lipped as he gave it; the handsome one was not happy at being forced into this. But he spoke to the injured girl and helped her up with great gentleness, he and his friend supporting her between them as before.

'Ten minutes and we're there,' Jesral assured them all.

oOo

The place where she lived was not much more than a shanty town; her mother's shack was almost palatial in this setting, with three separate rooms at the back that served as bedrooms. Unfortunately Jesral's mother was not in the best frame of mind this afternoon. The sight of her girl's paltry takings was hardly enough to encourage charity in her. But she brusquely ordered the men to sit Renia down because, money or no money, that ankle had to be put to rights.

Jesral was set to fetch this and that from around the

house, the handsome one to pump water; the other man sat with his sister. Jesral's mother undid the bandage firmly but gently, having to soak off the last layers to get to the wound. 'Yeughh!' remarked Jesral when she saw it. Renia's ankle was a mess of dried blood and puckered wound edges. The girl stared at it as though it was not part of herself – until Jesral's mother manipulated her foot and pulled and poked at the edges of the wounds, making them bleed afresh.

'This can be mended,' she pronounced. 'The tendon is partly cut, but will mend whole, and no bones are broken. But those wounds will not close on their own. They will have to be stitched.'

'Oh, God.' Jesral was not possessed of a strong stomach. Her mother rounded on her.

'Jesral, go away. You're worse than useless at times like this. Go and make dinner or something – and take one of these men with you. I don't want you all cluttering up the room while I work. I'll need one of you, though. You, what's your name?' She tapped the handsome one on the knee, since he'd put his foot on the bench near her. She tapped a second time, harder, to show she wanted his grubby boots off her furniture, thank you.

'Roker, Ma'am. Roker O'Connell.'

'Sit there, Roker.' To Jesral's surprise, he did so; to his surprise as well, from the look on his face. She judged his mood and her mother's and deemed it wise to leave quickly before anyone blamed her for anything. Cramming some vegetables and several scoops of barley into a cooking pot, she seized it in one hand and the tall man's arm in the other, and left.

This man, the one Roker called Vel (if those were their true names), had been more spoken to than speaking himself; so far Roker had done most of the talking. He had let little slip. It was not certain that they had anything to hide, but Jesral's intuition was nagging quietly at her. Perhaps there was more to be gained from talking to Vel on his own.

'We cook communally here,' she told him conversationally. 'It saves fuel, and means there's one building we can all go to that's warm.' A Godsend, this last winter. 'Same as they do in Federin, I think.' She looked at him and he realized the last statement was a question. No doubting that he judged his answer cautiously, from the look she got back.

'I wouldn't know,' he said haltingly.

'Oh, you're not Federinese then?'

'No, Mhrydaineg.'

'But Roker is from Federin?' Again the turning of the thoughts in his mind was plain on his features.

'Yes.'

'He has the look of a gentleman,' she observed.

'Yes…' Oh, my, she thought, now we've struck true. Look at him trying to steer *that* away from trouble.

'He's a soldier. A captain.'

'I see.' And what I see is a man who doesn't want to let anything slip, beyond the story the three of you have already put together, she concluded.

She judged it wise to let it drop now, so as not to push him too far. They had crossed the grassy area in the centre of the village, on to which her house opened, to mount the steps of the long low cookhouse on the far side. She pushed the door open and led Vel over to a table, acutely conscious that the building, pre-catastrophe brick and concrete, had been shoddily patched up. Even the furniture had seen better days – like most of the village.

'This was the generator house once. Lots of people think they're a myth, like machines that flew, but not me. The machinery's long gone now but look, you can see where the cables went to the lights in the ceiling.'

'Yeah, I see. There used to be a steam engine running the hammer in our village smithy, but everyone thought the man who ran it was crazy. When he died, no one could make it work. They tried, but it blew up the smithy and they had to build a new one. That was generations ago, of course.'

He was looking around now, noticing himself watched by some of the others there, and their topic of conversation would be frowned on if they were overheard. Damn it, she had to make him fit in.

'Two pints of water in here, please. The pump's over there.' He took the cookpots she thrust at him and did as he was bidden, which took him away from her neighbours. She smiled an acknowledgement at them, which they returned before going back to their cooking.

Before long he was back beside her with the pot. He stood and watched her, but when she glanced up, it was clear his mind was somewhere else.

'She'll be fine. My mother's good,' Jesral reassured him. He nodded hastily, to make it clear he had no doubt of that.

'I was wondering how long until she's recovered enough to travel?'

'I couldn't say, you'd need to ask that of Mother.'
Men in a hurry, she added to her list of known facts.

She was finished; the vegetables were crammed
tightly into the cookpot, enough to simmer down with the
liquid and some borrowed seasoning to make a nice thick
broth in an hour or so. They joined the neighbours at the
fireplace, making introductions and finding a hook above the
fire for the pot. The risk remained of the others asking too
many questions of him; this time she resolved it by sending
him out for more firewood. Ideas were seeding themselves in
her mind, some interesting possibilities…

They were still setting seed while she gossiped, but
she was distracted from them by a tap on her shoulder. She
turned to find her cousin Alessi, looking very pleased with
himself. He drew her away from the others.

'Greetings, Jez. And how has your day been?'

'Interesting.' Oh, if he only knew the half of it…
'And yours?'

'Profitable!' he announced. Not good for someone
else, then – but live and let live. They had to eat, after all.

'Profitable, and serendipitous. I have something I
think you'll be very pleased to see; consider it a gift from me.'
From behind his back, he produced a pair of boots.

'Oh!' Her heart leapt; decent boots too, well made
and meant for a woman's feet.

'They might be a little big, but you can stuff the toes
with rags,' he said magnanimously. 'Ah, we've had a great
day, Jez. Three horses, all their tack, three nice full purses…'

She was inspecting the boots, the wonderful boots,

when her joy crashed around her. All of a sudden she could see only one set of feet that would fit in them. She clutched the boots to her chest and stared at Alessi as he enumerated their haul. It took some time before her expression penetrated his enthusiasm.

'...the oilcloths will do to patch that leak at the back of the house and... what? Jez, what's the matter?'

'A girl with light brown hair. Two men, one tall, one good-looking.'

'That was them. But how did you...'

She dropped the boots and put her head in her hands.

'Oh, God! They're here, Alessi! They're in our house!'

'What!' He went a colour she had never seen on anyone, ever before. 'Oh, *Uffern*!'

'What were you thinking of? Robbing people on their way *to* the Three Villages!'

'They were in the forest, up on the High Plains. How were we to know where they were going?'

She struggled to get her thoughts straight. There had to be a way out of this.

'If the gang gets out of the village tonight, they may not see you. You'll need to move the horses without being seen and...' A horrible thought struck her, and her gaze dropped to the boots. 'You've just walked across the square with those in your hand, haven't you?'

'Ah, but I put my head round the door at your

mother's and saw no one but her, so they can't have seen them.'

'Except the one outside here, picking up wood for the fire. You didn't even notice him, did you?' She sprinted for the door and pulled it open; he was not at the woodpile. There he was, his back to her, going into Mother's house. She slammed the door shut.

'Oh, Lord.... You have to find Talenn, Alessi. You have to give it all back.'

'Tal'll never agree to that,' he said doubtfully.

'Well, his only other options now are running or the assizes, unless he's prepared to consider murder. I suggest you point that out to him.'

He shrugged desperately. 'I'll find him. That's all I can promise.' He contemplated using the front door, decided the back was better, and slipped out through the storeroom.

She ran back to the house, the incriminating boots under her arm, straightened up and went in, with never a clue as to what she might say to them. Her mother turned from tidying the table; no one else was to be seen.

'Where are they?'

'In your bedroom, checking on the girl. Puts up with the whole business of stitching her leg up, then she faints, poor soul. But she's set to mend well now. That tall chap looked out of sorts when he came in…'

'Mother, we have trouble.'

'Oh. What kind?'

'The Talenn and Alessi kind.' She set the boots on the table. 'Guess whose.' It did not take her mother long.

'Lord and His angels. My brother bred idiots! And the tall chap knows they're here?'

'And that they know us. Alessi thinks Talenn will baulk at giving the stuff back. What do we do, Mother?'

'I have no idea. I can't find the knife I left on the table, so I think it safe to say they intend to make a fight of it. It strikes me this Roker would be trouble even without a weapon.'

'At least we can use these to show good faith.' Jesral took up the boots again, not without a pang at the thought of giving them back.

The opening of the bedroom door made them turn. Her mother had been right about the knife; it was in Roker's hand. The two men shut the door behind them and stood there.

Jesral moved first. She went up to Vel and handed him his sister's boots. His look reproached her, questioned her, and she knew she should say something, but for once words wouldn't come. The best she could manage was a silent dialogue of apology with her eyes; and his acknowledged it, even if they did not accept it.

'And the rest?'

No such look in Roker's eyes. He asked the question of both her and her mother, who folded her arms and met his accusing stare.

'You'll get it. They're my nephews; they'll do as I tell them or regret it. I should probably apologize for them, but I'm not going to. This is not an easy place to make a living.

They try to do their best by us – sad effort though it is. But I doubt they'll come back here now.'

'So where do we find them?'

'Ioni's place. Near the stables. Shall we go and resolve this?'

'One thing, with respect, Ma'am. They may be your family but they are not honourable men. They didn't scruple to threaten Renia's life while robbing us. I would not leave her alone for that option to be tried again.'

'Oh! I have an idea.' Jesral turned to Roker. 'Alessi didn't see you or Renia when he called in earlier, did he?'

No, nor we him, or you would be short of a cousin by now.'

'And you didn't tell him how badly she's hurt?' Jesral asked of her mother.

'It didn't come up,' she replied.

'Then this should work. Mother, can you stay with Renia like Roker asked? If any of the men should come in, tell them she's not here any more.'

'What do you intend?' Roker spoke with all the trust of a man with nothing but a fox to guard his chickens.

'We have to call their bluff. Please, I know these people. Let me speak, back me up, and we may all get out of this in one piece.'

The men looked at each other, came to a silent agreement.

'Fine,' said Vel, 'but I'd still appreciate a knife if you have one, Ma'am.'

Jesral's mother strode across the room and pulled one out of a drawer. 'Jesral, you tell your cousins if they come back bleeding they're not stepping across my threshold. And the others can whistle if they think I'll doctor them when they get cut up.'

oOo

All six of the gang were at Ioni's; they rose and spread out across the room as Jesral pushed open the door without ceremony. Roker moved to her left as she crossed to face the tallest of the gang; Vel stayed back to guard the door.

'We don't want any trouble, Jez,' the man in front of her said. Her response was to set her mouth more firmly and raise her head more. Her eyes smouldered at him.

'Neither do they, Talenn. Give them what's theirs and they'll go. That's an end to it.'

'Can't do that, Jez.'

'Can't or won't?'

'If you must, won't. They should cut their losses and go. They can fight if they want, but at three to one I don't give them much chance.'

She looked baffled for a moment. 'Three to one? Someone's maths is wrong.' Her knife was magically in her hand. 'I make it two to one.'

He swung the astonished look from her to his brother; Alessi was suddenly looking elsewhere. He turned it back on her.

'Why, Jez? Why would you betray family? What have they promised you?'

'They've promised me nothing. Not like you Talenn, you've promised me so much. But what you promised wasn't to be trapped in a life like this, forever scraping an existence from other people's misery. It's always been, "After this one we'll settle down, buy into a trade, make something of ourselves." Never seems to happen, though.'

'You have to give us time!'

'How long do you need? I've been back a year; you were at this when I left three years before that. It's not going to happen. Anyway, now your hand's being forced. While we've been talking the girl's been saddling up. She and a spare mount are well on the way to the town militia by now. With a change of horses she should ride fast, and unless one of these two gets away in time to catch up with her on the other horse, I dare say she'll be back with the militia before nightfall.'

Another of the gang on the right started forward, the swarthy youth who had got a kick and a cut from Renia.

'M'neighbours said the girl at your place was hurt. She can't ride that fast.'

Vel stepped into his path.

'We'll buy her all the time she needs,' he promised darkly.

A flurry of movement on the left and suddenly Talenn and another were disarmed, nursing stinging wrists as knife and sword skittered across the wooden floor. Roker retrieved the sword and shrugged cold reason at Talenn.

'We could carry on with this. Better if we took the

time to call her back, surely?'

A look at the others was enough for Talenn to see the fight had gone out of them. He nodded to them; weapons were dropped and slid across the floor to Roker. The lost packs reappeared from under beds and out of cupboards.

'Vel, get to the stables, saddle up and fetch her back. The rest of you can take a seat while I check everything's here. Be sure you are comfortable: this could take some time.'

Chapter 9 – The Eagle Gets a New Owner

Kerin's diligent stocktaking gave Vel ample time to visit the stable and make it look as if all the horses had been out and returned. 'Stable' was an ambitious description; it had probably been a byre once, though no animals other than their three horses looked to have been there in some time. A small sack of oats and an old half-barrel of water had been found somewhere. Vel made sure the horses ate the rest of the sack of oats before any of the gang thought to retrieve it, and then using the back alley to ensure he wasn't seen, he went to check on his sister.

She was sleeping, but fitfully, Jesral's mother told him, and encouraged him to let her be. She expressed no opinion on the outcome of the visit to Ioni's house. He sat and fretted a little longer, reckoning in his mind the time it should have taken him to have saddled up, caught up to Renia on her non-existent journey, returned and seen to the horses; he was about to head back to Ioni's when he was saved the effort by the arrival of the others. Alessi and two of the gang sheepishly carried the packs in – mindful that Kerin was on their tails; they stowed them where Jesral told them to and quickly disappeared.

Jesral scowled after them, arms folded, till the door shut behind them; she allowed enough time to be sure they were well away before letting go her breath and dropping on to a stool, radiating relief.

'Well, what now, Roker? I recall setting a meal to cook about two hours ago. Is it safe for us to go and get it?'

Kerin glanced at Vel.

'All's well in the stable. The tack was all there, and I've moved the horses round as if they have been out. The lie should hold for tonight, at least.'

'Maybe, but I am reluctant to leave the packs alone. No reason for you not to get a meal in you though,' he told Jesral and her mother. 'Vel, you go too.'

Vel did, and settled at a communal table with them, but only for as long as it took him to eat. He got two more big bowls of broth and some of the rough bread, and made his apologies in order to take food to his sister and Kerin.

Renia slept still; she was curled up, covers wrapped around her head so that just her face showed, the curve of her eyelashes dark against her pale face. Vel quietly pulled the door to, covered her bowl and set it on the stove lest she wake hungry later. Kerin had eagerly started on the contents of his own bowl as soon as Vel had handed it to him: by the time Vel turned from the stove he was almost finished.

Vel felt dog-tired, but it was the kind of sleepless weariness that demanded some other activity. He drew the map out of his pack and sat at the kitchen table to review their journey. His mind tried to fathom how Renia's injury might affect the routes they chose and how fast they could travel, and where to replan their halts to allow more resting time for her. Both terrain and distances swam in his head. He couldn't calculate properly. This had been the wrong task to pick when he was tired; but it had to be done.

Kerin's empty bowl clinked gently on the table. Kerin's hand rested beside it as he leant over, studying what Vel was doing for a few moments.

'I want to go on tomorrow as planned. I want to leave

Renia here.'

'I see.'

'No, you don't,' Kerin sighed, turned and sat on the table edge. 'Vel, I grant you Renia could cope with the journey; she proved that this afternoon. When Jesral's mother stitched her up, she never made a sound. She could do it. I'm certain she would do it given the chance – but she shouldn't. That wound is deep and if it gets infected, it could be very nasty. Here, Jesral's mother can look after it properly until it's mended. I can't wait that long. What she's far-seen proves we need to hurry if we are to save Jastur. I trust her judgment that he's still alive. But Lemno must surely be involved still and, if he has anything to say about it, imprisonment will be a temporary state of affairs for Jastur. To keep him locked away cannot be enough. This vendetta runs deep in him; old history, reasons that even I don't fully understand. But I do know that he wants us dead, and now he has the power to do it. He thinks – please Heaven, he still thinks! – he's succeeded with me. If he succeeds with Jastur, Ilmaen will fall apart. The truth is, my friend, I seriously doubt I can keep my country together if I can't save Jastur.

'I must go on, and Renia must stay. That leaves you in the middle. I know the extent of the favour I'm asking of you, to leave Renia here and come with me. I've been loath to admit it, but I can't do this alone. Two men will attract less attention than one. If we are cornered, two swords are better than one. These are some of my reasons – the selfish ones – but I'm also worried about Renia. It matters so much to her that she should come, but this whole business plainly scares her half to death. It could be that she feels obliged to come, in some way. Perhaps this is the greatest kindness we could do her.' He sighed and frowned at Vel. 'Now you must speak your mind. Can you do what I ask?'

Kerin had to know full well that he had Vel boxed in,

finishing as he had on Renia's needs and fears. A low blow; but given the urgency, Vel couldn't blame him for trying it. 'You test a new citizen's loyalty awfully hard,' he said ruefully.

'I know, and I'm truly sorry. I wouldn't ask this of you if I didn't have to.'

'This is some turnabout.' Vel got up to pace the floor; Kerin watched him. 'It's only a matter of weeks since you tried to persuade me not to come, on the grounds that it was too dangerous. Now you ask me to come for near enough the same reason.'

Kerin said nothing.

'All right,' Vel conceded reluctantly, 'I'll come. So, we're to start out tomorrow as planned?' Kerin confirmed it with a nod. 'Well then, do you mind if I make a suggestion? That we leave early without letting Renia know. If we're gone, we're gone, there's not much she can do about it then.'

'I agree. Oh, this has been a long day. You'd best get to bed. We hold watches from now on, mark you. I'll not be caught again as we were this morning. I can manage five hours. I'll call you then.'

oOo

Kerin woke Vel as agreed, proffering a mug of beer that Jesral had brought while he slept; a strange drink for that hour of night but welcome nonetheless. While Kerin sank into the luxury of a warm bed, Vel settled on the bench near the stove, hoping in vain to find some remnants of warmth. Kerin, aware of their hostess's limited resources, had let it go out some time ago.

An hour or so later, the combination of the growing cold and the beer created an urge that would not be denied.

Vel unlatched the door slowly, conscious of the noise it could make and not wanting to alarm the others in the house. He crept out to the privy at the rear.

As soon as he stepped back on to the porch, he had a sense of something wrong. A movement just missed, a noise not quite heard. He stood still, watching and listening, but it eluded him. He waited a few moments more, but could detect no movement nearby. A thought struck him, and he re-entered the house with care.

His eyes grew quickly accustomed to the dark inside, and he could see nothing out of place, but the doubt still nagged at him. Some instinct told him to go back outside. He stood on the porch and listened. Then, far off, he heard the stable door being opened – the rattle of its dangling chain made the sound distinctive.

He ran back in and threw open the door to Kerin's room. To his credit, Kerin was already out of bed.

'They're after the horses again! Come on!'

They hurried back into the main room where they tore their swords off the packs – and the door to Jesral's room flew open and she flew out, knife in hand. When she saw only them she ignored the fact that they had their blades up and ready to strike, and rubbed the sleep out of her eyes with her free hand.

'Lord above, what are you two playing at?'

'Keep your voice down. Your cousins are trying for the horses again.'

'Oh, please stop reminding me I'm related to them. You'll want to sneak up on them from the back alley. Come on.'

She led the way. They had no lamp, but the waning

moon lit their path; this was fortunate, for as Vel had learned earlier the alley was largely composed of muddy gullies, privies and midden heaps. The smell was not sweet. They stepped carefully over and around the obstacles until they were at the back of the stables. Between the ill-fitting slats they could make out lamplight inside.

Somewhere across the far side of the village a dog barked, and a voice harshly silenced it. The air seemed still and yet charged, as though any sound would carry through it as sharp as a whiplash. Jesral's breathing and the sound of her careful steps came to Vel's ears with painful clarity; yet he knew she couldn't try any harder than she did to be silent. His own breathing was set to deafen him.

Jesral beckoned them, and they followed her towards the stable front. Kerin caught her arm before she got there and overtook her, so as to be the first out into the street. He readied his blade and stepped forward, expecting to meet at least one lookout. There was no one there.

He went on to the stable door, the others following; he repeated the procedure.

Still no one. The others joined him; all they could see was Bluey standing in his stall, saddled and patient in the lamplight, his tail idly flicking at the insects the light had attracted. Beyond the horse were sounds of something being dragged and the laboured breathing of the person dragging it. Kerin stepped forward silently and brought up the blade he had lowered. Ready, Vel judged, to close the open space before his adversary had time to react. Then the person moved into the lamplight.

It was Renia. She came backwards, holding the stall edge for support with one hand and pulling some wooden mounting steps with the other. She had to hop along on her good leg. Kerin cast Vel a look; in an instant it was apparent what had happened. She had overheard the two of them talking earlier and now she was either going home or, more likely, trying to prove she could go on.

Kerin beckoned the others in and set his sword point down quietly; he crouched down behind it and rested his hands on the handgrip, watching her.

When Renia turned to mount up she saw them. For an instant she looked startled, but straight away she composed herself. Throwing the reins up on to the pommel and using Bluey for support, she hopped up the steps, leant across the saddle and swung her bad leg over. It looked uncomfortable, but she managed it. Then she shuffled herself upright, put her good foot in the stirrup and coaxed Bluey out of his stall. Turning him so that she could look down on the others, she stated tersely, 'You're not doing me a kindness. Leaving me isn't an option. I should only have to follow.'

'You heard us talking.' Kerin made it a statement rather than a question.

'My leg kept me awake. It's quite all right now,' she added hurriedly, lest he should seize on her comment. 'I'm going,' she declared again, tenacity written all over her.

'Clearly my plan to leave you causes more hurt than the leg does. It was meant to help, not hurt you. Nonetheless, I apologize.' At Kerin's words she relaxed her stiff shoulders and stared at him; first in astonishment at his apology, then doubt, then conviction that his remorse was genuine.

'I know your reasons for leaving without me,' Renia said. 'You haven't hurt me.' The emphasis was on the word 'you', and a sideways look towards Vel hinted at who would bear most of the blame for the intended deception. 'I *am* going,' she insisted.

'Yes, you are going.' Kerin stood up and sheathed his sword. 'I can see it would be impossible to leave you behind.'

Vel shrugged and stepped up to Bluey's head.

'All right, you're going. Now will you get off this horse and let us go to bed?'

Renia let him help her down, but immediately shook off his hands and hopped unsteadily to the door. Kerin came to her rescue; his support she accepted. That fact was not lost on either man, and Kerin glanced at Vel, feeling guilty for putting him in the wrong. Vel just sighed it off and started to loosen Bluey's girth.

Renia remembered her mount and half turned to tend to him herself but Jesral shooed her off.

'Oh, get back to bed. We'll do it.'

oOo

Renia hopped and hobbled halfway back down the street before Kerin, exasperated, stopped and declared, 'This is ridiculous. Vel and Jesral will be done and back before us at this rate. Let me carry you the rest of the way.'

She tensed up as he reached out to pick her up.

'Won't I be too heavy?'

'Hardly, there's nothing of you. The way it's distributed could be a problem, though. You're all arms and legs.' She was still hesitant. 'That was a joke,' he added. Renia was off the ground and in his arms before she had a chance to protest any further. He bounced her into a comfortable hold and strode on. She had automatically hooked one arm round the back of his neck and now she was unsure what to do with the other. She did not need to worry, his grip was sure enough. Tentatively she laid her hand across his chest. It rested on the bag holding the Eagle; she moved it hurriedly to his shoulder.

He shifted her in his arms to redistribute the weight.

'What did I say? All arms and legs.'

Now she was contrite.

'I'm sorry. I know I'm being a nuisance. I don't mean to be, but I couldn't let you go without me. I *have* to come, though I can't explain why any better than I already have. There's something I have to do, something only I can do. I wish I knew what...'

Kerin had once thought it might be infatuation that made Renia so eager to travel with him, remembering how she had behaved towards him in the first few days of their acquaintance, before the existence of the Eagle had come out; but now she was stiff in his arms, even nodding with tiredness as she was. Politely keeping him at a distance, as best she could in the circumstances.

'You've made your point. You will not be left behind,' he reassured her. 'Can you open the door for me?'

Renia bent forward and fiddled the latch open; he pushed the door with his shoulder, set her down briefly to take up the lamp and light it. Up again, with the lamp in Renia's hand; latch and shoulder again at the door to her room. There was no sign of Jesral's mother having got up. Either she was a very sound sleeper, or she had more sense than to run around in the small hours of the night like the rest of them.

Kerin put Renia down carefully and took the lamp off her to set it by the side of the bed.

'Are you hungry?' he asked. 'We brought some broth back earlier, it can soon be heated up on that little stove.'

'I'm so famished I'll have it cold. Can I also have the willow bark powder from my pack? It'll help me sleep.'

He fetched both for her. Renia measured out a portion of the powdered bark, took it dry with a grimace and washed it down with the broth. When she had finished it all she set the bowl down and started to settle under the covers.

'A moment longer, Renia, if you don't mind?' Kerin sat on the edge of her bed as she pushed herself up on her elbows, looking at him enquiringly.

'You felt sure there was a reason why you should make this journey. I think I may know what it is. This.' He opened the pouch, lifted the Eagle out and laid it on the blanket. In the dim room it caught the lamplight, shadow and sparkle. 'This marks me. Hardly anyone will know my face, but they will know this. We were lucky today, stopped by opportunists who grabbed the first things they saw. In Ilmaen, if my enemies find me with the Eagle on me, it will mean death for me, and possibly all of us. From this point on I dare not carry it any more; yet on the other hand it must be safe and within my reach. It is the only proof of my identity I have, until we find someone who knows me well enough to recognize me. That is true of very few people, in the highest circles in Ilmaen, and you know who one of them is. If Lemno gets hold of me first, only the Eagle can prevent me from being laughed at all the way to the gallows as a pretender. So I need you to keep it safe for me, and to put it in the right hands if fate dictates.'

Renia stared at the Eagle. He guessed she still associated it with her vision and shrank from the idea of even touching it. 'Must I? It wants to be with you, not me,' she said, faltering as she realized that made no sense.

'It's a piece of metal, Renia. It can't *want* anything.'

'You know I'm not good at explaining these things, but there's something about it that's keeping you safe… like a talisman. I'm scared that if you give it to me you'll lose that protection. Can't you keep it in your pack?'

'If they suspect me, they will search my pack. It's still a risk even if you have it, I know. In extremity it's better that you should run with it and leave me than that we should both be caught. But I need to have it near enough to back up my story with the right people, and if you have it I know exactly where it is all the time. Your hands are the safest. Please, Renia.'

He was determined, that was plain. And she was too tired to argue any more tonight.

'Very well. But promise me, the moment it's safe to do so, you'll take it back. The very moment.'

'I promise.' He took off the pouch, put the Eagle back in it, hung it round her neck. She lay down again, testing the weight of it. If it were possible, she looked more unhappy about this than she had about being left behind. It couldn't be helped.

He closed the door gently behind him as he left. Turning around to find someone beside him, he only just checked the instinctive reaction that could have broken an innocent neck; Jesral blocked his path. How long she had been there he could only guess; he had not heard her come into the house. 'Is Vel back?' he whispered, recovering himself. She shook her head. Her face was pale and serious-looking. She held one finger to her lips and beckoned him to follow her to the settle on the far side of the room. Once seated there, as far away as they could get from the bedrooms, she leant forward to speak in a whisper.

'I know about the Eagle.'

'What are you talking about?' His voice was all innocence.

'The walls are paper-thin in this house. A lesson you seem slow to learn, sir.'

His expression turned dangerous, and she had the sense to fear it. She took a deep breath and continued carefully.

'Perhaps you found his body and took it off him. Perhaps you *are* him. Either way you should know that – how shall I say it? – unofficial but highly authorized people from Ilmaen have been in the village in the last few weeks and are after both the Eagle and its owner. And given the conversation I just overheard, sir, I'd say I'm looking at the owner now.'

'Supposing your assumption is right, it could be a very dangerous piece of information for you to hold.' Despite the implicit threat in Kerin's words she returned his gaze calmly; so she still had some other card to play. It must be a good one, for her to take such a risk.

'I know. What choice would the real owner have other than to kill me? The only other option I can think of would be for him to take me along on his journey too. Now that would be difficult if I was unwilling to go – but very easy if I was willing. After all, by going along freely I'd be making myself part of the conspiracy. I couldn't betray the Eagle's owner without condemning myself.'

'The Eagle's owner might simply choose to leave you here,' he observed. She thought that one through.

'Mmm, possibly. But it's risky. He knows my family are thieves and vagabonds. We might conspire to turn him in for money. Worse still, if I am in fact to be trusted and he leaves me behind, he'd face the risk that his trail has already been picked up and could lead to me. He knows they are not fussy about how they get information out of people, so even if he could face the risk to himself, could his conscience stand the pricking?'

'You assume he has a conscience.' Kerin gave her a half smile, so cold he could sense the fear rise in her. *I have misread him!* he could see her thinking. He softened the look, sure now that she understood the limits of his tolerance. 'But he would be either a coward or a fool to signpost his route with corpses.'

Her sigh was one of relief. 'I think so too.'

'Remember, there are three in my party who must make the decision,' he said, dropping all pretence now.

'No, you will decide. You know you will.' A moment's thought, and he acknowledged this. 'Now we really must get to bed,' she concluded. 'And if I am not dead in mine by the morning, I'll assume I should pack.'

Chapter 10 – Gwrach

To Kerin's relief, neither of his companions said anything next morning against the latest change in plan. Renia simply listened and nodded as though she would have done the same thing in his place, and limped away to finalize the packing with Jesral. Vel looked troubled; understandably, with three changes forced on him in one night. Perhaps he was beginning to doubt Kerin's command of the situation. Kerin wouldn't have blamed him but cold reason assured him that, given the change in their circumstances, he had made the right decisions.

It was not exactly a pre-dawn start that they managed, but they were up before most of the village. There was a further delay while Kerin rigged up a blanket saddle for Jesral behind Vel, who followed the procedure with a keen eye; Jesral paid it only desultory attention, something else preoccupying her.

'Ready to try it?' Kerin asked. She started, nodded, tucked her hair behind both ears and gave him her full attention. Vel mounted up and proffered his hand; Kerin stood by to offer her a boost. She worked out which hand and foot to offer to each of them, then used the crupper to help straighten herself up. There was some awkwardness while she worked out where to hold on to Vel, and how tightly, given her natural curves. Some chemistry was at work between them. Kerin almost smiled, but was sobered by the thought that anything coming of it would only complicate things.

'That'll be fine,' she pronounced, swinging her leg back over and sliding down the horse's flank. 'Time I said my goodbyes.'

Vel watched her go. 'How far do we trust her?' he

asked when he was sure she was out of earshot.

'We do not. One of us watches her at all times, until we have good reason to do otherwise.' The frown that drew from Vel was expressive, as was the glance backwards at his sword, slung mercenary-fashion on his shoulder at present. Kerin signed Vel to unstrap it and demonstrated how to hitch it to the pommel so that it was within his reach, but not Jesral's. Vel's frown remained in place.

oOo

They set out. Jesral, keen to contribute, showed them an ancient lane which led north-east to the river. In places it was so overgrown they had to use their swords, but it cut several hours off their journey time along the more-travelled but less direct main road.

Midday brought them to a hay meadow on a bend of the river. The lower half of it had been recently mown, leading up from the river bank; young bullocks grazed at the far end, and with fresh grass and water to hand were unlikely to need any attention from their owner. The other half was still untouched meadow, colourful with spring flowers. There was no farmstead on this side of the river, so it must be an extension of the farmlands on the other bank. There a field of young grain stretched away, making anyone's approach easily visible. In unspoken agreement they made their rest halt there.

Renia slid carefully off Bluey, anxious not to jar her ankle; Vel was quickly there to ease her down. Kerin and Jesral tethered the horses with plenty of slack to let them make the most of the fresh grass; the animals needed no prompting. The riders chose a spot near the bank, and food and drink were distributed.

Afterwards, Vel persuaded Renia to sit and soak her leg in the river before he redressed it. As soon as he mentioned changing the dressing Jesral decided to go for a walk across the meadow.

Her mother had done a neat job, and it was not so terrible a sight as it had been the day before. The flow of the river, icy cold and clear, plainly soothed it. 'Ten minutes,' Vel ordered, and Renia raised no objection. With a glance to Kerin, Vel confirmed that he was off to keep an eye on Jesral. Kerin acknowledged it, and began to pack up their things.

He finished before the others returned, so joined Renia on the bank. It was warm in the sun and he lay flat out, jacket off and hands beneath his head, eyes half lidded. Through them he could see Renia moving her leg against the cooling water and glancing round at him. Her hand went briefly to the pouch around her neck and away again. She sat gazing across the river.

Coarse grass stems stabbing him in the neck made Kerin sit up eventually. Renia was still staring at the far bank.

'Look at that field over there,' she said. 'Doesn't it look just like the sea? Light greeny-grey, and lighter still where the wind puts waves into it.'

'It is very like the sea,' he agreed.

'I miss it already, even though we'll see it again soon.'

'Ilmaen will be tough for you then. It takes weeks to cross, and everywhere we need to go is inland.' He sat beside her, relishing how still and calm it felt in this place, despite the waves running through the grain, the flow of the river. He could hear the faint whisper of the wind all around and a skylark rejoicing in springtime far above them. He could just see it, seeming impossibly high to be singing so loud; the sound grew louder still as the bird swooped back down to earth. It stopped abruptly as it landed, deep among the meadow flowers. With no song and an empty field before him, it was possible to imagine he was utterly alone in the world.

The sudden sense of isolation unnerved Kerin; then Renia spoke and the sensation was gone as fast as it had arrived.

'Jez is keen to help us with the language,' Renia told him. 'Have you heard her speak Ilmaenese yet?'

I have. She has a good grasp, though a strange accent, to my ears. Probably best for you to get tutoring from us both; her accent may be safer than mine is nowadays.'

'She thinks we'll find it strange over there. Is Ilmaen so very different from Mhrydain?'

'In many ways it is very like. In others it could hardly be more different. Every province has its own style – in houses, clothes, food – and the people differ vastly, from of the colour of their skin to the traditions and beliefs they hold, having come originally from lands far to the north, east and south. I wager you will pick up more in your first two days there than I could tell you in a month.'

'But you must tell me something more! What about this thing with surnames… how changing the way you say it changes what you mean?'

'Well, that is to do with family and inheritance. Jastur and I are Hedsarollen; that is, the children of Sarol; but Jastur alone is Hed Sarol, the heir of Sarol. You will hear Hed used a lot, and also Lak. The words strictly mean male kin and female kin, but they are mostly used about children. Think of it as a narrower version of the system in Mhrydain, where you are a member of a clan, a wider community; Jesral Ty'r Plethu is Jesral of the Plethu house, the same as most of her village are.

So, let's imagine your Ilmaenese father was called Horben, Vel would be Velohim Hed Horben – two separate words and the emphasis on Hed, to signify he is the eldest son and heir. Both of you – and any other siblings if you had them – would collectively be known as Hedhorbennen – and you yourself would be Renia Lakhorben, a younger daughter. I had a sister, and she was Jastia Laksarol...'

He lost the thread of what he was saying. Old memories welled up, memories that hurt.

'I'm sorry,' Renia apologized, on hearing him use the past tense. His attention was recaptured.

'She died a long time ago.'

'But you still miss her.'

'I do. She was much younger than Jastur and I - eight years younger than me; our mother was ill for a long time when I was very young. Then all in the space of a year she seemed better and was expecting a baby. But it was too much for her. She died having Jastia.

'You know how good sometimes comes out of bad? That was Jastia. She was so lovely, inside and out. In looks she was a little doll, all dark hair and big dark eyes; in character she was such a serious child, five going on fifty we used to say. I never saw her squabble over a toy, or lose her temper, and she always seemed to understand how the world worked much better than I. People would do things that baffled me; but she always made sense of them.

'There was fever in Ilmaen about five years ago. Jastia caught it, and she died. She was six.'

'Oh, Kerin…' He gave a wan smile.

'I took it badly. Worse than when Mother died even. But Father – it was the end of the world for him. He always had to be tough with Jastur and me – we were the men of the family, it was for our own good. So he spent all his affection on Jastia. The last time I saw him, he was a shell of a man though I failed to realize it at the time, too busy wallowing in my own misery. That was why he sent us to Federin, Jastur and me, so that we would not fall prey to the fever as well – and rather than thank him for his care, I hated him for it.'

He looked over to see how she reacted to such a confession, and felt the hairs on his neck rise. Without thinking he made the sign for a reincarnationist's dearest wish: rebirth with loved ones. He looked down at his hands, fingers interlaced against his chest, and laughed in astonishment.

'What is it?' she asked.

'You. That look was Jastia to the core. You must have had the same nurse when you were babies,' he joked, trying to recover his lost composure.

'I doubt ordinary children over there would have a nurse. If it's like Mhrydain, I was probably tied to the kitchen table by my baby reins, and fed raisins soaked in gin if I was gripey.'

He had to laugh. 'I had no idea Melor had such inventive ways of raising you! We grew up in very different worlds, didn't we? Ah, here come the other two. Up with you now.'

oOo

They made good use of the journey, practising their Ilmaenese as they rode, while at some of their rest stops Kerin and Vel would work on their sword skills. Since Jesral was helping with the language tutoring, brother and sister had a tutor each, and could then swap to try their skills out on a fresh set of ears. The surprise was how much Vel grasped, considering he had, by Melor's reckoning, only been five when he had left Ilmaen. Renia's progress was not so fast; but she was dogged about it.

Jesral had given Kerin a severe dressing down for having so far taught them what she called 'Court Ilmaenese', when the object was to blend into ordinary society. Now they used common speech patterns, and the one who struggled with that was Kerin.

They were two days out from the Three Villages and it was late morning. Kerin and Renia were riding level. The bridleway, for it was not big enough to be called a road, passed along a causeway above the marshy river valley. The river traced a curve northwards here, but the causeway passed straight to the east across the marsh to meet the river where it looped back again. The height of the rushes in the surrounding marsh lessened the feeling of being up high, and fair weather and birdsong made the place seem less lonely than a lowering sky would have done. They had seen no sign of anyone tending the causeway and Kerin suspected it was of ancient building. Beneath the horses' hooves long-forgotten earthworks must be standing up to the elements, impervious to Nature's onslaughts.

Behind Kerin and Renia, Vel and Jesral rode together. Renia, Kerin noticed, was trying to follow what Jesral was saying – she was berating Vel for something; Kerin had not picked up all the conversation. Renia was doing too much listening and not enough speaking. He had made her ask questions, to keep her talking; occasionally he was forced to do the asking if she dried up or, as now, became distracted.

'So, Renia. Tell me what you're going to do when we

get to Ilmaen.'

She answered hesitantly, trying to remember the future tense.

'I'll buy some clothes, so that I'll look like an Ilmaenese girl. And… we'll find where... where your brother stays – I don't know the right word there – and we'll... show him the way out?'

'We'll rescue him.' Kerin gave her the phrase she was looking for.

'Mmm. We'll rescue Jastur. You'll do it, and Vel and I will help you, because Vel is brave and I'm your friend.' She must have got the words for 'brave' and 'friend' from Jesral, he had not taught her them yet. He certainly would not have taught her the emphasis she put on 'friend' – unwittingly, he trusted, unless this was Jesral's idea of a joke.

'No, no. You must remember where the emphasis comes on words in Ilmaenese,' he explained in Mhrydaineg. 'It makes a difference; you can get yourself into real trouble if you don't pay attention. You wanted to say 'tamaani', 'friend', yes? You put the emphasis on the last syllable, and it should have been on the second, 'ta*maa*ni'. Swapping the emphasis to other syllables is used on a lot of words to alter the meaning, slightly twisting the sense in which the word is used.'

'Ta*maa*ni. Tama*ni* . What did I say, then?'

'Emphasis on the end implies a more intimate meaning. You said, 'Vel is brave, and I'm your bed-mate.'

She coloured up, cheeks flaming. 'Better you say it to me than to someone else on the other side of the water.' He returned to Ilmaenese again. 'Try it once more.'

'Vel is brave, and I am embarrassed,' she said in a tiny voice. He laughed at that, but not unkindly.

As they rode on he turned to easy things she should know by now, listing the months and numbers up to one hundred, to give her a chance to get over her mistake. After a while she fell silent again, staring off into the middle distance as the horses plodded, and a look of vacancy came over her face. Kerin thought she must have forgotten the next numbers, but when she spoke it was in Mhrydaineg again.

'East and south – a long way away,' she said, head tilted as though she was listening.

'Use Ilmaenese,' he instructed, but she did not.

'He's in the east, where the mountains start.' She cocked her head the other way, and looked confused. 'Somewhere high up, but... deep? That doesn't make sense.'

Kerin suddenly grasped that she was somehow in communication with Jastur. He took her reins and stopped Bluey, waiting for her to say something else to give him more clues.

Vel and Jesral caught up with them. 'What's wrong with her?' Jesral asked.

'Quiet, Jesral,' Kerin snapped. 'Renia, this place... tell me more about it.'

'He knows it so well, he's not thinking of the name. It's rocky and barren, and there's rock all around him – and no windows. It's cramped and so dark there. But there's something else wrong too. There's food on the floor for him, but he won't eat; it makes him worse. He's trapped and desperate and he can't see any way out. No, you can't give up, not now! Please, hold on a little longer.'

Kerin grabbed her arm when he saw that this last was spoken to Jastur and not to himself, but she said no more. Her eyelids fluttered and she started out of her thrall.

'Oh. It was him, wasn't it?' she asked, as though he had been party to both sides of her dialogue.

'You tell me! But something is wrong with him. What is it?'

She shrugged worriedly. 'I don't know. I just caught a snatch of his thoughts. He felt so weak, so desperate! He thinks there's something wrong with the food and he daren't eat it. Could they be trying to poison or drug him?'

'Never mind that, Ren,' pointed out Vel. 'Do we still have enough time to reach him?'

She never got a chance to answer, as Jesral distracted them by starting to sob. The terrified expression on her face was all too familiar to Renia and Vel.

'That is not normal! That is definitely not normal.' Jesral slid quickly off Vel's horse and tried to tug her pack from Renia's baggage roll, but it was too firmly strapped on. She backed away, crossing herself, throwing a look containing both apology and fear at Renia.

'Give me my stuff. I don't want anything to do with this. I'm sorry, but no. No.' When they did nothing she decided not to wait, turned and stumbled back the way they had come, glancing over her shoulder at them as if she thought they would try and stop her.

'Hell's teeth!' Vel shortened his reins to turn his horse after her. Kerin stayed him.

'Best go on foot or you'll panic her,' he advised, so

Vel did.

oOo

Jesral quickened her already fast pace when she heard his steps approaching, determinedly not looking back. Vel was well able to keep up.

'Jez,' he called when he was about three feet behind her. She spun round so suddenly it stopped him in his tracks.

'Just stay away from me, d'you hear?' she hissed. Her eyes blazed with anger and fear. He put up both palms to indicate assent, but he was not going to give up.

'Jez, it's all right. I just want to talk.'

'Don't waste your breath,' was her recommendation as she carried on walking. He quickly caught her up and grabbed one wrist.

She snatched it away.

'Don't touch me!'

'Jez, this is mad…'

Her panicky laughter cut him off.

'*This* is mad?' she asked incredulously. 'She's having a conversation with someone in a cave somewhere, while you two expect her to ask questions of him, and you think walking away from the three of you is mad? *You're* the ones who are mad – or bad. I'm not staying to work out which.'

'Oh, come on, you've been with us for days, you know that's not the case.'

'Normal people don't do that,' she said, looking back at Renia who still sat on Bluey, making no effort to move either toward or away from them. She looked very ordinary, sitting there. 'Oh, God. You believe her, too… believe she really can hear someone.' Jesral did not know what to think any more, struggling to keep a grip on her sanity. 'She was pleased I joined you. She said so.' She couldn't drag her eyes away from Renia. 'Mama used to tell me: Be a good girl. If you aren't the *gwrachod* will know, and they'll come and take you away because they'll think you're one of them.'

'She's not a *gwrach*, Jez.' There was warning, as well as understanding, in Vel's voice. He had heard the same himself as a child. In front of him, he realized, was someone who had dismissed such stories long ago, but now found herself fearing they were true after all, and wondering how far caught up in one she was.

This was not a thing you could reason with people about. Past experience had shown him that. So he saved his strength.

'Look,' said Vel with a sigh, 'we aren't going to make you come with us. If you want to go back, that's fine. You can take your stuff, and enough food to get you home.'

'You won't get me round by pretending to be nice.' Jesral said it without much force, but it was still enough to irritate Vel.

'Then let's assume you're driving me beyond endurance and I'm contemplating throttling you and throwing you in the marsh. Would you care to make a decision? I think it's plain other lives than yours depend on us getting on with this journey.'

'Vel, I'm sorry! I don't know what I'm saying at the moment, I'm too scared.'

'Well, don't be. Ren can't hurt you; she wouldn't hurt you. None of us would. You've got to come back for your stuff anyway.'

She followed him back apprehensively. Vel laid a hand on Renia's pack, and turned to Jesral as she trailed up behind him.

'Well, should I unload your stuff?'

She glanced at the other two. Kerin still held Bluey's reins; the stare he gave her held a mixture of anger and contempt. Renia's gaze was steady and unaccusing, and she was careful not to lean over Jesral when she spoke.

'It doesn't matter, Jez. Everyone feels this way when they first find out.' Kerin made a little movement; Renia looked at him, challenging him to deny that he had felt something. He could not hold the stare for long.

Impulsively, Jesral steeled herself and seized Renia's skirt.

'How do you do it?'

Renia shrugged.

'I don't know. It just happens.'

'Often?'

'Not very often.'

'What do you want me to do?' Jesral finally asked of her. The question startled Renia and she looked to the others, but only she could answer it.

'I want you not to be scared of me,' she said simply.

'I want you to go with us, if that's what you choose.'

Jesral wrestled with the alternatives, looked up at Renia again.

'If you don't do this, I won't be scared of you,' she reasoned. 'You've just done it, and you say you don't do it often, so I'll take my chances. I'll go on with you.'

Renia looked relieved; so did Vel. Jesral looked as though she was still not sure it was the right move, but managed a nervous smile. Kerin's relief was inward, and partial; this momentary alarm might be over, but its cause, the news about Jastur, had renewed the tension in him. He wore his most intense frown.

'Repeat what you can remember again, Renia,' he said, so she did as accurately as she could. He nodded as she spoke, eyes shut, trying to fit the facts together – high, but deep, where the mountains start, in utter windowless dark...

He opened his eyes.

'Karn. He is in Karn.'

And even with an army, he could not see how he could ever get his brother out of Karn.

Chapter 11 – Keep Your Enemies Close

The estuary of the river opened out before them the next day like a great lake; the Pool, it was called. At its south-eastern end lay Greatharbour, where the depth of the water was sufficient to berth long-haul ships of substantial draft.

They wore their best clothes to ride into town, so that they would not look too out of place on horses. First thing to be done was to visit the Harbour Control House, where notices of sailings were posted outside. Kerin fretted as he scanned the lists; he wanted to sail within a set time, or he was ready to go to another port. By good fortune, there was a ship sailing late next morning for Beloin, well to the east along Ilmaen's coast. But the *Dawn Wind* could not carry livestock, so as they had suspected they would have to sell the horses before they left.

They found an inn with stables and took two rooms. With the horses settled in, brushed down and fed and watered, they went to sit in the girls' room and discussed their next steps.

Kerin drew them a map of Ilmaen on a large scrap of cloth, laid it on the floor between the two beds and outlined the route to Karn. He sat back afterwards, frowning. 'This will be a long journey east, almost to the borders, and then we must go far south to find allies. Even with Melor's generosity and the price of the horses, we may stretch our funds to breaking point.' Jesral looked at the map on the floor and read into his words what he did not say; another passage to pay, another mouth to feed, for as long as it took them. She said nothing though, overawed by yesterday's experience and more cautious now with these people.

'What if you and I work our passage to Ilmaen?' suggested Vel. The idea appealed to Kerin.

'You think they would take us on?'

'Well, I know my way round a ship, and you have all your eyes, arms and legs, and that's more than many they get to choose from. But it would need to seem as though we can only scrape together enough to pay the women's passage.'

Kerin nodded.

'So, ladies, are you agreeable?' They both looked surprised to be consulted. Jesral shrugged absently while Renia asked, 'Who goes to book the berths, and who takes the horses to market?'

'We should leave the horses until we know we have the berths. I'd prefer to do it tomorrow morning. We've paid for stabling till then – and I like to cover contingencies, when I can. As to our passage, best if the captain meets those of us with least experience of the sea, then he can't say he didn't see the worst.' Kerin turned to Jesral and said bluntly, 'I presume that's you and me.'

They dressed down and left the Ty'r Athres to wait; Vel started a game of patience with himself, while Renia settled to some repair work on her good wool skirt. Jesral and Kerin's shadows passed the window of the ground-floor room as they walked down the road. Renia craned to watch them, but the glass was too opaque for her to see anything. She sat back, resisting the urge to scratch at her ankle where the skin was mending itchily, lest Vel saw.

oOo

The quayside was huge, and in total chaos. Cranes and people and packages filled it. It took Jesral and Kerin half an hour to find the *Dawn Wind*, and then they had to try and make themselves heard by her captain over the din. He was busy bellowing out orders in Ilmaenese as his main cargo was loaded – regardless of the nationality of the dockers and sailors he was shouting at.

'Oi! Go gently there! That stuff's fragile. And be shiftin' that loose rope, sailor, 'fore someone falls over it.'

'Ho, captain!' Kerin had a reasonable voice on him, but the other man must have been deaf, or else standing where the wind did not carry the sound. A second try did no good either, and as Kerin stepped back to yell again he bumped into one of the stevedores loading goods into the hold. No damage was done; indeed, the man was helpful enough to tap the captain on the shoulder as he passed and point out the two new arrivals.

He hung over the bulwark and peered at them in none too friendly a fashion.

'Wha' d'you want?'

'There're ourselves and two friends, a brother and sister. We men seek working passage as crew, and the women will pay for their berths. We saw you offered both options on your bill at the Control House.'

'Aye, we have both, but you don't get guest berths as passage-workers. I'm runnin' a business here. You and your friend would be in the crew's quarters.'

'Understood.'

'Hmm. Any experience?'

'Myself, I can only offer a keen will and a strong body, but my friend's sailed extensively, mostly trawling for fish further down the coast.'

'Hmm. Hmm. You appreciate that passage-workin' means you do as you're told twelve hours a day, get three meals and a hammock each for eight hours – and you stay out of the guest berths?' Kerin nodded as humbly as he could, but looked a little offended. The captain peered at him closely.

'You're Ilmaenese, yes? Wha's the purpose to your voyagin'?'

'I'm Ilmaenese, but my friends aren't. They go to Ilmaen to find their fortune. Me – I go to be home again, I suppose. I've been away too long, I need to see the old country.' Kerin flashed his disarming smile at the captain, and nearly received one in return, if the man was capable of smiling.

'Well, well.' Kerin could see he had his doubts, but was apparently weakening. The captain was measuring up Jesral now, though she was unaware of it; since Kerin did not seem to need any input from her in this discussion, she was looking around the quayside. The captain made the mistake, in the light of what Kerin had said, of interpreting this as a sign that she did not understand Ilmaenese.

'One thing though – how're your womenfolk for travellin'? You know how ladies are. I don't want any wailin' about the passage bein' too rough... or any, er, mess in the cabins.'

'We're paying good money for the berth, sir. If I wish to be sick I shall be, and at my own leisure. And you won't get any wailing from me. A good tongue-lashing, maybe, if it's your navigating that's bringing us a rough passage...'

The captain stared at Jesral, then roared with laughter. She stood with arms folded and an angry pout on her face.

'Enough! Enough with the black looks! You have your berths, and your workin' passage. For the berths it's cash on embarcation. I want you on board and stowed away afore eleven tomorrow. And don't you be late! I'll miss your money sooner than miss the tide.'

He was out of sight before they could say goodbye, and before Jesral had got all she had to say offloaded. The grin Kerin wore was as good a reason as any for her to thump him hard on the arm.

oOo

In a proper bed again for the first time in days, Jesral still found it hard to sleep that night. She tossed and turned, sighing to herself.

'Jez?' A match was struck, and the lamp blazed into life. She sat up. Renia was sitting up too, one knee pulled to her with hands clasped round it and her other, bandaged leg resting on the covers. The lamp's warm glow lit her face – which was worried-looking, as it almost always was.

'Sorry, Ren, I didn't mean to wake you.'

'No, I was awake anyway. I wanted to ask you a favour.'

'Yes?'

'In the morning, will you make sure Vel sells the horses to a trader who looks after his animals? You don't have to go to market with him or anything, just ask him. So it comes from you and not me.'

'Yes, of course. You're rather attached to Bluey, aren't you? But why not just ask your brother yourself?'

'I need to toughen up for this journey. They can't

keep making concessions to me, Jastur doesn't have time for that – but where Bluey's concerned, I'm not quite ready to be tough yet.'

'Mmm.' The mention of Jastur brought back unpleasant memories of yesterday for Jesral. She'd chosen her path but still wasn't comfortable with everything she was encountering on it. On the one hand, Renia had a power that let her far-see the business of the ruling classes; on the other, she was a soft-hearted soul who loved horses… Jesral shivered and sought to cover it.

'You're sure of where Kerin's brother is?' she asked.

Renia rested her chin on her knee. 'Kerin seems sure.' Her head came up again. 'I'm sorry, Jez, I know what I do has frightened you. It's not something I can help.'

'I gathered that. No, I got myself into this; my own fault, for eavesdropping and then letting Kerin know what I know. It seemed such a good chance to make an escape from the Three Villages. Oh, I don't know – is it just me, or do you find you jump on to life's ships, thinking you know where they're bound, only to find they're going somewhere completely different?'

'Yes, something like. Only life press-ganged me aboard this particular ship, and then handed me a chart that says *here be rocks* on every course I can steer.'

'I don't understand why you didn't take the chance to get out of this when you had it. We'd have taken you in; they'd have left you enough money to get by.'

'I couldn't. I'm needed, in some way – oh, damn it, I can't explain. I've tried so hard to make it make sense to them, but it clearly doesn't, not even to Vel. I'm not sure if I'll ever forgive him for being prepared to leave me behind.

'But they were right about going on; Kerin's urgency isn't misplaced. Time is running out for Jastur. Since that last vision, I have this picture of him stuck in my head, shadowy and far away. It's like something you can only see out of the corner of your eye, not if you look straight at it. But it's getting dimmer all the time, and I know that can't be good...'

'Please, can we talk about something else?' Jesral pleaded uncomfortably.

'Sorry, sorry.' Renia was silent for a while, searching for another, safer topic.

'What did you do, when you were in Ilmaen before?' she asked eventually.

Jesral brightened: 'I was with a travelling show. We went all round the country; toured the south in autumn and winter, north in spring and summer. I danced, I sang a bit, I did knife throwing, I juggled...'

'Oh, that must have been wonderful. You are lucky. I've always wanted to juggle.'

The other girl gave Renia a quizzical look. 'Why would you want to juggle, of all things?' Renia seemed not to have thought about it before, but it didn't take her long to reach a conclusion.

'I think it's because I can see no earthly use for it. There's a point to almost everything I do; it would be nice to do something pointless, just for its own sake. Just because I could.' She yawned and sighed deeply, and so did Jesral.

'Now you've set me off.'

'Best to give in to it. We're supposed to be up early. Goodnight, Jez.' Renia smiled, a genuine, friendly, trusting smile, before she blew the lamp out; Jesral heard her turn over and settle down. Her level breathing a few minutes later told Jesral she was already asleep.

Jesral's yawn had been a false hope. Sleep didn't seem any nearer. She mulled over the events of the last few days again.

It was strange how Renia really seemed to trust her, despite yesterday. She had thought that would be the final nail in her coffin with all of them. Kerin she had no illusions about, and Renia was right about Vel; her brother or not, he was Kerin's man now. She waited, patiently but joylessly, to be proved right. It was perhaps ten or fifteen minutes before the floorboards outside the room creaked ever so slightly. She shut her eyes and feigned sleep as the door opened a crack. The surveillance was a long one; so that would be Kerin. Vel had the decency to be brief, in his guilt over the deceit.

She wondered if she'd ever succeed in making those two trust her. Loyalty was a quality she prized, and she gave it very rarely these days. But yesterday, after she had got over the initial shock, had fixed something in her. These three were so close, sharing their dangerous secrets, and she had a sense that the bond between them would be unbreakable. That provoked something very like jealousy in her; a desire, not to break the bond, but to share in it. She felt as though Renia had seen it, and had offered her a welcome, even now, but that didn't fit with the way the others watched her. Yet they clearly trusted Renia's judgment, had faith in her vision, so surely they'd trust Renia to know if Jesral was a threat?

Perhaps she was being neurotic. Perhaps they only watched her because they were worried for her. It made little difference. She'd thrown in her lot with them, and that was it. Nothing else to worry about now but getting on the ship tomorrow.

And, of course, being sure to avoid a certain travelling show that would be touring the northern ports of Ilmaen at this time of year…

Chapter 12 – The Crossing

They were mindful of the captain's warning and careful not to
be late. Vel and Kerin took the horses off early to market,
returning with the proceeds in Internationals, and they split the
money four ways. Back into their travelling clothes then, and
the swords, the only remaining signs of affluence, were
wrapped in blankets and strapped to the girls' packs.

Vel persuaded a passing barrow boy to give Renia a
ride down to the fish market, so they arrived at the quayside
closer to breakfast than sailing time. It was busy there, but not
as busy as yesterday; nearly as many people came and went,
but there seemed to be more order, less bustle and hurry, for
yesterday the ships had been eager to catch the imminent tide.
Doubtless it would be busy again soon, as people took
advantage of today's late morning tide.

Jesral and Renia sat and waited outside a quayside inn
while the men took all four packs to the *Dawn Wind*. The
captain might not want the women to board until just before
sailing, as was the habit for passengers. However Vel was
soon back to carry Renia to the ship; it seemed the captain did
not concern himself with the usual practice.

The gangplank on to the ship came as a shock to
Jesral, for it was nothing more than a set of planks, barely two
feet wide, with cross timbers to give a foothold in the wet, and
no handrail. The nonchalant way Vel strode up it with Renia in
his arms did nothing to help because from where she stood,
Jesral could see it bow under their weight. Kerin followed and
they all disappeared on to the deck, lost to her sight beyond
the bulwark.

Jesral edged nearer the quayside and looked over it.
Grey-green water swirled sluggishly and menacingly, hinting

at strong currents dragging between the ship and the piles
below the quay. She backed off and the sick feeling it had
given her subsided a little. She tried again and got one foot on
the gangplank before a wave of fear hit her. She stood there,
eyes riveted to the side of the ship; it was too far away, and the
gangplank was too narrow. Her heart was racing, she could
feel it right up in her throat.

'Are you coming aboard?'

Vel's tone was impatient, but by the time she looked
up, he had worked out what the problem was and his
expression had changed to one of concern.

'I'm trying,' she informed him. He jumped on to the
gangplank, making her shudder, and came down it. She
backed off to let him on to the quayside.

'How did you get on the ship last time?' he asked.

'On a nice, solidly built gangplank, four feet wide,
with proper handrails.' She decided not to mention the added
assistance of two large shots of gin before boarding.

'I see. Well, what if I carry you up?'

'What if you don't?' she responded tersely. She
wasn't abandoning what little dignity this sorry situation had
left her.

'Then I'll go first and you can hold my hands for
balance.' She eyed the swirling water again, then Vel.

'Oh, dear… all right then.'

Vel took both of her hands and stepped backwards on
to the gangplank. 'No!' she squealed, pulling him back on to
the quay.

'What?'

'You might fall in, going backwards.' His grip on her hands tightened enough to hurt. 'Ow!'

'I'm going up.' He glowered at her. 'I'm going backwards. I'm going now. Are you coming, or shall I tell the others to come and wave you goodbye?'

That earned him a glower in return. 'You're a brute. I hate you and I'm only coming to keep Ren safe from you.' She gave him a half-hearted shove with the crushed fingers.

He led her as before, still going backwards himself, all reassurance now and encouraging her to keep looking at him and feel her way with her feet. At the top he stepped down on to the deck, and she rushed the last few steps after him as if she expected the gangplank to vanish now he was off it. She grabbed on to him as the nearest solid object.

'That wasn't too bad, was it?' The note in his voice was different now. It was a moment or two before she was aware of Kerin and Renia looking at her curiously, before she realized how tightly she was clinging to Vel. Jesral extricated herself – since it was his hold as much as hers – with what composure she could muster.

'No. Thank you for your help.' She took up her pack from the deck where it lay and stuck out her chin. 'Where's the cabin?'

oOo

Captain Harrat had given the women his own cabin, not the more basic accommodation that passengers normally used. Jesral's willingness to stand up to him had gained his respect and he seemed very taken with Renia, who was shy in most things but comfortable on board a ship. Kerin had at first thought the captain might suspect who he was and be sympathetic to their cause, but the colour of the man's language at Kerin's first crewing mistake suggested otherwise. He steeled himself against the abuse and tried again. Vel showed him how to bind his hands against the chafing of the ropes, the cause of his error. At last all was ready aboard and in the bright light of late morning the *Dawn Wind* cast off, swinging out into the Pool towards the open sea.

Kerin hauled on a rope as more sail was put on. His thoughts were elsewhere, fixed on Karn; south, and east, far across sea and land, where the mountains began. Granite Karn, a fortress second only to Lestar; a spur of rock riddled with passages, and cryptlike chambers tunnelled deep into its heart. It was like Lestar but without the beauty; more honest for that maybe, but no more forgiving. From his stays there as a child he knew the stories about it. Dark tales of oubliettes: chambers where people were thrown and then forgotten. His mind raged at the idea of Jastur abandoned in one of those, and his heart sickened. The puzzle of how to rescue him lay heavy on Kerin's mind, and no answers came to him.

Part of his malaise was genuine seasickness. No answers would occur to him while he had that to contend with, so instead he got on with the job in hand. There would be more than enough time between Beloin and Karn to formulate some ideas.

oOo

Jesral was suffering too, and once the ship was out of harbour Renia persuaded her up on deck. There were steps up to the poop deck from the captain's cabin. They were steep but with an effort Renia could manage them, and at least being up there kept her and Jesral out of everyone's way. It put them above even the helm deck where the captain now stood, so they sat against the deck rail and breathed in fresh air and had a good look around the ship.

The captain came and joined them from time to time, his brusqueness reserved now for his crew, it seemed. As they passed a dredger he explained how it cleared the main channel into harbour for deep-draught ships such as theirs. The two crews exchanged greetings before they quickly left the dredger behind.

Renia watched Kerin and Vel working side by side, Vel explaining the purpose of each order. Kerin looked a little ill, wearing a set expression on his face most of the time as he listened and worked. But occasionally he would smile, deriving some pleasure from the way the ship reacted to their efforts. The *Dawn Wind* flew through the water, quickly leaving Greatharbour behind. She ran with the wind and the tide past the vastness of Slope Island and the towering cliffs of its west coast.

The day wore on and the sun began to lower. Now cool, slow-moving cloud shadows mingled with the golden light crossing the deck. Beam and rope and sail strained to pull them ever eastwards. Full sail was on, and the wind steady; watchful sailing but little hard work. The low hum of conversation down on the main deck barely reached the poop. The girls sat there, soaking up the remaining afternoon warmth, undisturbed by the creaking of ropes above them and planks below. Even Jesral seemed to feel better, to the point of lying down and falling asleep on the bare planks.

While she slept the sun sank out of clear skies into the heavy grey bank that was building steadily to the west of them, and by the time she woke she had been in shadow for some time. The wind had become ragged and more biting. Renia prodded her and offered her a sweater; she already wore one herself, and held some more – the men's, brought up from the packs in the captain's cabin. The men had taken only the bare minimum with them into the cramped crew quarters where they were to rest.

Jesral pulled hers on and rubbed the sleep out of her eyes. Renia stared off to starboard, watching what she knew to be storm clouds. Jesral gazed that way too, unconcerned until she realized she could not see land anywhere. She looked all round, saw the coast hazy with distance behind them.

'It that Mhrydain? What's happening? I thought we were to follow the coast up, not cross the water yet.' It was plain any change of plan would serve to make Jesral nervous, and worse than that, the change was making the vessel pitch and roll more.

'Wind's changed,' Renia told her, as honestly as she could without alarming her. 'We're having to tack – zig-zag – to maintain our course.' She couldn't help staring off to starboard still. She tried to keep it hidden, but feared the expression on her face would tell Jesral there was more to it than just idle curiosity.

'May I join you, ladies?' Captain Harrat was as good as with them anyway, already on top of the steps from the helm deck, but Renia nodded him on with a shy smile. She gestured to the sky.

'The weather seems to be setting in. Could you get these to our friends?' She held up the sweaters, which the captain took. He looked at her closely.

'Your brother tells me you've sailed too. What d'you make of this?'

Renia frowned off to starboard, toyed with the idea of lying to protect Jesral but abandoned it. She didn't want to be dishonest with her, and the captain looked to be the sort of man who would just say how things stood anyway. 'I don't know these waters, but I know bad weather's building. Do you plan to make for a port?'

Harrat shook his head. 'No chance of that this side of the water. We need a port with a good nine feet of draught to be safe. That one back there,' he indicated a harbour almost directly behind the ship but too far away to be seen, 'has a bar you avoid at all but high tide, so we've missed that. The next nearest deep-draught ports are twenty miles off, either way.' He indicated up and down the coast, back the way they had come and where they had planned to go. 'That storm will hit before we make a port this side, and we'll be in its dangerous quadrant. But the wind's comin' round with it; my best option's to run south sooner than I expected and hope it stays north of us, so the eye passes behind us. It'll take us to landfall in Ilmaen further west than I'd hoped, but if we're fit to carry on we can take advantage of the tide stream on that side then. Safe to say, ladies, it'll be rough goin'. I'd be below and get everythin' put away, if I were you.'

Jesral, already a deeper shade of green than ought to be possible, seemed incapable of speaking. Renia set one hand on her arm reassuringly. 'Can we wait until it really turns? My friend gets sick below deck.'

'Ah, well, hmm. Try her on a drop of spirits when you do go, eh? You'll find some down there.'

Renia's forecasting was accurate. Yellow-grey clouds sped in over them from the west and headed for the eastern horizon, and the ragged gusty wind increased. Driving rain was not far behind, and sent the girls scurrying for their cabin. The storm lamps had already been lit all round the boat. Renia could see the rain sheeting down like a gauzy curtain in front of one as she and Jesral sought a firm footing on the slippery boards. They headed down into the cabin below and slid the hatch across tight.

Jesral had found a couple of blankets. One she wrapped herself in as she threw off her wet clothes, kicking them into a damp pile in one corner. She rubbed her hair dry with a corner of the rough fabric as she searched out a dry shirt from her pack, and was struggling into that as Renia followed suit with the other blanket. Jesral was still damp, and the shirt was sticking to her as she tried to get it on. 'God damn it, I'm no warmer!' she cursed. She checked the blanket, turned the driest side of it to her and wrapped herself up in it again.

Renia found the spirits, in a little cupboard over the bunk. She poured them both a tot of liquor and they huddled together, sipping until the shivering stopped.

'I feel sorry for the others,' Jesral remarked. 'They're still up on deck in the cold and wet doing the work, while we get the cabin, the spirits and the warm bed.'

'I feel bad about it too, but there's not much we could do up there. Since we have the good end of the bargain, let's make the most of it.' Renia threw off the blanket, slid into her dry shift and clambered under the covers.

Jesral heaved a deep sigh. 'I can't see me getting any sleep in this weather, even given a comfy bed – bless the captain's heart. No, I think you'd best take the inside, and leave me within reach of the bucket. Move over a bit.'

As they settled into the shared bed and, surprisingly, drifted off to sleep, Renia's thoughts about the captain were equally kind. She had seen him watching Kerin, was sure that he suspected his new deck hand's real identity, but felt no qualms about the man. She and Jesral had kept their mouths shut and he seemed the sort to keep his suspicions to himself and let other people go about their business. It was likely, from what he had said to her as they chatted on deck, that if his sympathies lay anywhere it was with their cause anyway. The weather might be against them, but she felt safer than at any time since they had started the journey.

oOo

Many hours later, as what should have been dawn drew near,
Kerin tied off the rope he had been set to hold and took a
moment to rest. A lull in the driving rain gave him a chance to
look back to the helm deck, and he saw the captain approach
his helmsman. The wheel was lashed now, and the helmsman
slumped over it more asleep than awake, just hanging on to it
for support, not to control it; he and another sailor had battled
to tie it down as the storm reached its head, more than an hour
since. The damned storm had followed them across, Vel had
explained earlier; luckily it had not overtaken them, but there
was no evidence of it lifting yet either. Kerin watched the
captain shake the helmsman and shout into his ear. Clearly the
sailor was being ordered to go down below for a rest and a bite
to eat, with the captain intending to cover the helm himself
until the next watch came on. The end of this one could only
be an hour or so away now. On their first watch they had
avoided the worst of the storm but then it had really taken hold
and the captain had called them back on deck early, so that
even the hardiest sailor among them was short on his sleep.
The crew had been wrestling the storm these many hours, and
were all exhausted.

After a check of the compass and the lashing, the
captain surveyed the rest of the ship through the endless rain.
He saw Kerin looking up, and signalled him to send the
boatswain over. On the helm deck high in the stern, the
captain was well placed to see any problem that arose. Just
enough sail was set to keep them off the lee shore, except for
one stubborn one that had jammed despite all their efforts to
wrench it free. It was catching every squall. The boatswain
worked his way over to the captain, clinging to handholds as
the ship rose and fell. Three of them were left hanging on
below the sail, trying to make out in the flashes of lightning
overhead what was jamming it. The storm was so severe it had
blown out most of the storm lamps.

After an urgent conversation with the captain, the boatswain worked his way back and they all four put their heads together. Vel, Kerin noticed, looked as exhausted as he felt.

'Captain reckons it's the strengthening ring,' yelled the boatswain, gesturing with his hands to demonstrate what he meant. 'A band of metal, eyes where each end of the band overlaps, and a rivet through the eyes. Rivet's worked loose, that's what's catching. We need someone up there to free the sail, but also to see if they can sort the rivet out to stop it catching again, at least till the storm's over.' He turned and selected a marlinspike from its fixing nearby and handed it to Vel. 'You're mast monkey, boy. And I want a man either side to hold that yard and canvas steady as they can, or the wind's liable to flip the yard and knock the mast monkey off. Get to it… and be careful.'

The slippery wetness of the rigging made it a slow climb, and the yard creaked and swung threateningly. Kerin took the same starboard rigging Vel was climbing, until he could grasp the yard itself and haul it aside, out of Vel's way. On the port rigging, the other crewman climbed level and braced the far end of the yard. Thankfully it had jammed close enough to where the rigging joined the mast that Vel didn't actually need to be on the mast or the yard to reach it. Eventually he made it to the nearest point, leant out from the rigging and yanked at the canvas; folds came free, and more crew below hauled in that section. Kerin could just see the rivet that had been snagging the sail; it looked to have almost worked its way out. Unless it was removed or knocked in, it would only catch again.

Vel used the pointed end of the marlinspike to try and tease the rivet free, but it was not going to come. Careful not to drop it, he reversed the spike and used the wider end as a hammer. When he was satisfied, he raised his arm; Kerin and the other crewman carefully released the yard and two men below them hauled it in again. To Kerin's relief the yard began to move, away from where he and the others clung to the rigging. None too soon: up here above the towering waves he could see the coastline by the lightning flashes. They had been driven within half a mile of it. He moved to the outside of the rigging to give Vel room to come down, and started his own slippery descent.

The ship suddenly started to turn sideways on to the waves and wind. The loose sail billowed and suddenly tightened as it filled and the ship heeled crazily, dropping the starboard side perilously close to the waves. In the rigging they were suddenly flung at an angle of forty-five degrees. Kerin hung on and tried to wind his feet further into the mesh of the rigging, but Vel was thrown just where Kerin's feet were scrabbling for a hold, and knocked them away. There was an audible crack, the yard hitting something, and Kerin winced despite his own struggle for safety; Vel had been within reach of the yard. Something fell silently past him then; the other crewman, he realized. Vel was still on the rigging, clinging to what for him was now a mesh floor, looking down at the fermenting sea only fifteen feet away.

Kerin's hands had binding on them still, or he would have gone overboard as fast as the other man. Even so, as he struggled to swing his feet back up into the rigging, he could feel the wet rope working its way inexorably out of his grip.

Vel was on the right side of the rigging for his own safety, but slightly below Kerin now, trying to see where the crewman had fallen. There was not four feet between them.

'Vel!' Kerin almost screamed in panic. 'I can't hold on!'

Still aghast at the other crewman's fate, Vel registered the grimace on Kerin's face and started working his way across, but Kerin could not measure his progress; he had to strain to keep his grip. His entire soaking weight had slid down past his knuckles, past the binding, and on to his fingertips. His arms, exhausted from hours of work, had barely been able to take him up the rigging just now; on the inside of his wrists, where tendons met flexor muscles, it felt as though someone was trying to rip everything out with red-hot pincers.

Kerin felt Vel's hand closing over his but it was too late; he slipped from Vel's grasp. He fell backwards into the boiling sea, incredibly slowly it seemed; he had time enough to see lightning illuminate a huge wave that struck the traitor sail, splintering the yardarm and the mast and dragging the canvas, rigging and Vel with it.

oOo

The sudden yaw of the ship tossed Jesral out of the bunk with a scream of terror. Renia, on the inside and half awake, just managed to hold herself in by jamming an arm and leg against the framework. It was her bad leg; she gave a scream to match Jesral's.

The ship heeled even further, with a great shudder and a noise that sounded like it was tearing in two. 'We're sinking!' Jesral screamed again, clutching the side of the bunk in near hysteria.

'No!' Renia yelled back, her mind made clear by the pain. She could hear shouting under the noise of the storm and the agonized groaning of timbers. 'Someone's trying to control her. You feel it?'

She clambered out of bed and nearly fell on top of Jesral, such was the tilt of the cabin floor. She found the blanket from last night, and wrapped it round both of them as they huddled together. But the floor was wet; in the wild twirling of the shadows thrown by the swinging lamp she could see the hatch was leaking. That scared her. She knew it had originally sealed well, so the stresses on the ship must be enormous. She swallowed her fright.

'I'm going to fix the hatch. Might have known it'd leak. There, the ship's straightening up again. We just hit a wave wrong, that's all.' She worked her way over to and up the steps, ankle still screaming at her; for lack of anything else, she used a piece of their discarded clothing to bung the leak. Voices shouting out on the helm deck carried through as she forced the hatch open then shut again on the bung. They carried as far as Jesral, still clutching the side of the bunk.

'Man overboard? That's what they said, didn't they? There's a man overboard, Renia!'

That was indeed what they had been shouting. Just yesterday afternoon, in warm bright sunlight, she had laughed as Captain Harrat and one of the off-watch crew had gone through a pantomime to illustrate this and other nautical Ilmaenese phrases. No sense in denying it, thought Renia, struggling with the hatch that continued to leak and her own feeling of rising panic.

'There's thirty crew on this boat, including our two. There's not much chance it's one of them.' That sounded harsh, as if the rest of the crew did not matter. More shouting from above, as she wrestled the hatch open and shut again, informed the captain that three were overboard now. That paid her back for her unfeeling comment. It shortened the odds frighteningly, if their men's shift was on.

Renia had a strange feeling as if she were being strangled. She caught at her neck and found the pouch the Eagle hung in had worked its way round to the back and the cord had twisted tight. She remembered what she had said about the Eagle to Kerin, about its power to protect him if he wore it, and began to feel real foreboding.

Chapter 13 – Taking It In Stages

When morning came and the storm had abated, charts could be properly checked. The bad weather had driven them farther west and closer to the coast of Ilmaen than they had realized. With their position re-established, Captain Harrat set a heading to the nearest deep-draft port, Wistram. The *Dawn Wind* limped towards it under the ragged remains of the storm clouds.

Jesral and Renia called the captain into the cabin as soon as he knocked. They were up and dressed, sitting on their bunk. He looked briefly round at the storm damage and their efforts to repair it. The floor was still wet and the clothes wedged in the hatch dripped slowly. Jesral looked drawn and sallow – ill as well as upset – and Renia knew her own face must show the apprehension she felt.

He came and stood before them, an expression of misery on his face. The stare Renia gave him was piercing before she shut her eyes and turned her head away.

'Which one?' she asked. He did not answer, and after a moment she looked back at him in bleak comprehension.

'Not both of them?' Harrat looked down in assent. At the edge of her vision she saw Jesral's face folding in distress. Strangely, Renia found she didn't even have the urge to cry. 'They can't both be gone. I'd know,' she said to herself, once out loud but repeatedly in her head.

Harrat sat beside them and quietly described what had happened. Renia found she wasn't listening, her mind filled with that single repetitive thought she couldn't shake. With an effort she granted the thought permission to exist, if it would only sit quietly in the back of her mind and let her focus on

what he was saying. She heard what he said now, she
understood it all, but it was just words to her, not real, not fact.
Not until he described the smashing of the yard and mast, and
how the rigging and sail must surely have trapped and
drowned the two men. It still wasn't belief, but the words
reached out and touched something; a thought older and more
compelling still.

'What did you say?' Harrat's voice broke in, startling
her. 'You said something, but I'm afraid I didn't hear,' he
added kindly. 'It sounded like "ropes" to me.'

'I'm sorry. My thoughts were wandering. Please go
on.'

He explained where they were in Ilmaen compared to
where they had intended to be, and offered to find some
lodgings in port for them, at his expense, for a few days while
they got over the shock and decided what to do next. Renia
heard herself accept the offer in a dull voice. Her
concentration was elsewhere, her 'thank you' as much a signal
for him to go away as any expression of gratitude.

She knew she was being rude. She heard Jesral
thanking him volubly as he left. And when she cried
afterwards Renia hugged her, understanding her grief but
feeling none of it.

They couldn't be gone. The thought just wouldn't be
dismissed.

oOo

The lodgings Harrat found them had thirty-five stairs. Jesral
knew, because she had counted them as she laboured up with
two of the packs, following the captain who carried the other
two, and a crewman who helped Renia. She had counted them
again when, on their own at last, she set out to get some food

and other basic necessities for them both. She was in no doubt as to their number when she had carried it all back up them again.

Renia was no help. In shock, Jesral surmised. She just gazed out of the window all the while Jesral unpacked and put things away. It was a pretty view to be sure, over slate roofs and back towards the harbour – but it led the eye to the *Dawn Wind*'s shattered mast, just showing beyond the rooftops, and that she could do without. Renia was so knocked sideways by the loss that she couldn't take it in properly, that was it. Not a tear, not a word of anger or grief. It couldn't be good for her, and it was stopping Jesral from grieving properly herself. God knows what would happen when Renia finally came out of shock.

Jesral remembered her dad's death when she was twelve, after some stupid drunken brawl about nothing at all, from a head wound that had seemed superficial but had caused him to die in his sleep. She must have been like this then, she supposed; she only really remembered from the point where they buried him in a shallow grave in a mean little wooden box, and the villagers carrying it had stumbled and dropped it, and she had shouted and screamed at them and at the unfairness of it all because, drinker though he might have been, she'd loved her dad so much. She doubted that she would witness such a performance from Renia, but it did not mean the girl would not feel the same way inside. Jesral wished she knew what to do to help her. It all added to the physical and emotional draining that left Jesral, like Renia, unable to do anything more than pick at a cold supper and fall into bed to a sleep of exhaustion.

Jesral awoke late next morning feeling no better. Indeed it was beginning to sink in that they were in a far more difficult situation than if they had truly been at the mercy of Harrat's hospitality. Neither of them had really given much thought to what would happen when they got to Ilmaen; Renia had expected to follow Kerin's lead and Jesral had not dared to do anything else, given her precarious position among them. If they just sat here now, however, they might sit until doomsday. They could afford it for a while, thanks to the not inconsiderable amount of money they had hidden away in their packs; but Jesral for one had never been a sitter.

They might try to find Renia's relatives, but they had little enough to go on there. Another alternative was to go back – which was not actually an option at all, Jesral decided, shuddering at the thought of ever setting foot on a ship again. Or there was the crazy notion Renia came out with as they broke their fast on what was left of their supper. Came out with it so calmly, too, sitting there on her bed with her good leg folded under her, as though the idea of the two of them trying to get Jastur out of a fortress on their own was obvious. It clearly surprised her that any other option had occurred to Jesral. Dear Lord, she was so calm it was not normal. Still no tears at all, after losing a brother and being stranded in a strange country to compound the misery. Either she was bottling up her grief masterfully, or she was still refusing to recognize her loss. Or Renia *was* possessed of some evil spirit, and Jesral had followed the wrong instinct in not running all the way back to the Three Villages while she had the opportunity.

No, she thought, dismissing the last idea. It was not that kind of unhinged calmness. It was more as though Renia was waiting for something to happen, patiently adamant that they must help Jastur – not that she had a single practical suggestion as to how to do it.

It's suicide to try it on our own, Jesral had argued.

Maybe, but we must do it, came the reply.

Someone else must be trying to help him, Jesral's next tack.

We can't know that – but if there are others then we can help them and increase the chances, was Renia's retort.

It's too far away, you can't walk or ride hard enough.

We'll find a way.

We'll draw too much attention, two women travelling alone.

A shrug only to this last objection.

It was Jesral who saw an improbable solution slowly take shape in her mind as Renia sat, patient and stoic. Nothing will happen unless I make it happen, she concluded, and jumped up to rummage through her pack. The money they had got for the horses was in Internationals, deliberately so: being notes they weighed less, for a start, and though they might be difficult to use in the smaller towns and villages they would travel through, they moved so fast in a port like Greatharbour that in any transaction you could expect to get Internationals from a dozen different countries of origin. There was no way to trace them back. More of Kerin's forward planning. Shame the fool had not thought to survive himself. No one was going to suspect anyone like herself and Renia of planning a counter-coup, so whatever they did next, local currency would be a lot more useful to them now than some complicated plan to cover their tracks. She ferreted out the few Ilmaenese coins Harrat had exchanged for the last of their Mhrydaineg coinage. She took those and an International, in case she found somewhere that would be prepared to take the note and give her back local currency in change.

'Well, this is getting us nowhere fast, and this garret is making me claustrophobic. I'm going out. Lunch needs buying anyway.' Renia did not appear to be listening. Jesral sighed and pressed hard on her browbone; she could feel a headache coming on.

'While I'm at it, I'll ask about to see what rumours are flying. Jastur can't have just vanished off the face of the earth, if he's still alive.'

'He's alive.'

'Fine, fine.' At least that had got a reaction. Jesral increased the pressure on her browbone, gave it up as a bad job and snatched up a drawstring bag. 'Could you at least sort out the packs while I'm gone?' She faltered a little, softened her tone and chose her words carefully; doing so as much from her own grief as from sympathy for Renia. 'There's no way we can carry all their stuff too. We'll just have to take as many useful things as we can manage.'

oOo

Renia continued to sit on her bed for quite some time after Jesral had gone. The other girl's judgement was accurate; Renia was in shock, but trying hard to fight it. The absent calmness on the outside might look like complete denial, but it disguised her turmoil. She had stopped telling Jesral it could not be true about Vel and Kerin. It did not stop her feeling so, though she knew that was against all reason. She stared over the rooftops towards the harbour and the broken mast of the *Dawn Wind*, running a scene through her mind again and again; Vel turning Kerin over that day on the beach, and the blueness of his face. Somewhere during the last day someone else had done that to Kerin, and to Vel as well, only this time there would be no faint flush of pink to the cheeks, no spark of life to rekindle. They were gone. They must be.

But they could not be: not Vel, at least. Surely she should feel it inside, somehow? But there was nothing, nothing at all.

No. They were gone. Jesral was right to tell her to face facts. If they were going to follow the original plan, if things were still going to happen, then she and Jesral had to make the decisions. There was no one else to make them now. And she could not let Jesral do everything, not when this was more Renia's fight than Jesral's.

Her fight. She fingered the pouch around her neck, feeling the Eagle's shape within like an oath between herself and Kerin. It was clear now what she had promised him by accepting it. She had thought only of it saving him; he had seen its power to save Jastur also, and so Ilmaen, by corroborating his claim. Was that why she had felt the compulsion to come? Had she known at the back of her mind of the fate the others had faced, known all along that they were going to die? But if that was so, if it was her destiny to rescue Jastur, then why had she seen a noose for him as well? What was driving her on, if it was all for nothing?

Such thoughts were unbearable. She pushed them aside. She should take a positive step. Sort out the men's packs for a start.

These were both upended in an unceremonious hurry on to the middle of Jesral's bed, and sorted to either end, stuff to be kept or disposed of. They had no need of two more sets of cutlery and dishes, so those went. But the small cooking pan from Kerin's pack could be used, and Vel's little knife with all the extra tools, and some rope. Their water bottles were discarded too. Then she remembered Jastur. If he had to travel with them for any length of time, he would have need of such things. So she took one of the water bottles back, and one set of dishes and cutlery.

Something was caught between the dishes in that set, and she separated them to find a fold of cloth, and inside that a single flower. The dishes were Vel's; the flower was from the water meadow they had stopped in, that day back in Mhrydain. Jesral and Vel had been gone together over the slope above the meadow for a while, she recalled. Vel must have kept this flower, planning in future years to use it as a memory of a day long ago. Plans come to nothing; but the memory of that day still survived. It was a memory for Jesral really, so Renia replaced the flower in the cloth and laid it aside in the 'things to keep' pile for her.

Vel's kit for repairing leatherwork was kept, and his sealed tinderbox as a spare lest their matches got damp. She also put the swords and an oiled cloth to clean them in the 'to keep' pile. They would be useless to her and Jesral, but Vel's in particular had meant so much to him it would seem a form of betrayal to leave it behind or sell it – unless the need was truly desperate.

Soon only clothes remained, rather creased now in spite of careful packing, even their best which had been at the top to avoid getting crushed. There lay the shirt Kerin had briefly worn the day they rode into Greatharbour. It still bore the faint smell of him. It reminded her of the busy night they had all had at the Three Villages. The smell conjured up the sensation of being carried by him. Never again, she told herself; nor another bear hug from Vel.

She was on the verge of tears but of frustration, not grief, for still she could not make herself believe they were gone. There ought to be grief by now. Why was there no grief?

All the clothes went in the 'to go' pile in a frenzy of blind activity, but when she turned again to the 'to keep' pile she had somehow put that one shirt of Kerin's there.

She sat down on the floor this time, which put the stuff on the bed at eye level. She had long ago run out of nails to shred and was forced to tear at the cuticles instead. The shirt sat on the pile where it had no right to be, and she stared at it.

It had to go. This was stupid. One minute she was refusing to admit that they were dead, the next she was clinging with desperate sentimentality to their things. She got up again and stood over the shirt.

He should not be more important than Vel, no matter who he was, not to her. It was not right, not respectful to her brother. She put her hands on the shirt – but she could not discard it; and tears fell in earnest now, the first shed in grief. She realized what the problem was. Kerin had been way beyond her, always. She could never have had him, but like an addiction she could not give up the wanting, not just like that, to the point that her mind wouldn't let her think him gone. Given time, perhaps...

She wiped her eyes on her sleeve and calmed down a little. Jastur came back to mind again then. He might need clothes, and from her visions she knew little of his height or build. So, she put aside clothes from Kerin *and* Vel to keep, including the troublesome shirt. It covered her weakness to others, if not to herself. She could only hope Jesral would not guess at the truth.

The things that they would be taking with them would not fit into two packs now, so she made up a smaller pack to carry by hand. Finally she set the packs aside and lay down on her bed, miserable beyond words.

oOo

Fate had given Renia a good companion in Jesral. She would often panic over unimportant things. But she could be a rock in a crisis, and she knew a crisis when she saw one. Abandoning Renia never even entered her mind. Renia was in shock of some kind, so Jesral planned to stay around while this continued, to keep things moving, and then to pick things up when it finally sank in for Renia. Less nobly, she saw it as a matter of her own survival also. She did not care to travel Ilmaen on her own, not like before. Such risks had seemed nothing when she was seventeen; she shuddered now to think

of the dangers she had put herself in. Going home she had
ruled out already. The more she thought about it, the more
certain she was she would never board a ship again! But there
was more to it than these practicalities: this adventure she had
joined in through chance opportunism had become as much
her mission as theirs. She had never really felt a strong
commitment to anything – except to one person, and he had let
her down badly. Since that time, she supposed, she had been
avoiding commitment. Yet in just a week she had become
entranced by this powerful friendship between the other three.
With it they had faith that they could pull off this crazy task, a
faith so strong that even on her own, Renia was not going to
let it go.

With an effort Jesral pictured how Renia must see
things. She had this special vision; to her Jastur was someone
she had met, a creature of flesh and blood. He was Kerin's
brother, so Kerin would have stood Hell on its head if it would
help him. And Vel – well, he was after adventure, like Jesral.
Or had been, until the adventure turned awry. He would have
made the journey fun, she knew, all long-limbed and keen-
eyed and so full of life...

Enough, she told herself. Leave the grieving to his
sister. She walked on through the streets, slowly but
purposefully, scanning street-corner noticeboards and
neglected, flyposted walls for the poster she wanted to find.
She was looking for the familiar, but with an eye open for
other possibilities too. It was over a year since she'd last seen
them, after all; they could have changed the colour, the
picture, the words, anything.

To think that two days ago, she had been praying
heart and soul *not* to meet them. Now all she could do was
look and hope. Hope that their route hadn't changed and they
still travelled the north coast in May and June. Hope that she
would receive a welcome, given the things she had said when
she left. Hope that she could persuade old Atune to take the

entire caravan east to give them cover. And finally, and probably most unlikely, that the old woman would agree to the Company actually helping with the rescue. *We don't touch politics with a midden shovel,* Atune used to say to any song or act or joke that could imply any kind of political bias. Jesral could see her now, tiny birdlike eyes glinting in the lined, laughing face. *You can insult their morals, their family, their looks and their town, but mention politics and like as not there'll be a riot. And even if we didn't start it, it'll be us they run out of town, and the wagon wheels won't touch the ground.*

Jesral was most of the way to the marketplace when she saw a flash of the distinctive blue paper on a wall and hurried over. Yes! The old woodcut was still being used, so the little printing press the Company carried must be working yet. But the poster was in tatters, part torn off and someone else's poster over the top of it. The date they had performed here was lost. Biting back her disappointment, she walked on.

She kept looking, but what little optimism she'd had for the idea was fading. From the state of the poster they could easily be too far ahead to catch up with, and she had no other ideas. She'd pinned more hope on this than she had realized. There didn't seem any other way they could make the journey without drawing attention to themselves, two women travelling unescorted. And the idea that the two of them alone could get Jastur out of Karn was ridiculous.

But Renia wasn't going to accept anything else.

Jesral wandered through the food stalls, brought fruit and bread and preserved meat and a few bottles of the weak beer she knew Renia would drink. She could have done with something stronger herself, but this was no time to be without a clear head.

If they were going to head east on their own, the best thing would be to move as fast as they could. That meant staging coaches. To pay for the whole trip they'd need to use the Internationals, large-denomination money. Should she buy enough journey stages for the whole trip or just a few at a time, as though only going to the next big town? Which would draw the least attention, leave less of a trail? She tried to think what Kerin would do.

The whole journey, as open stages. Then you stay out of the staging company offices. Only the coach hands and other passengers will ever see you and they won't know where your next stage takes you. It will help if you cover that hair up, and Renia wears her long skirt to hide the bandage.

But remember, you will be the one buying all the stages at that first office, not me. Can you carry off such a transaction convincingly? One of his honest, look-you-straight-in-the-eye questions. The type where even if he was implying nothing, you inferred everything.

She stretched her neck and pinched the bridge of her nose, feeling the headache still. He was gone. It wasn't his decision any more. It was hers. She'd check the staging timetables and charges, see how much was needed, then make the call on what she felt she was capable of.

She mounted the town hall steps, threading her way among the other folk there. It was through a chance gap in the crowd that the vivid blue of a poster to her right caught her eye. She rushed over. It was complete and undamaged, being on an official board, and those were changed weekly; she recalled Atune telling her so. They were less than a week away! She scanned the performers in the picture fondly, especially the girl juggler Atune had said was her, when she was first accepted into the show. Good memories flooded back and Jesral clung on to those, knowing that in another mood she'd remember the bad ones and this was not the time. She checked the date of the shows they had given, here in Wistram.

Three days ago, the last performance. They would have come up from Corsay and set up the night before; rehearsal in the morning; shows at three and seven. Pack up at dawn and on the road to Cabuc. That had been the route for the three years she had been with them. If she was wrong, they could only have gone inland to the next nearest town. They were no more than two days away, probably less than that, as the coach could outrun them.

Hope renewed, she walked across to the staging notice boards.

The trip to Cabuc was listed as one stage, and a reasonable sum. But the next coach was leaving from the market inn at two o'clock that afternoon. Christ, it was gone one o'clock now! She almost elbowed people aside in her haste to get into the stage office, bought two tickets, and ran hell for leather back to the garret room.

Chapter 14 – Routes East

On the coast road ten miles north-east of Wistram, a covered wagon pulled up.

Naylan and Partners

Cutlers and Tinkers

the painted canvas sides read. It was driven by a swarthy thickset man of some forty years, who spoke to the boy who sat beside him and jerked his chin towards the beach, swept last night by the storm. The youth jumped nimbly down; maybe fourteen but slightly built and as dark-haired as the man, but even darker-skinned. He crossed the sandy beach to where a long bundle lay some way above the high waterline. It hadn't been thrown there by the storm; marks in the soft sand showed the movement from where it had originally lain in the surf. The boy prodded the bundle with one foot; it groaned and rolled over, sand caking blond hair and one side of the face. The eyes flickered open.

'Uhhh... a beach. Hell has beaches?'

The boy grinned at him.

'Mebbe it has but you gon' have put up wid Ilmaen a bit longer. Come, tamaani. You feel like hell now, but you soon be glad you alive.'

'Bighur!' roared the man on the wagon. 'I don't need you to get all his details including date of birth. Just get him up here!'

Bighur pulled a face and helped the man on to unsteady feet, and then back to the wagon. There were steps to the rear; Bighur walked him up them and, on hearing yet another rumble from the driver, unceremoniously tipped him inside. Arms caught and steadied him, lowered him to the floor gently.

'Hello, Vel.'

He was looking into a face upside down and having trouble focussing, but he recognised both voice and face as Kerin's.

'Uhhh. Hello again. No, don't get me up. It was a long, tiring swim and I drank a lot of seawater on the way. I think I'd best lie on the floor for a while.' The wagon started up, and took away any benefit lying still might have given him. He continued to lie there though, while Kerin helpfully moved to where Vel could see him the right way up. That did a little to settle Vel's stomach. Only a little.

'That boy tells me I'll be glad to be alive soon, but I have reason to doubt him. Kerin, please – if you're going to make a habit of falling off ships, do the rest of your travelling by land.'

oOo

Vel fell asleep far sooner than he'd expected his sick feeling would allow. When he awoke, in one of the wagon's cots and covered with a blanket, the light from outside suggested that evening was coming on. The wagon had stopped. He got up, aching and disorientated for a few moments before he remembered where he was and why.

The door of the wagon stood open. He could hear the crackle of a fire outside, and voices; one of them was Kerin's. But what really brought him awake and suggested to him that he was feeling better was the smell of food.

The taste confirmed it. Kerin was solicitous and relieved to see him set to his portion, strange though the meat was. It was some kind of bird, presumably a sea bird as the meat was decidedly fish-flavoured; certainly something new to Vel.

Kerin had adopted a new false name in Greatharbour, Anken Hedgresten. Vel had struggled to remember it on the *Dawn Wind*; but it fell off the others' tongues now as if it had always been his name. Vel listened to him asking skilful questions of their rescuers, in between teasing out their life stories. Naylan was a big, friendly-mannered man despite his weathered, almost fearsome looks. A few days' stubble, black shot with grey, sat on his cheeks. He had travelled the roads of Ilmaen and beyond most of his life, mostly tinkering but occasionally turning his hand to smithing, where there was a forge to work at. The life clearly suited him; he was a man happy with his lot.

In comparison the boy Bighur had not had much of a life, though he beamed as Naylan told them what he had been able to piece together of his story. Naylan did not speak the boy's native language, and for a bright lad Bighur had never managed or else had never chosen to speak Ilmaenese very well. As far as Naylan could work out, Bighur had been thralled by his parents to pay a debt when he was no more than six – a custom still too common in the lands both north and south of Ilmaen. Bighur's master had been a hedge bandit; to him the lives of others were expendable. The man had not even been prepared to halt to pull one of his own gang, this mere boy, out of a bog. It was pure chance that Naylan had passed by in time and got him out. Despite so many years spent living that kind of life, Bighur had, in Naylan's opinion, still turned out a good lad.

'I one lucky bastard, to meet Boss,' Bighur told them earnestly.

'Language!' retorted Naylan, rolling his eyes at the others. 'How come kids always master the swearwords before the grammar?' He chatted easily with Kerin, answering his questions and asking his own without apparently noticing how little real information Kerin was passing on. Vel sat half listening, but something else was nagging at his attention. An uncomfortable, unprotected feeling. Unable to give a name to it, he dismissed it and continued listening.

Kerin was trying to find out which way Naylan was travelling, but without asking directly. He was subtle and Vel's Ilmaenese was still limited, but knowing Kerin's need to head east showed up his intentions. Naylan appeared unaware.

From off the sea, the breeze quickened. Vel felt the skin on his back tighten at the cold, sharply aware all of a sudden of the lack of Jesral's presence behind him, as it had been for so much of the previous week. She had been a nuisance at first, clinging on round his waist with a grip fit to crush him, until she had got used to riding double. She had been a nuisance at second, come to that, either leaning out to see round him and complaining how it made her back ache, or else sitting upright and frequently banging her sharp chin into his back at that sensitive point right between his shoulder blades. He'd raised her makeshift saddle after a day of that, which had improved both their tempers considerably. Now he missed her light hold on his beltloops, the unconscious sensuality of her tucked in behind him, covering him like a cloak. Even her cursing as she tied his long blond hair back with a piece of rag to stop it whipping in her face would not go amiss now.

He looked at Kerin again. Bighur was talking now and Kerin watched the boy, but once again he had that frown on his face that indicated his mind was elsewhere. Vel knew where.

All Kerin's questions had been geared to getting underway again, getting to Jastur. Even in his concern for Vel's health he was just establishing how soon they could be on their way to Karn. Karn, where Kerin might never have thought to look had it not been for Renia. He had taken great interest in her welfare when her presence had been a potential delay to his plans. Now she and Jesral no longer figured in his thinking. It probably did not occur to Kerin that they had any obligation to go looking for them. For the first time Vel looked at him with some dislike, and wondered if he had done the right thing in accompanying him.

Eventually Kerin succeeded in his aim; Naylan asked him about their own travel plans. Kerin named the province, carefully avoiding naming the town, but dismissed their chances of getting there now that they had lost everything, and pondered aloud on alternative plans. He didn't even mention the existence of Renia and Jesral, let alone raise searching for them as one of those alternatives. Naylan, ignorant of the manoeuvring, countered by pointing out that his own route would at the least get them part of the way there and offered them the ride, in exchange for their work when he set up stall in the markets on the way. Subtle as ever, Kerin didn't say yes and didn't say no; he said the two of them would sleep on it.

Vel didn't sleep so much as fester, sheltering under the wagon on a borrowed blanket that night. When they exchanged watches Kerin came and lay down where he had been with a cheery goodnight and never a suspicion of Vel's feelings. He was sleeping like a baby in minutes.

oOo

'It seems our luck has turned at last,' Kerin declared as they put the blankets away in the wagon the next morning. Naylan and Bighur had offered to share their breakfast, and though two meals between four would not be filling it would at least take the hunger away. Naylan expected to make the next town in time to set up stall by midday; an afternoon's work would earn the cost of their next few meals. For now he had just enough left to buy them all a bite of lunch before they started work.

'You've decided then.' The bitter note in Vel's voice startled Kerin; the look he saw on his companion's face dismayed and bewildered him.

'He'll take us south-east, Vel. It may not be perfect but we will not find better cover, not in our circumstances.'

'Our circumstances may not be good, but at least we know what they are. In the meantime the girls could be anywhere, in any state – but they'll be on the coast, we know that much. Naylan was travelling the coast road up to now. I couldn't say where he was really planning to go before he met us, but you charmed him and now he goes south-east.'

'You want to go and look for them?'

'Quick, aren't you?' Vel taunted, making Kerin bristle.

'Vel, they could be in any of a dozen ports along this coast. In fact, I dare say they are no longer in any port; they have the money and the gear, they will be on their way to Karn by now, on Heaven only knows what route. We cannot take the time to search for them! Renia made that clear. None of us came all this way just to see Jastur's life slip through our fingers.'

'We didn't come expecting to be abandoned by our friends either,' retorted Vel darkly.

'They will not think we have abandoned them, Vel, and they will not be looking for us. No one could have expected us to survive that storm. But you saw how determined Renia was to carry on at the Three Villages. That is what she will be doing now. I will lay you odds she is at Karn before we are.'

'Before you maybe,' Vel replied bluntly. He got up and started looking around for stuff for his journey that Naylan might be able to spare. 'Stay,' Kerin protested mildly, but Vel rounded on him.

'If you're going south-east, you're going without me. Since I know you won't change your mind, you'd better get used to the idea.'

Kerin got up too, watching him with a heavy heart and searching desperately for a way to change his mind. 'Vel, I don't think I can save him without you.' Vel's rummaging among the shelves continued unabated. Kerin leant back against the cupboards. He had finally pushed his companion too far, and in his arrogance he had not even noticed. 'My fault, Vel. It was unreasonable of me to assume you were my man in these circumstances.'

Vel paused, then asked, 'But you still won't come and look for the girls?'

'No.'

Vel used the blanket to bag together the few things he intended to ask Naylan for. He shouldered past Kerin and set his hand on the door, but turned back before he opened it.

'Your assumption, it was no more unreasonable than mine about you. I hadn't realized you were such a *haliwr*.'

Kerin hauled him back at that and slammed him against the cupboards, but their affray was halted by the sight of Bighur as the door swung open. His eyes were round as he looked from one to the other of them.

'You gon' fight?' He looked quite enthusiastic at the prospect, then his expression changed, dismissing the idea.

'You no fight. You friends, yeah? The boss man, he sort this. You ask him. Boss!'

The call was made before they could stop him. They glared at each other as the boy bounded off, exasperated at this turn of events and each blaming the other for it. Vel walked down the steps, dropped his bundle and stood with his arms folded, waiting. Kerin sat on the wagon steps, no less sullen. Naylan appeared, carrying the water can he had just refilled, and Bighur danced round him, telling him as much as he knew of the row. How much did he know? Kerin tried to remember the angry words, what they had actually said to each other in the heat of the moment. He could tell nothing from Naylan's expression as he approached.

'Dey were gon' fight for real, you know. Dey not practise.'

'All right, Bighur. Don't push your luck.' Naylan set down the water can. 'So who's going to tell me what's going on?'

He looked at Vel, who said sullenly, 'Ask him.' Naylan turned with a look of patient enquiry; Kerin stopped glaring at Vel and sat up a little straighter.

'When we sailed from Mhrydain we were travelling with two women. One is his sister. Although they have all the money and gear, he feels they are not safe or able to look after themselves alone, and wants to look for them in the ports ahead. I, on the other hand, think they will shift very well for themselves. What I haven't told you, but what is certain, is that my brother is in mortal danger in the east, and that if we make a search here, we will be too late to save him.'

'Hmm. And do you want to add anything to that?' Naylan asked Vel, who unfolded his arms briefly to spread his hands, *no more to say*, and folded them again.

'Well, a pretty dilemma, to be sure.' Naylan furrowed his brow, took up the can and walked over to the fire, where he set about filling the kettle and putting it on the flames while he thought.

'Well...' He got up from the fire and walked back to them. Bighur had settled into a crouch nearby and gazed up at Naylan, looking strangely like a dog watching its master.

'You know that my route takes me south-east.' Vel's shoulders slumped a little. 'I go that way for good sound business reasons. It's busy. Lots of towns. Lots of people on the road. Lots of reasons for them to stop me and give me money. It'll be a slow route, unless we want to draw attention to ourselves by turning business away – and something tells me that, whatever your reasons, you don't want that.

'On the other hand, the coast road is well made but less busy. There will be fewer stops, and it turns inland in forty miles anyway. When we part company you should be able to pick up a bridge over the Sen that much sooner, and make your way north of the citywild. How about we try the ports between here and the Sen and then go inland?'

Kerin calculated distances in his head and tried to estimate the number of stops.

'Forty miles, you say?' Vel asked.

''Bout that,' Naylan replied.

'How many ports would that take us to?' cut in Kerin. Naylan screwed up his face.

'For a ship the size you said, two or three. If it happens that she's hove to in deeper water off a shallower harbour, the land's flat and clear from the road to the sea, all along the coast. You'd soon spot her.'

'Vel?' Kerin prompted tentatively. Vel raised his head, still thinking it through; Kerin waited. After what seemed an age, Vel gave him a curt nod.

'Right, breakfast then,' Naylan concluded, and returned to the fire. Vel picked up his bundle and started back to the wagon. Kerin got off the steps to let him pass; they weren't ready to look at or speak to each other, not yet. He crossed to the fire to help out there. Bighur followed him over with a smile that split his face, and it was an effort not to smile along with him. Vel rejoined them, still silent but no longer angry. Bighur's smile stayed put all through the meal, and the washing up they shared.

'So you missed a big fight, but you're happy?' Naylan asked him eventually, his own face all seriousness.

'Eyah. You did real good, Boss. You damn' clever bugger.' They all wore grins now. On Naylan's face it made all the stubble stand to attention. He thumped the boy across the shoulders with rough affection.

'And you're a damn' cheeky one, bog rat. I suppose you want to drive as well.'

'I first there, I drive.' Having declared the rules of the game, Bighur scampered off.

Chapter 15 – The Company

Jesral watched Renia trying to sleep against the shaking of the coach, and wished she hadn't pushed her so hard. It had only just occurred to her that there might have been another staging coach the next day. They had made it to the inn by two o'clock, by the skin of their teeth, despite the extra pack to contend with as well as Renia's ankle. The pace Jesral had forced had been too fast. Even Kerin had not pressed Renia so hard.

She had spent a bad night at their overnight stop, despite her homemade medicine. And this morning she continued to fret because they had left without even a note to Captain Harrat, despite the handful of Internationals they'd left him in the room for his trouble. Kerin would have been livid with them for doing that, it screamed out the deceit they had practised, but they'd have to take their chances. Even if Harrat had harboured any suspicions about Kerin, who would imagine that two *Mhrydainaidd* would take up his cause once he was dead?

When had she made Kerin her spiritual mentor? Here she was, trying to think like him, still feeling uncomfortable about breaking his governing principles – this was ridiculous. What worked for him would not necessarily work for her. That was why they were on this route.

And she knew their route so well. That was thanks to Atune's teaching. God knows why she had thought it so important Jesral should learn it, but it stood her in good stead now. Posters in the last town had confirmed the Company were on this road. She and Renia would probably overtake them before Latuc. She had toyed with the idea of getting off at one of the minor halts along the way, if she should spot them, but had decided to carry on to that port even if it meant a day's wait for them. It had to look like a chance meeting, an accident – or serendipity. She had to be careful; Atune would be angry if she sensed she was being played, and if Cedas smelt a rat, he could make things very difficult. As if things wouldn't be difficult enough for Jesral anyway, with him around.

So… get there ahead of them. Be somewhere a chance meeting could happen – the marketplace, probably. Just bump into one of them – so long as it wasn't Cedas, anyone but Cedas. Tell them our tale of woe, accept a ride, and…

And then what? Oh, Hell. It'd come. Give it time, the right idea would come. Let's get that far, at least.

She glanced at Renia again, still with her eyes closed. Jesral felt bad about deceiving her too, implying she had the answer to their problems when her plan was so full of flaws only an idiot would have considered it. She herself went into most things in life full of optimism, and right now *she* doubted this plan's chances. But it was the best she had to offer.

The coachman's assistant sounded three blasts on his horn, the signal for slower traffic ahead to pull aside for them. Jesral tucked herself in behind the blind just enough to see but not be seen. They passed two covered wagons, then several caravans. The angle was too tight for her to see any of the drivers – but that vehicle, she knew. It had been given a fresh coat of paint, but it was Atune's beyond a doubt. Jesral settled back while the stage passed the remainder of the caravans then shut and rested her eyes, readying herself for the work ahead.

The staging office stood next to a boarding house, where they took a room for the rest of the day and overnight. It had a little parlour, book-lined on one wall: she selected a few volumes and settled Renia in their room with them. For practice, Jesral told her. She left Renia frowning over one, trying to fit the spoken language she knew to the written word she had not, apart from a few place names, ever seen before.

There was the usual range of food bars and drinks shops at the top end of the town square. Jesral ordered herself a hot drink and a sweetroll at one and settled down at one of the tables scattered before it. She wasn't hungry; in fact she had no appetite at all. She was just delaying the next step while she worked it through and through in her mind.

There was so much that could go wrong, it was almost bound to. What did they do then?

Carry on to Karn on the staging coaches, she supposed. But nothing she and Renia could do there would get them into the fort proper – short of being arrested themselves, in which case they wouldn't be of much use to Jastur.

She stirred the hot drink absently. There must be some organized resistance to this man Maregh. She had overheard conversations at the inn last night, and today on the coach and in the square as she had idled her way up here. Everyone agreed that things were going badly, be it trouble on the southern borders or local taxes and lawlessness both going up. Surely some of the people at the top were prepared to do something about it, even if only to further their own ends. But Kerin had been the one who would know who to contact, and how. She had been over this ground before…

'Hello, stranger.'

She glanced up, and stopped stirring the drink.

'Good Lord… It's been a long time, a long time. How are you, Nina?'

Bright, confident mahogany eyes looked at Jesral from a pretty oval face. There was the old remembered smile, if a rather guarded one, as they had parted on such a bad note; but it was enough to maintain the conversation. Thank you, God, thank you for interceding like this, Jesral acknowledged fervently.

'I'm well enough, thanks,' Nina told her, and settled on the nearest chair, staring at her with an expression of wonder. 'Where have you been? We thought you'd crossed the water, it's been so long since we saw you.'

'I did. I only got back the day before yesterday, but it's been a bit of a nightmare so far. I came in a foursome and there's only two of us left now. The others drowned in the crossing, we hit an almighty storm. We have a desperately urgent task in the east, and have to get there as fast as possible. My friend who made it, she's in a daze; one of those who drowned was her brother. She has a bad ankle too, which doesn't help. Fact is, Nina, I'm at my wit's end as to what to do now.'

'So nothing changes, then? You really do get yourself into some situations.' Nina thought for a little. 'We may be able to help. But you haven't asked after the others.'

'No, I'm sorry. How are they? How's Atune, and Cedas?'

'Well, Cedas is in charge now. Age has finally caught up with Atune. She has had a couple of bad winters, especially this last; we thought we might lose her. She still insists on having a say, you know how she is, but she realizes the organizing is too much for her now. Cedas and I do most of it. We're still together...'

'That's good. Really, it is, Nina. Cedas and I are old history. I'm long over him. The only thing I hold against him now is that he came between us – and we were stupid enough to let him. Things are different now; we're different. It would be nice to start again, wouldn't it?'

Jesral cringed inwardly, for this was not the total truth and it sounded false and grovelling to her ears. But Nina smiled at her again. It was more natural than her first smile, but also more wry. She knew Jesral well enough to see there was an element of acting in this, knew she had a knack for extricating herself from almost any situation – almost as good as her knack for getting into them.

'Look,' she told Jesral, 'you know the Company is going up the coast road from here. If you want to go east that's a bit out of your way, but if it helps you're welcome to come. Usual rules: if you travel with the show, you contribute to the show. We're camped outside the south gate. It's just an afternoon show here, we're to be on the road again tonight. Can you and your friend get there by five?'

'Of course!' Jesral declared excitedly. 'We'll get the old routines going again, and Renia – oh, she can tell you what she does when you see her. Look, I've got to get our things sorted. I'll see you there later. Give Atune my love, eh?'

oOo

They received a cool reception from Cedas, as Jesral had anticipated. Luckily he had been too busy striking camp to pay them too much attention, but had simply directed them to a particular wagon. Jesral was glad of that; there would probably be Hell to pay when he discovered that Renia was not merely injured, but totally inexperienced. She must let her friend know about that part of the bargain, of course, but not now. Renia sat on her pack nearby and was gingerly flexing her ankle – they had been in less of a rush this time but again the journey had taxed her. She was tired and in discomfort, and that bit of news could wait.

Cedas was going to be a problem. Jesral had seen the controlled anger in him when they arrived, upsetting his schedule. It was written all over him, in the way he moved, the way he spoke. He was even short with Nina. The ambitious bastard: he wouldn't let anything affect the Company's performance. She had always suspected that the Company had come before her, back when she had reigned in his affections, and he hadn't even been in charge of it then. Well, let Nina have that painful knowledge now; she was welcome to the disadvantages as well as the advantages of a relationship with Cedas.

Jesral was only seeking to fool herself, though. There was no denying that little leap inside she'd felt on first seeing him, followed by unspeakable depression for the next ten seconds at the thought of going through all that pain again. The anger that followed had been her defence mechanism and it was working well now, but even with defences in place Cedas's magnetism was overpowering. Granted, when you looked at him closely he was not conventionally good-looking, but something about him… the rich dark glow of his skin, those fluid brown eyes that could be hard as coal or sweet as dark honey… all this had once enthralled her. And then there was the way he moved and held himself. He was a short man, but with his natural, effortless grace he projected a presence as proud as a lion amongst the biggest men. The next few weeks looked set to be the longest of her life. Jastur had damned well better be at Karn, after all this!

oOo

The wagon Renia had been sent to was fairly typical of those the Company used, consisting of a cabin ornamented by painted decoration and fronted by a fancy driver's box. It was backed by a short veranda with a bench and steps down to the road, and that was where she and Jesral now sat. A young man of about seventeen had clambered up to drive, and Jesral and Renia watched the port fall away behind them as the convoy of wagons moved north-east along the coast road. It was a warm day, but the sea breeze buffeted them on the back of the wagon and irritated Renia, blowing her hair into her eyes. It was long enough to tie back, but wisps always escaped anyway, and she had not got round to combing it that morning either. It was a mess and a nuisance, and Renia decided to get inside out of the wind.

She had realized they were sharing with someone but had assumed it would be the driver, and that had discomforted her enough. It came as a shock to her when a bundled up heap in one of the bunks squawked shrilly at her. Eventually she understood that the squawks were an instruction to shut the door she had come through and she did so hurriedly. That kept out the wind, while the unshuttered windows still let in enough light for Renia to see by. At one end of the heap she saw the grey hair and rheumy eyes of an old woman. Half her face drooped out of shape; Renia recognized the marks of a stroke. With her lack of Ilmaenese and the old woman's difficulty in expressing herself, it was a wonder she had understood anything at all.

Renia dumped her pack and herself into the lower bunk opposite and leant forward to the old lady. The old eyes were bright and alert in the seamed dark face, suggesting the damage done by the stroke was physical only. Still Renia spoke as slowly and clearly as she could, allowing for the possibility of bad hearing and for her own poor Ilmaenese accent.

'Hello. My name is Renia. My friend and I will be sharing your wagon. I hope it is not too much trouble to you. Can I get you anything?'

The rheumy eyes glared back determinedly, and the old woman said something. Renia had to get her to repeat it twice more.

'Someone else's right half. Stick it on to the side of me that still works.'

Renia had to smile. It was bitterness, but at least it was fighting bitterness. This old lady had some chance of making a recovery. 'Anyone you'd prefer?' she asked, encouraging the fighting spirit. The old woman's left hand wavered a little way off the coverlet.

'Ah, not important. Just make sure they're under twenty.'

'Oh, but your poor left half, having to keep up with that!' Renia pointed out.

The eyes sparkled as the old face twisted into a parody of a smile.

'Hah! If it can't cope, you can replace that too.'

Jesral came in, hearing the conversation. She screwed up her nose fastidiously at the faint dirty linen smell, dropped her stuff on to the top bunk and sat down next to Renia, who explained the old woman's condition. Jesral must have stared at the sagging features for two minutes before she jumped up from her seat with a start and went to kneel by the old woman.

'Atune! I didn't recognize you. I thought you'd be in your old wagon. Nina said you'd been ill. It's good to see you again.'

The way she looked didn't bother her now, Renia noticed. There was worry but also unfeigned affection in Jesral's smile, and she took hold of the woman's clawlike hand without a qualm.

'It's good to see you too, Jesral. Your friend here, she's *Britillaainen* too? Ah. Thought I recognized the accent.

'Well, it's a nasty turn this time, Jesral. Not a little one, not like I was when you left. You see my right side? Useless. It's frustrating. So much I want to do...'

'It's about time you had a rest, you crazy old woman. Rushing about getting up to the things you did, at your age. Cedas can manage perfectly well, from what I've seen. I'm sure Nina has told you so.'

'Yes, she's a good girl. She looks after me; moved me to this wagon when the other one got impossible to manage. She comes over here often, makes him pay some attention to me. But he's a cocky sod. He needs keeping in his place, you know. Yes. You know.'

When they had made camp that evening, Cedas came to the wagon. Atune hurled a mixture of advice and abuse at him the instant he stepped through the door, even if half of it was unintelligible. The bits that weren't proved her mind was still alert. Cedas's replies were ostensibly polite and courteous, until you stopped and thought about them, when you realized he was jibing back at her. Atune caught the meaning of every veiled insult at once and loved it, her cackling laugh making all the china in the wagon reverberate alarmingly. They finished their exchange, happy that they had struck level, and Cedas turned to the other two.

'You still doing the same acts, Jez? Never mind, they'll fit in. You'll have to see Nina, she wants to have a go at some of your old double acts again. And what about you - Renia, is it? What do you do and can it be worked around with your bad leg?'

She looked at him blankly.

'I'm sorry, I don't understand.'

'Your act,' he snapped, impatient with her slowness. Then he fathomed it.

'You don't have one, do you?' Renia looked at him: they both looked at Jesral. She was suddenly engrossed in picking fluff off her skirt.

'Jez, you know the rules. What was the point of bringing this girl along when you know we're going to have to dump her?' He turned back to Renia then, his explanation blunt: 'You perform or you're out. That's the way it's always been, that's the way it still is.' He made for the door, stopping by their packs.

'Which is yours?' he asked Renia, plainly intending to throw her out right now, in the middle of nowhere.

'Wait! Give her a chance at least. You gave me a chance – or have you completely forgotten those days?'

'No, Jez, I've not forgotten. There are long parts of them I try not to remember.' Jesral started and looked hurt at that. Renia sat uncomfortably, holding herself responsible for the tension between them.

Atune's crackly voice broke the atmosphere.

'Go on, give her a chance, you miserable *perse*. Always complaining about the lack of new blood in the show. I'd have given her a try in my day.' Atune's glare would have burnt holes in the best blanket, but then so would the look Cedas threw back at her.

'In your day, I recall, you spent six months giving me hell for landing you with a certain complete novice not a thousand miles away.' Jesral raised her head at this mention of herself.

'Aye, and as it happened, right you were. She took some work, but I got her there. But I told you then, I expect the favour back some day. I like this one so I think I'll call the favour in now. After all, it's less of a challenge than the one you set me. She's not half as silly, and she has the language better – gets her grammar right, at least. She can't possibly be as hard to teach as Jesral. No one else could be that difficult.'

'Thank you,' said Jesral testily.

'You mean, you expect me to train her?' Cedas protested.

'You expected me to train *her*,' Atune retorted, referring to Jesral. She almost had him now; a proud old woman, no pleading in her voice, she made a request seem like an order.

Cedas blinked uncertainly under her gaze and turned away to think. Doubt looked to be an alien emotion for him and it did not last long. He did not turn back to face her, but flung out one finger behind him. A theatrical gesture; she was starting to get the measure of him.

'You… are you a quick learner?' He fired the question at Renia.

'Yes,' she shot back her answer when normally she might have given it some thought. That was due to nervousness. It was an honest answer nonetheless.

Cedas turned now, lifting his head to make a pronouncement.

'You'll learn a mind-reading routine then. All it takes is a quick brain and a clear voice. I used to do one with Jez.'

'Oh, yes! I can teach her the codes,' put in Jesral.

'You will not! You'll have forgotten them all and teach her wrongly. Besides, I've refined the code system since then.' Then to Renia again:

'First I want you to attend tonight's rehearsals. You must watch the performers. Watch how they carry themselves; watch their gestures. It's all part of the act. Then tomorrow I want you on my wagon at ten o'clock for an hour's study, and again straight after the afternoon show to check what you covered in the morning. The same times the next day, then we'll see.'

He started to go, but swung back angrily at a chuckle from Atune.

'This pays for all, old woman, you remember that.'

Atune only chuckled harder.

'Cedas, I give you leave to make my life hell for as long as it takes to train her. After all, we want the exchange to be fair, don't we?'

He was almost out of the wagon by now, but Atune's comment to Renia must have carried to him.

'Now, girl, you need to get this act right by the end of the week, do you hear?'

Chapter 16 – A Raw Deal

Renia tried to concentrate, but it was hard. The blindfold on her eyes was too tight and the elaborate costume she wore, encrusted with paste jewels, was oppressively heavy and hot on such a close evening. It was one of the Company's prized stock of costumes that served for many roles, and was supposed to make her look like an exotic Eastern princess. It was the right size for Renia's figure but not her height; still, Cedas had liked it and wanted it in the act somehow.

It was not the only problem to work around; there was also Renia's bad leg. She'd taken her stitches out now but still limped badly and would for a long time, which hardly made for a regal entrance. In a stroke of inspiration Cedas had found the answer to both problems: a litter. She sat cross-legged on it and two suitably dressed 'royal retainers' bore her in, shoulder-high, and set the litter down on a high platform. There was no reason for her to stand, as the crowd could see her clearly, and appearing too proud to rise fitted the role she was playing perfectly.

Renia hated the role. She hated trying to pick up the key words that Cedas used as prompts, certain that she would remember them all wrong. She hated using the voice projection she had been taught to make her voice carry to the back of the crowd. Granted it worked but afterwards it made her hoarse, and it sounded to her as though she was shouting, although the others kept telling her she had proper control of her voice now. She hated the stiff-shouldered stance she had to keep up while pretending to be in a trance, though for that she had only herself to blame. What with being so uncomfortable and nervous when they began and having the ornate headdress to balance as well, she had adopted the stance automatically, and now Cedas would not let her fall out of it, claiming it added to the effect. All she could see that it did was give her a stiff neck. And above all, after the last week, she hated Cedas.

The trouble had started that first night, when she had attended the rehearsal as Cedas had told her to. They had camped in a dell off the road, far from any villages, and set up for a full rehearsal. As the night looked set to stay fine, they had not bothered with awnings for either the stage or the audience, merely set out the benches. At rehearsals the players who were not on stage or preparing to go on were the audience, which made it small enough to be intimate and inclined to be friendly. Renia might have enjoyed it if it weren't for the knowledge that in a few days she would have to perform herself, in front of a paying audience. Jesral, on the other hand, loved it and sat with her pointing out everything the players did, be it right or wrong.

Renia found she could quickly work this out for herself, simply by watching Cedas. She could not pin down precisely what it was he did, a look or a gesture, but she could tell what did or did not please him, and to what degree a mistake irritated him. She was a quick learner, and bright, but she was not sure if she would be able to overcome her nervousness sufficiently to avoid any mistakes. She was also in terror that she would have a fit onstage – mainly now because of what Cedas would say or do if she wrecked the show. But she would have to put up with it all; she certainly couldn't tell him about that risk. Jesral had grabbed a lifeline for Jastur here, if they could only persuade Cedas to take the caravan east. Renia dared do nothing to threaten that.

The rehearsal finished, the last act came off: but despite the late hour everyone then gathered on the benches where they all reviewed the show, praising and criticizing as they saw fit. They could be harsh in their criticism, though to be fair only where it was due, and no one took offence but listened to each suggestion for improvement. Cedas took the chance to introduce Jesral and Renia to the others, and they received a friendly welcome: most of them already knew

Jesral and greeted her as an old friend. The review put Renia much more at her ease.

That lasted only until they returned to their caravan. There they found Atune in a state of high agitation. Once they had calmed her down, she revealed that Eddir, the boy who drove their wagon, had come in during the rehearsal and, thinking Atune was asleep, had rifled through their packs.

Atune was more outraged by the boy's stupidity in assuming she slept than by his crime. It seemed he was some distant form of blood kin and she took it as an insult to the family pride that his pilfering had been so inept. It was the loss of the money needed to ensure Jastur's safety that concerned Jesral and Renia most, and they grabbed the packs and turned them out at once to see how much was missing.

It was all there still; the best part of three hundred Internationals, and anything else that might have been considered of value. Puzzled, they asked Atune if the boy had been disturbed in his snooping. She was adamant that he had taken his time, repacked the bags carefully, and left with no apparent haste.

It made no sense; even worse, soon afterwards they heard their would-be thief scramble back on to the wagon bench and settle down to sleep. He plainly had no fear of discovery. They decided that they would not leave the packs alone with Atune again in case his plan was to come back for the money later. Settling down for a night when they knew they would get no sleep, they resolved to tell Cedas next morning. If it rubbed him up the wrong way, so be it. They could not afford to lose that money.

oOo

Jesral elected herself for the task, on the grounds that she was better at being self-righteously angry than Renia was. Renia was too nice. She probably had difficulty even imagining how it felt to be that angry, Jesral concluded as she arrived at Cedas's wagon the next morning.

Cedas always exercised for an hour before most of the camp was even up, then had his breakfast. He was still eating when she arrived; Nina was cooking for him. Jesral took in the whole scene at a single glance: Nina in only her shift and skirt, the rest of her clothes scattered around the floor, the smell of cooking thick in the air. However well they might be turned out when they were in public, indoors neither of these two could be called house-proud. Still, Jesral had to admit she and Cedas had been no better in her day...

Long past now, and best forgotten. If only there weren't so many reminders here. Cedas had not changed his wagon much; he still lived with a minimal amount of furniture. His life revolved – a raw irony for Jesral - around the mattress in the centre of the floor. Anyone who came in had to sit either on the floor or on that mattress. There was a little fold-out table on one wall, but it was hardly ever used.

The bedsheets were still rumpled, neither of them having bothered to smooth them yet. Cedas sat cross-legged on the mattress, his trousers on but nothing else; his plate was balanced in his lap and he was mopping up the last of his meal with bread, every little movement drawing her gaze to the muscle definition of his bare chest and arms. If he had known she was coming, she would have laid odds this was deliberate. Cedas's taste might have changed from redheads to brunettes, but he was the sort of man who would happily remind her what she was missing.

It took some determination to cast that thought aside and sit down with them. She accepted some breakfast, although it almost stuck in her throat. Nina would keep curling up against Cedas on the mattress and hanging around his neck. She might once have been a dear friend, but she could be a real bitch when she put some effort into it.

Even so, Jesral managed a few pleasantries before getting down to her real business. And it was not the rifled packs. Oh, no. She had something far more important to thrash out first before she brought that up. She wanted the caravan turned east and she was going to get the caravan turned east, because she had the trump card; knowledge of the one thing Cedas would put before the Company.

She knew that for years before joining it he had risked his life as a mercenary, and he had done it for money. It had never been clear to her why he'd given it up; she could only assume that, given a good performance (which Cedas always did give), the show life paid well enough, but with less risk. Goodness only knew what he wanted with money; he did not seem to live extravagantly beyond always being immaculately dressed in public. His reasons mattered little to her. She had money, and she was going to use it. Well, some of it. She knew they would have to hide Jastur if – no, she corrected herself, when – they got him out. There was no telling how long for: so at least half of what they had was emergency money for food, horses, bribes, whatever it took to ensure his safety.

She did not make small talk for long. Cedas had cunning but very little patience, and she was in no mood to play games of wit at the moment.

'Cedas, I know it's going to be disruptive, but I want to ask the Company to do something important. Very important,' she reiterated, as the other two glanced at each other with unreadable expressions. Nina untwined herself from Cedas and he turned to face Jesral full on, like a brick wall. Jesral had seen that stance before. She was not about to be put off by it.

'I told Nina, Renia and I have to go east. But we also

need help, and cover. In short, we need the Company too. I'm asking you to divert the caravan, and come with us. I can promise you, it will be worth your while if we succeed.' Again a look passed between the others, barely perceptible this time. Nina set about retrieving her scattered clothes and moved away to get dressed, leaving the business to him.

'How far east?' His question was non-committal, so she did not let her hopes get too high.

'To Karn. After that, I don't know.' Something flashed across Cedas's face, too fast for her to identify it.

'If it's going to be worth our while, that means it's going to be risky. So how much is worth our while?'

'I'm not in a position to give you a final figure – but trust me, those involved will pay any sum we agree and more.'

Cedas responded to her reply with a doubtful shrug.

'It'll have to be some amount: after all, if we turn east there's all the lost business up ahead on the coast, and the lost goodwill in the future. Then we have to send out notice ahead of us again, if we're to get any sort of crowd in the towns ahead of us. Takings are certain to be down anyway. At the very least, we have to secure that much for the livelihood of the Company. Can you supply anything in advance, to cover that at least?'

Jesral allowed herself a benign smile.

'I think I may. How much are we looking at?'

'One thousand, two hundred internationals,' Cedas calmly replied.

'*What?*'

It was a ludicrous sum, and four times what they had. She had certainly never seen that much money in her life, even in Cedas's hands.

'Are you mad? You can't make that much in a year, never mind the ten days or so to Karn! Where am I going to find that kind of money?'

Cedas made a show of being contrite.

'I'm sorry, Jez, but I've got to insist on a big advance, if only to keep the rest of the Company sweet. Let's say, a quarter of the sum I named.'

'But that's still... three hundred.' The penny dropped, and the expression of innocence on Cedas's face when she glowered at him was unconvincing.

'You had that boy go through our packs. You knew before I started how much I had to bargain with.' The corners of his mouth turned up a little.

'And you've just told me you'll have access to more,' he pointed out, 'or perhaps I've read you wrong. Perhaps you aren't going to Karn to try to rescue the Crown.'

Her jaw dropped. 'How did you know?' she asked, once she had gathered her wits.

'The rumours; swords and men's clothes in your packs when your companions are dead; above all, your secrecy. That's not like you. So, you believe the rumours?' Jesral set her jaw again, obstinate once more.

'I know he's there. Well, now you know why we need to go east, are you going to persist in blocking us with your impractical demands? Are Renia and I going to do on our own what you're too gutless to attempt?'

Cedas sucked in his breath as if affronted, mocking her.

'That was below the belt, Jez, even for you. And a bit of a cheek, when what you're asking me to embroil the Company in is not so much risky as damn' near suicidal. So what goes on? Who the hell is this friend of yours?'

'Renia? She's no one, Cedas. She's just a girl from Mhrydain, same as me.'

'Same as you?' he snorted. 'When did you last have three hundred Internationals and connections with the aristocracy?'

'I don't know where the money came from,' she said sullenly, 'but the connections are pure chance.' She was thrown by how much he had worked out already and couldn't decide how much more it would be safe to tell him.

'You mean it, don't you? Then she's no one important?' Anger and disappointment crossed his face – seeing his one thousand two hundred Internationals evaporate into thin air, Jesral guessed. Then something else occurred to him, and he turned a scrutinizing gaze on her. 'But she carries something important. That bag around her neck…'

'…is non-negotiable,' she told him bluntly. The smile and the raised eyebrow said he doubted that. 'Cedas, it is not. Someone will die before she gives that up. Leave it alone.'

'Fine. But you don't just need a ride there, do you? You need help rescuing him too. I'm not touching this job unless I know what we're letting ourselves in for. Why are two girls from Mhrydain trying to rescue Ilmaen's Crown all on their own?'

Jesral sighed. Kerin was gone, so what did it matter if

she told him?

'The men we travelled with… one was her brother, that's true enough. The other was the LandMaster of Lestar.'

'The Crown's brother? But he drowned.'

'No.' With a pang, Jesral corrected herself: 'Not when everyone said he did. He washed up on their doorstep, they nursed him back to health; and being at least part Ilmaenese themselves, they decided to come back with him to help. Then it all went wrong.'

'So, what she carries is something of the LandMaster's, to identify herself to the Crown?'

'And to others after. Cedas, if God willing we do it, if we get Jastur out, then we have to hide him, feed him, get him into safe hands. That three hundred is all we have. Look, we aren't part of a bigger group; we can't get any more money until we have him safe. There's me, and Renia, and that's it. If you take it all, he'll be helpless.'

Cedas leant forward, and at last to her relief he had a genuinely serious expression on his face. He looked at her, frowning, and softly said, 'He'll be out of Karn. He's Crown; he must have some wit. Let him use it.'

'Cedas…'

'Jez, I can't conceive how you got caught up in all this, but if you want to drag us into it as well, it's going to cost you. And that's to get you there, and to help you get him out. No more than that for the three hundred – and remember, it's just an advance. If we succeed, I expect more from our good Crown. A lot more. That's it, final offer. Now do you take it?' He held his hand out, ready to shake on it.

Jesral stared at him, dumbfounded and depressed. So much for being in control of the situation. Renia could have done as well, in her broken Ilmaenese. But Jesral knew her adversary in this battle of wits too well. He had scored enough points against her that he would not back down in any way now. She took his hand, but with as little contact as she could to convey her loathing for his tactics. The battle over, he relaxed quite happily and hailed Nina for more food. Jesral folded her arms, an automatic gesture of sullenness.

'Well, I see little point in prolonging my stay here,' she snapped, and got up.

'Tell Renia she doesn't need to bring the money over when she comes for her class,' he remarked. 'I'll send someone to pick it up later.'

Jesral turned in the doorway.

'I don't suppose you need reminding of it, Cedas, but you're a real bastard.'

He grinned in his usual infuriating way.

'Do you know, Jez, I'd lay odds my father would say the same thing.'

She slammed the door so hard that half the camp turned to look as she left.

oOo

She was in a foul mood still when she explained it all to Renia, back at Atune's wagon. Renia offered no criticism of her efforts, partly because she did not think she could have done any better and partly because she did not want to feel Jesral's temper. Atune, on the other hand, blithely labelled her every form of idiot under the sun, and a fearful row ensued between them. Before long Jesral had swung the argument round to direct the blame for the whole episode on to Atune, as it was she who had chosen Cedas as her successor in control of the Company. This sent the old woman almost apoplectic with rage – Renia thought she would have another stroke as she stormed in her bunk. But the old woman managed to frame her answer at last.

'You witless child, you ingrate! Take your addled brain back and think! Who did I confide in, who did I take through every step in the Company's yearly circuit? Who was I in fact grooming to take over from me, when she goes running home to Mama over an unhappy love affair? Oh, well done! So glad to see part of your brain still works when it's rattled hard enough.'

Jesral sat down hard in sudden surprise, mouth open like a fish.

'I had no idea. I really didn't see that, till now. Why didn't you tell me then?' she wailed.

'Because, fool, I didn't want Cedas to know. But as it happened, your pillow talk must have given it away. Yes, I should have told you – and told you to keep your mouth shut while I was at it. He's a crafty one. I often wondered if the business with Nina wasn't deliberate, you know. Cedas has never been one to play second fiddle, and you were the only one who could have matched him. Still, no use crying about it. He hasn't done so badly. He's as hard as nails, and that's probably been a blessing to us, this last year.'

That was cruel of Atune, Renia thought, unnecessarily so; at the comment about Cedas's affair with Nina, Jesral had momentarily looked as though she had been kicked in the stomach. However, when Atune had finished Jesral railed no more. She just sat still for a few moments. She had a cotton shawl under her hands, one that she and Renia shared. She picked it up and fingered it thoughtfully, realized what she was doing and looked at it with strange concentration. Then she turned to Renia.

'Can we do without this?' She indicated the scarf. Confused, Renia nodded. Jesral turned it in her hands until she found a weakness in the grain of the fabric and ripped it feverishly in half, then in half again, and again, until it was a mass of shredded pieces on her lap and the floor of the wagon.

When she had caught her breath and calmed again, she announced to the other two: 'When we have finished this, I will take Cedas by the hand. Yes, I will. And I'll rip his arm off at the shoulder and beat him to death with the ragged end. But until then,' she told Renia in a voice heavy with warning, 'I want him to think that we think the sun shines when he passes by. I don't want him to have any idea what's going to hit him.'

'I think he'll know once you've ripped – OK, understood,' Renia backtracked, which probably saved her life.

oOo

And so Renia had gone on with the lessons and practised the codes and the voice projection, until she was dreaming of shouting codes and getting some inkling of how likely it was that Jesral could mean her threat. The trouble with Cedas was you had to admire him while he incensed you.

She was not concentrating. When she registered Cedas's voice, it was because of its change in tone; she realized he had had to repeat himself. She reacted to the keyword automatically.

'You hold a cloak pin.'

'What more can you tell me about this particular item?' he asked. Particular – that meant it was blue, or had a blue stone. But item meant a man's property. That was wrong. Was he trying to trick her, or had she confused the signals?

'It's a woman's brooch, with a blue stone. It's very special to its owner.'

There was a slight pause. Her heart sank when she picked up the background tone in Cedas's voice.

'I was given this item by a man. Is the strain of communing with the Hidden Realms becoming too great, O Princess?'

A voice from the audience interrupted him.

'No, she is right. The pin was my wife's. And it *is* special. It is old, and made from a very hard metal, perhaps from before the Catastrophe destroyed the old world. My wife and son died of the fever and I had to burn everything they had touched in my house, all their clothes and possessions. I thought I would have nothing of them but my memories, yet when I raked through the ashes of the fire that brooch had survived.'

The man's voice was awed and sad. Renia suppressed the urge to tell him she was sorry: an entranced princess was unlikely to do that. Cedas took control again.

'And indeed, the stone set in this pin is cracked, where it has undergone ordeal by fire. Your property, sir,' he said as he returned it, 'and a thing to be treasured. And now, ladies and gentlemen, I must call the Princess back from the Hidden Realms. For the temptations to stay are great, and none dare remain in spirit there too long, lest they fail to return.'

That was a carefully veiled threat if ever she heard

one.

Cedas went through the awakening routine, and the recovered Princess was raised on her litter and borne away out of the circle of the audience. The next act slipped past her and she heard her parting applause blending into their welcome from the crowd.

Cedas reappeared next to the swaying litter and slapped her blindfold, which he was still carrying, into her lap. He was seething.

'Don't you ever do that again!'

'Do what?'

'Improvise. You could have got us into all sorts of difficulties there, with that cock and bull business. "It's a woman's brooch"… I told you it was a man's!' His impersonation of her was not flattering.

'But I was right,' she retorted, stung.

'No, girl. You were lucky. Now get this straight. I tell you what to do, and you do it. Word for word, gesture for gesture. Or you and Jesral are sitting on your packs by the roadside, looking for another way to get to Karn.'

He made sure Jesral, who was just walking up, heard that before he strode off. Once he had gone the reluctant litter bearers put the litter down, and none too gently. Jesral helped Renia up as the others ambled off without so much as offering her a hand.

'Hmm. What did you do wrong?'

Renia shrugged hopelessly. 'I got something right.'

Jesral shook her head knowingly. 'Bad move, that. You know, we could come to some arrangement over his fate.'

'Meaning?'

'Meaning *I* could sit on him and *you* could rip his arm off – as long as I get to beat him to death with it.'

Renia shook her head. 'I can't do that.'

'Why not? You know he's asking for it.'

'Because he deserves a lot worse,' said Renia darkly. 'You'll have to think of something far more unpleasant.'

'Give me time,' Jesral assured Renia, 'I'll come up with something.'

Chapter 17 – Something Lost, Something Gained

Kerin watched Vel lay out the last of the display wares on Naylan's stall and look them over. Mindful of Naylan's warnings about light-fingered passers-by, he then swapped a cheap item at the back for a more valuable one at the front. He caught Kerin watching him, and stared back to see if he was about to be criticized; he was still a little over-sensitive at the moment. Their argument was over; each understood the other's point of view, but they were not going to resolve the difference of opinion. Now that they had agreed a plan of action, honour bound them to it. Vel had the chance to search while Kerin chafed at the delay, but that would soon change. That was why Vel was so tense.

Kerin gave a jerk of his head towards the Harbour House. Vel followed the line of Kerin's nod, gazed at the whitewashed stone building at the bottom end of the market place with a degree of nervousness. Their third port; his last chance.

'Are you going, or shall I?' Kerin asked.

'Me. I need the practice in Ilmaenese,' Vel reasoned. 'Ah, well, here goes.'

He strode off across the market place with forced jauntiness. Kerin watched him go with pity and regret, knowing Vel was making an effort for appearance's sake. They had agreed; three ports and no more before they turned south and east for Karn. Kerin had reassessed his judgment of Vel after their fight and could not stop cursing himself for not seeing how Vel would react to that situation. Now he was

confident that he knew his man. If they got no news here Vel
would not press for them to carry on his search. The
knowledge did not make him feel much better. There had been
no news at the last two ports; no ships had limped in from the
storm, no sightings of the *Dawn Wind* were reported. Vel had
brushed off each new disappointment; at the most recent port
he had spoken at length to some seamen, and had afterwards
expressed optimism that he had misinterpreted the tides on the
Ilmaen side of the water, not allowing for the tidal stream
running the other way at certain times. That would mean the
Dawn Wind might have made port further south-west, behind
them. He had left it there; no hints or suggestions that they
should turn back, however he might feel. Kerin was all too
aware of what the lack of news meant to Vel. The fool who
said 'no news is good news' needed to live with the suspense
they had been under.

Even so, Kerin knew he still hadn't made Vel grasp
all of the repercussions that would ensue from Jastur's loss.
Renia seemed to understand even before he had tried to
explain, especially his more personal reasons; those he
doubted he would ever be able to voice to Vel. Probably not to
anyone else, either. No, if he could only get the practical,
economic reasons across to Vel that would be enough.

The chance would come; there would be some way to
talk of it, to bring it into a conversation in passing. He could
comment to Naylan on the state of decline all around them
here; he had seen the same in all the ports and coast villages
they had passed through. It was very apparent, when you knew
Ilmaen. This port was the biggest town they had been to, but
like the poorest hamlet it bore the marks of hardship and
demoralization. He had known the northern ports when he was
younger, and they had always been bustling and noisy. The
quayside market was like a graveyard today; and this was a
catch day, a trading day. The townspeople seemed wary and
suspicious, or else lethargic – both out of character. It had not
been going on for long though; it had not yet reached the point

where the buildings showed signs of neglect. A matter of months; about the time Maregh had been in power.

The market was so quiet and his thoughts so engrossing that nearly half an hour passed in this way. Then Naylan called him, breaking his reverie; he was attending to a man who was not happy about the balance of his sword. As they had travelled Kerin and Vel had borrowed from Naylan's stock of blades to practise with, and it had been impossible for Kerin to do that and hide his sword skills. While Naylan knew Kerin wanted to keep himself to himself, he was not about to waste that kind of knowledge if business could be made from it; Kerin could not escape that, in fairness to their benefactor. Once or twice should do no harm. He joined Naylan and his customer.

It was a fine sword, old and doubtless a family heirloom. Its owner watched anxiously as Kerin tested its weight as unshowily as he could. The sword was slightly unbalanced, although excellently kept.

'Either you've been fortunate not to draw this sword in anger or self-defence for a long time, sir, or it's been superbly looked after,' Kerin told the man.

'A bit of both, as it happens,' the man replied. 'It was last used by my father, who was a soldier; he taught me how to look after it. Now I've a mind to go soldiering myself. There's no trade you can make a living at round here any more. I just wanted to be sure I was as well equipped as I can be.'

'Well, it's in no need of sharpening, but I'll whet this edge here a little, just to balance it up. Look, this is how you can tell...' And he condensed a year's training in sword judgment into thirty seconds before grinding down and polishing the edge in question.

He charged the man five hundredths, quite a high

sum, but the customer did not quibble. Naylan managed to keep the surprise off his face until the man had gone, then leant across to speak to Kerin.

'Sure I can't interest you in joining the partnership, lad?' he enquired, eyeing the money meaningfully.

'I'm afraid not.' Kerin grinned as he reached for the takings pocket on his work apron. Naylan dismissed the need for it with a wave of his hand.

'Ah, go on, you pocket that yourself, lad.' Kerin did with thanks, mindful of their lack of cash. Naylan had talked this past evening about wages, but he clearly would not be able to pay much and Kerin was thinking of the future. He did not like to tempt fate, but they had to be ready to spirit Jastur away and lie low. He knew how to live off the land, and Vel would be able to add a few more tricks to his. Even so living like that was tough on a fit body; and Jastur seemed likely to come out of Karn in a bad state. He wished Renia had been clearer on that. Her concern for Jastur continued to nag at him.

Naylan leant across him, ostensibly to tidy the goods on display, and murmured, 'Laddie is back.'

To Naylan, Kerin was 'lad' and he used 'laddie' for Vel. 'Laddie' usually involved more decibels, as though Naylan thought Vel was deaf rather than unfamiliar with his language. This time Naylan simply nodded Vel an acknowledgement of his return and turned away. Kerin looked at his friend's face, and saw why; there were no words to bring comfort to such complete distress.

He will ask to go on to the next port, Kerin suddenly thought, his previous faith in his friend gone and his heart sinking; and I must tell him no. He stood and waited for the question to come.

'Kerin –' Vel forced the words out '– what's the one possibility we didn't allow for?'

He tried to fit a possibility to Vel's expression, and horrible realization dawned.

'The ship foundered?'

'*A* ship sank, the night of the storm.' Vel clarified the doubt, but his face spoke of hopelessness. 'About a mile south-west of here. There were no survivors, no positive identification of the ship by the authorities.'

'It might not have been the *Dawn Wind* then.'

'The flotsam that's been thrown up: it's the same cargo as the *Dawn Wind* was carrying.'

'You still can't be sure. Look…' Kerin nearly made the offer, stopped himself. He couldn't do it.

'No. You were right; we've wasted too much time. Let's not lose Jastur as well. We should turn east now – I think we should start today.'

Kerin went and asked Naylan quietly if it would be inconvenient to move on. Naylan shook his head; business was slow here. He gazed keenly back at Kerin.

'It's more than just not finding them, isn't it?'

'Yes. He found out that a ship sank near here, the night of the storm.'

'Your ship?'

Kerin shrugged in angry uncertainty.

'Hell only knows; the harbour authorities don't. But it had the same cargo. Damn, I don't know what to think. But he's upset, and wants to get out of here.'

'All right. I sent Bighur for his lunch; as soon as he's back, we can start winding down. We'll eat at an inn before we go and get a good stiff drink down Laddie, eh? Ah, talk of the little devil, here comes Bighur now.'

They broke the stall down and left Bighur to mind the wagon while they went to eat and drown Vel's sorrows. Naylan offered Kerin a drink too, and to his surprise found himself asking for mulled wine. He never drank mulled wine. Except that one time...

Renia had been a comfort to him that night, just sitting there. But she had thought he had asked her to stay to talk, and so she had felt obliged to say something. He looked at Vel, a picture of misery, and felt the same urge to talk himself. Yet there was nothing he could think to say or ask that would not be painful, so he did not. If it *had* been the *Dawn Wind* that foundered, and they were gone – the thought hollowed him out, and he could not get past it.

Naylan brought over a tray of meat, gravy and fried vegetables, and a trencher each to eat it off. They picked at it wordlessly, pushed most of it aside. The landlord came to clear away, and Naylan ordered another round of drinks, which seemed to go down far easier.

'Gentlemen, do you mind if I make some observations, and a suggestion?' Naylan said at last. 'We seem to have done all right together, the four of us, but it's not much farther till we're due to split up. You seem to want to keep out of sight of the authorities, and I'm not going to ask why; what I don't know can't hurt me. I know you've got this business in the east that won't wait and you don't want to talk about it too much, but if we can keep things going as they are, it's worth our while for Bighur and me to go east too. If that's any use to you?'

Kerin took in what he said, and started to turn to Vel, who put out a hand.

'Don't even waste time asking me. I'm a fool and the reason we're not halfway there already.' He turned to Naylan. 'I'm sorry I can't act more grateful for your offer due to the circumstances, but we accept.'

oOo

Four days later it was a relief to all on the wagon when they started up out of Parri Citywild. It had reduced the journey time a little, cutting across it rather than going around it; still none of them had enjoyed it much, conscious that they crossed a land of ancient tragedy. A place where once men had built a city so great it held people beyond numbering and then other men had eradicated all life and sign of the city in the Catastrophe, scouring it down to bedrock and beyond. It was a place harmless in itself, but inhospitable; the topsoil was so fragile it would not tolerate farming, and so the area remained a wilderness, one vast boggy heath populated only by herds of wild horses and sheep. The River Sen flowed from it; they had followed the river upstream until it turned to fenland where the Catastrophe weapons had disrupted its course. Vel knew of other Citywilds; Melor and the villagers had spoken of Hampton, which had once been a great port. This was the first time Vel had seen one, and the size was numbing. Up ahead you could, at a distance, make out the transition point where trees began to grow again and know the Citywild was ending. They were within an hour's journey of the edge now; the wild herds did not venture out to graze this close to man and that meant bigger shrubs could grow to either side of, and sometimes on, the barely visible track through the gorse.

As Naylan followed it, Vel looked back. It was a fair

day and seeing was clear, but the edge they had come from was far out of sight, a day and a half's travel away. And they had only clipped the northern edge of the Citywild; it must be two, three days across the middle. He tried again to envisage how many people it would take to fill it, and then crowded that number on top of itself hundreds of times, just as the city had piled storey upon storey. How terrible, to live like that; how awful, to have so many lives snuffed out in an instant. It felt, as Naylan said, as though this place resented humans after such unchecked destruction. Vel had been to places where the people had made him feel unwelcome, but never before to one where the land itself did.

Naylan certainly had not wanted to come, doubting the chances of a ferry across the river this near the Citywild and voicing grave concern about how passable the track would be. Kerin had been firm and was proved right. To have taken a more northerly road or headed for the better but more travelled road to the south would have added time he was not prepared to spare. Cutting out a few stubborn bushes blocking the track was a job that Kerin and Vel took upon themselves to do, and Naylan joined them for the last few, seeing how much travelling time had been saved. In the end they had endured no worse than a sobering experience, one they gladly put behind them now.

Once past the Citywild, they headed north-east to rejoin the main road. Time had been saved, but now they had next week's meals to earn. They stayed a full day at one town, a day and a half at the next, and stocked up the last afternoon with the intention of making a long run before the next stop. However Naylan's wagon was feeling the strain of the route, the extra passengers and additional stores. They had to stop again at the next town for parts to repair a wheel, and that took all their spare money.

Since it was a bright day and a small, quiet town they took the chance to do a little more business after the wagon was repaired, but it looked as though it might have been a mistake.

'Ho! Is caravan coming,' sharp-eyed Bighur announced. Fifteen or so brightly coloured wagons entered the square and made a circle nearby. 'They circus people! We get some fun tonight?'

'No, Bighur,' Naylan replied. 'We need to stay ahead of them. If they're going our way, they'll hold us up for too long. We'll shut up shop as soon as we get a chance.' He turned to Kerin, aware of his hurry if not his purpose, and pointed out, 'It'd look odd if we passed up the chance for their business, and caravanners do gossip. Hopefully they won't want much doing, but if they do, you two stay on the stall and keep yourselves to yourselves. Stand around and have a beer or something; the more you make business look slack, the slacker it'll be. I'll manage them.'

Two of the caravanners were eying the wagon and came over. One was an eye-catching man, smartly dressed: dark and lean with flashing black eyes. Naylan stepped away from the stall to greet them; they spoke for a while, then Naylan and the man shook hands before the man strode away and Naylan headed back to the wagon.

'Bighur!' Naylan roared, and Bighur trotted obediently after him as he went up the wagon steps. There was much clattering and cursing inside, until they emerged carrying a portable grindstone.

'Who'd have a knife-throwing act and nothing to sharpen the knives?' Naylan muttered grimly. Bighur said nothing, too busy struggling with his end. They staggered over to the ring of wagons and began setting up. Caravanners approached them from all directions; there looked to be a score or more knives to sharpen.

Vel sighed. 'I'll get us some beers, then,' he murmured and ducked under the stall counter.

He returned with two bottles from their stores; opened them both deftly and passed Kerin one. He had just taken a pull from his when he stopped short and looked back at the circle of caravans.

'What is it?' Kerin asked.

'It's Jez!' said Vel in disbelief.

'Where?' Kerin tried to follow where he was looking.

'Just going into that blue and grey wagon.'

Kerin found the wagon he meant, just as the door shut. 'Ah, I didn't see. Vel? …Vel!'

He had put the bottle down and was striding purposefully towards the wagon. Kerin dared do no more than that fierce whisper or he would risk drawing attention.

Too late. Vel was managing to draw enough attention on his own. He had barely entered the ring of caravans before he was challenged by the dark man. Naylan had seen what was going on; Kerin lipread his silent oath as he hurried over to intervene. There was a brief conversation, polite on the dark man's side, urgent on Vel's. The man suddenly drew himself up, offered Vel entry to the circle with a flourish and watched him hurry to the blue and grey wagon. Then he turned and the flashing black eyes looked directly at Kerin for several seconds before glancing away.

Kerin cursed roundly, ran his eye over the stall's contents and palmed a long knife.

oOo

In Atune's wagon, Jesral was tidying up while Renia finished giving Atune a wash, the old woman holding the bowl on her lap so Renia had both hands free to work. She brought Atune a rag and, not having the words in Ilmaenese, mimed that she wanted Atune to blow her nose on it. Atune muttered something indecipherable and doubtless rude, but when Renia would not give way the old woman forced her weak hand up to take the rag off her, rather than suffer the indignity of having her nose blown for her.

'There,' Renia declared triumphantly, 'you can get your arm up if you try. So you can brush your hair yourself as well.'

'Tricksy child. You've been in that one's company too long.'

Jesral heard, and poked her tongue out at Atune.

'Jez, have you seen Atune's brush?' Renia asked.

'It's on the shelf above you. Did someone outside just call me?'

'I'm not sure, you spoke over it,' Renia said, listening hard because the call had caught her attention in some way too. Jesral shrugged and finished folding the last blanket. 'They can wait till I'm done.' Then the call came again, much nearer, and the van swayed as the caller ran up the steps and flung the door open.

Jesral found herself face to face with Vel. The sight struck her dumb. He grabbed Jesral by the shoulders, proving himself no ghost.

'You're all right!' he gasped. 'And Ren?' He caught sight of her then and beamed at her.

'Oh, my God,' Jesral said in a small voice. 'My God. I thought you were dead.' And she burst into tears, flung her arms round his waist and pressed her face against him to try to stop her tears. When it did not work, she let go and caught him a thumping blow across the arm.

'You bastard! Don't you ever do anything like that again, you hear me?'

'I didn't do it on purpose, Jez,' he pointed out reasonably. He got his previous treatment in reverse order, a sideswipe first before she hugged him again. He held her uncertainly and looked in bemusement at Renia before noticing Atune with a start.

'My apologies, Ma'am, for bursting in like this, but I'm so pleased to see them again...'

Atune waved his apology aside.

'You carry on, they need cheering up,' she told him, so he turned back to Renia. She just sat where she was, the little half-smile on her face starting to turn into the question she desperately needed to ask.

'Yes, he's all right too. He's outside,' said Vel. Jesral disentangled herself from him.

'Oh... I have to go and hit him, too,' she declared tearfully and hurried out of the wagon. Vel went to sit by Renia, and looked at her in a mixture of wonder, relief and happiness.

'Well, here you are,' he said. 'And here are you,' she responded, and they both smiled inanely, until her eyes started to fill. Her brother patted her hand encouragingly. 'Hey, don't you cry on me too. You've done well, and we're fine... everything's fine now.'

She struggled against the tears, unable to say anything. He wasn't very good with her crying, she knew. He looked around in desperation, stood and bowed politely to Atune. 'Ma'am. Velohim Ty'r Athre, at your service.'

'Ahh. The brother! Nice manners,' she said in an aside to Renia, who had taken the chance to compose herself. 'I am Atune Lak Sumin, retired leader of this Company. Sorry this stupid body cannot greet you properly. Stroke, you know. Ah, and Jesral brings the other one…'

They stepped through the door, Kerin closing it behind them. He surveyed the room, took in Atune in the bed, her birdlike eyes boring into him, and gave her a brief acknowledgement before turning to the others.

'It's good to see you both again. However, we have a problem. We may need to get out of here quickly.' He lowered his voice beyond Atune's hearing. 'The man you spoke to, Vel. I don't know him, but he knows who I am.'

'No. No, it's all right,' Jesral interrupted. 'He's… friendly. His name's Cedas, he heads the Company. He's agreed to help us, but he… had to know a bit of background first.'

'You told him,' Kerin interpreted.

'We thought you were dead,' she defended herself, and the reminder nearly set her off again.

'Well, it's done now; as long as you're happy you can trust him,' He looked to Renia, who sighed. 'He's kept faith with us so far,' she assured him, wondering how she would ever explain the rest.

Kerin sighed and tried to relax, giving them a tight but genuine smile. 'It's truly good to see you again. We had all but given up hope that we would. I dare say it was the same for you.' He caught Atune still watching him, stood and gave her a more formal acknowledgement than before. 'Madam, we are disturbing you. It would be more polite of us to take our business outside.'

A final parting bow and he led the others out of the door and on to the verandah to continue. Atune caught Renia's sleeve before she followed, jerking her chin towards the door.

'His manners are a bit slower than your brother's. He seems to have more on his mind,' she observed. 'He's a handsome lad, isn't he?'

'Oh, yes, he's very handsome.'

'Nice to have a good-looking man in my bedroom again, though I can't help thinking he's a bit too young for me.' Atune's laughter at Renia's shocked expression was shrill enough to break glass.

The others were sitting or standing around the wagon's verandah when she limped outside.

'She won't hear us,' Jesral was telling Kerin, low-voiced. 'Even if she did, we can trust her. I mean, who's she going to go and tell? She's bedridden, for God's sake.'

Kerin's doubt was angering Jesral, aimed as it was at a friend. Renia wanted to defend his cautious approach, because she understood it – but having come to know Atune herself, she was inclined to agree with Jesral. Kerin resolved the problem himself: 'I am sorry, it is my job to be the suspicious one. I trust your judgment. Sit now and tell us how you two come to be here.'

They had left space on the verandah for Renia, and she settled there as Jesral related their side of the tale.

'I suppose we're doing the same as you – trying to get to Karn. These people are the ones I travelled with before. We got them to turn away from their normal circuit to take us to Karn. Cedas – he's the one in charge – says he'll help us get Jastur out.'

'So he knows about Jastur too,' Kerin concluded, one of his statements she could read as an accusation.

'We didn't tell him. Apparently there have been rumours that he is in Karn.' She glanced at Renia, wondering how much to say about Cedas. 'We were hoping he would come up with a rescue plan. He was a mercenary some years ago, I thought he might know the best way to storm a fort. I don't know about you, but I had no idea how we were going to get Jastur out.'

Kerin spread his hands in a gesture of uncertainty.

'I don't think you could have done it, not without inside knowledge of the fort. But that you were prepared to try… I can't thank you enough for that.'

Jesral admitted: 'Ren's mad idea, not mine. But you've got to tell us how you got here. I still can't believe you didn't drown in that storm.'

'Fate must not have been ready to give the two of us a new life yet. We were up in the rigging fighting with a jammed yard when the wind hit the ship badly and it heeled over. Vel tried to save me; I lost my grip, and the next big wave brought him in after me, along with half the rigging.' Jesral nodded, tying that in with the Captain's story. 'How we avoided being trapped in the wreckage I have no idea. But the ship was further inshore than we thought, dangerously close – I was upon sandbanks almost as soon as I began swimming. Though swimming is probably not the word for whatever it was I did to get ashore; still, I made it somehow. I started walking, and the next thing I know I'm stumbling through a copse and nearly getting a knife in the ribs from some tinkers when I barged into their camp.

'They took me in; we found Vel next morning, further down the coast. We have been tinkering this past week, part for cover, part for a living. We looked for you in a couple of ports but then we had to give up and turn south-east. And that brings us to here.' He paused, story finished, and frowned apologetically at Jesral.

'Forgive me, Jez, but I would feel better if I had the chance to talk to that man who knows me – Cedas, did you say?'

'Yes. I'll come with you.'

'Fine. Vel, can you keep an eye on Naylan and Bighur? It's time they knew what this is really about, and I would sooner it came from one of us.'

Renia was left alone as the others wended their way through the cluster of vans. Not needed, not able to help. She sat there a few moments longer, puzzling over one thing.

They were all safe and well and together again. So why didn't she feel happier?

oOo

Jesral knocked on Cedas's wagon door; Nina opened it. She stood back to let them in, casting a knowing glance at both of them. Cedas stood at the far end of the wagon, waiting for them. Once they were in Nina picked up a shawl.

'I'll go help Tamli buy stores,' she told Cedas, and left.

'This is Cedas,' Jesral introduced them. Both men

eyed each other. Cedas gave a bow that Kerin matched.

'You honour us, my Lord LandMaster,' Cedas said.
Kerin straightened up sharply at the honorific.

'The last time you should use that title, my friend. It
will bring trouble with it. Call me Anken.'

'Anken it is.'

'Do any others here know the other name?'

My woman who you just saw, your two; that is all.
Oh, there is a boy who knows how much money your women
have on them; but he does not know your name, and he has
sense enough to keep his mouth shut.'

'Yes, about the money,' Jesral started, and hesitated,
not sure how Kerin would react. Cedas stepped in.

'We came to a financial arrangement about your
brother's rescue. I was assured it would be honoured,' he said.
Kerin looked levelly at him.

'You assume the money was mine.' He glanced at
Jesral; she had probably assumed the same thing. 'I have been
off the side of a ship twice in the space of three months, and
both times came out with nothing but the clothes I stood up in.
Everything I have, I owe to the generosity of those I travel
with. But do not doubt that if Fortune favours me I will repay
that generosity, a hundred-fold. Now,' he continued, 'how
many here know where we are bound, or why?'

'Know? The same as before. Suspect… well, they
aren't stupid. We're off the normal circuit, and rumour has the
true Crown in the dungeons of Karn. But then, it also has him
in the tallest tower in Lestar, under Maregh's personal guard;
or in Federin still, being held for a great ransom by a renegade

clan. I understand to some, he never left the ship; he has travelled to northern lands, in search of a pure-blooded Northern bride. And those are the least fanciful of the rumours I have heard.' He dropped the wry smile. 'But you, I understand, are certain he is there?'

'My source is very reliable. The only question remaining is whether we can get there in time.'

oOo

Further meetings with Cedas and Naylan (when he had recovered from the shock of discovering who one of his workers was) established that they would all continue on the same route to Karn, but that Naylan's wagon was not effectively part of the Company. This was due to Cedas's insistence on the rule about all members of the troupe contributing. Kerin, even if he had been able to do anything, would not draw attention to himself in that fashion. Naylan and Vel avowed themselves devoid of any performing skills, and Bighur was persuaded that his light should stay under a bushel for a little longer. Cedas took it no further. Kerin could see he was wary, understandably. Cedas treated him with respect, but he was also cautious of him, doubtless in case it was all a ruse. Here was a man, claiming to be LandMaster of Lestar, as good as telling him what to do in his own camp. Cedas did not look to be a man to take kindly to that, but he said nothing. Kerin conceded to his insistence on Company rules to give the man some of his ground back.

Whether Cedas believed in Kerin's identity or not was immaterial, so long as Kerin had convinced him that Jastur was in Karn, and that Kerin was not fool enough to try and get him out if it couldn't be done. The days spent on the journey had served that one purpose at least; a plan had formed and been checked and rechecked in his head. At last, improbable though it had seemed till now, it looked like it was possible.

No further mention was made of payment. Jesral was thankful that Cedas did not raise the matter again, fearing Kerin's wrath when he found out that the arrangement had taken care of all their funds. Little did she guess what would really set light to the tinder.

Chapter 18 – A Little Learning...

At first, despite an offer of seats from Cedas, Naylan's party stayed away from the shows. Bighur's disappointment was salved by the promise that he could watch a rehearsal further along the way. If they were going to get to Karn in six or seven days there could only be four public shows, but to Cedas that was more reason than ever to have rehearsals at every evening halt, to keep everyone fit and their acts up to standard. Each day they set out early and travelled as long as they could; and on show day afternoons, while the Company set the show up, Naylan traded to curious townsfolk who came to see what entertainment that evening might bring.

Kerin stayed out of sight now in all the towns and villages they passed through, unlikely to be recognized but unwilling to risk the possibility this close to Karn. Even if his face was not known, his good looks drew attention; there was always the danger that these would be remarked on and the connection with Naylan and the Company made later, when Jastur was out and the hue and cry got under way.

Despite his self-imposed isolation it was not long before Kerin found out the full extent of the agreement between Jesral and Cedas, but if Jesral had hoped for an argument, given that Kerin's concerns were the same as hers, she was to be disappointed. He conceded entirely to Cedas his rights to the full sum, but quietly negotiated a compromise. Kerin could name large and plausible amounts he could lay his hands on – but only if Cedas gave Kerin's party what they needed to spirit Jastur away. He made an offer Cedas could not refuse, the balance to be paid in Lestar in October as long as Kerin or Jastur were alive to do so. So they had their emergency funds, but Cedas was a hard bargainer; it was only just enough. The whole business made it clear to Kerin that he and Cedas were never going to like each other, but so long as they could respect each other's skills they'd be able to work together.

The skills were what mattered. The second night together, after the show had finished, they held a meeting in Cedas's wagon. Kerin knew who he wanted for the rescue and why, and he made sure they were all there.

He began by telling them of Karn, fortress and town, and how impregnable it was. He painted a bleak picture of intense security and formidable architecture, built on a site with command of the surrounding area. He ended his summary with a smile; most of them thought him gone mad at the sight, but Cedas laughed and propped his head in his hand.

'So, we've all dismissed the impossible options, and no time wasted arguing over them; now what's the improbable one you're left with?'

The improbable one sounded as impossible as the others. Vel protested against it, as did Jesral and Naylan; Bighur, Nina and Renia sat silent and uncomfortable along with Eddir, Cedas's youthful spy who had rifled their packs. But Cedas asked question after question, probing round the edges of their protests, aiding Kerin in proving his idea viable, suggesting alternative skills that were available in the Company. Kerin welcomed the former but turned away from the latter, proving to each in the meeting that they held all the skills needed, and that to include others in this was to increase the danger to the Company and themselves. Each of them was a lynchpin in his eyes, no matter how small their role. The lure of money was mentioned but it was Kerin's oratory and enthusiasm, his honesty in admitting he was uncertain on some points but seeking their suggestions, drawing and redrawing plans and coming back to the key points to reinforce his conviction that the plan could work; that was what fired them all. Even Renia left the meeting happy.

Kerin waited until the others had left before he spoke to Cedas.

'My thanks for your support.'

Cedas's expression dismissed his pleasantry. 'It's what you're paying me for,' he pointed out. Then he regarded Kerin steadily. 'Mind you, I'd dispute your claim that you could do nothing for the show. I could use a man like you.'

'In what way?'

Cedas kept his tone light as he replied, 'You have all the skills of a confidence trickster. I'd lay odds you could talk folk into anything, after tonight's performance. I suppose it'd be less offensive if I said the skills of a politician or military officer, but from my experience they're all the same. Look at them: you told them the truth about Karn, yet they've gone away happy to attempt this lunacy.' Kerin's look darkened as Cedas continued, 'I told Jez when she first suggested this that it was damn' near suicidal. After this last two hours I know I was right. I know you think so too.'

'So what are you saying? Do you wish to withdraw your people, or are you trying to raise your price?' Kerin's tone was level, trying to hide his resentment and disappointment at this change of heart. Cedas shook his head.

'I shook hands on it, with Jez and with you. Even if you were to agree to it, from her point of view I couldn't withdraw and hope to keep my – well, let's be polite, and say my honour. There is bad blood between us. She only sought my aid because she was desperate, thinking you and Vel dead, and I can't say I didn't take advantage of it. The others of the Company, Nina, Eddir, they aren't bound like me; it won't be me who tries to dissuade them though, not so long as you're honest with me in one respect. Tell me why you're attempting this madness.'

'I would have thought my reasons obvious. Jastur should be Crown; for Ilmaen's sake he must be Crown. I made a pledge to him and Ilmaen, to be his Champion. I consider it no less binding than your pledge to Jez.'

'Ah, but which binds you more, him or Ilmaen? If one's a lost cause, shouldn't you think about the other and keep yourself safe? You're the only other heir – without one of you two, the choice is between keeping Maregh or having civil war, isn't it?'

'Jastur is not a lost cause. If you think that, then I would sooner have you out of this business now. With you or without you, I will go ahead.'

'The point is, you can't go ahead, not without two of us. The rest are replaceable, but you need me to scale the wall and Naylan to pick some locks. You won't replace yourself either, even if you could, despite the risk. You see, Kerin, I know you've not been completely honest with me. But I'll let it go, because I see the reason.'

'What other possible reason can there be?' Kerin asked scornfully, but carefully. Ready to fetch Renia back with the Eagle if doubt as to his identity was voiced; ready to laugh it off if Cedas told him what he knew to be true, that he was scared to be Crown. The obviousness of Cedas's reply he had not prepared for.

'Because he's your brother; because you love him.'

Kerin kept his self-control and met Cedas's eyes with little more than a blink to register his confusion.

'You think me too human, sir.'

'On the contrary, *you* forget how human you are. I, on the other hand, am a mercenary in this. I'll go in there because

I'm paid to. I'll look to achieve our aim, I'll be a killing machine if need be, but I'll not throw my hide away for nothing. Nor yours, since you're paying the wages. You'd best know now that if push comes to shove and we can't get him out I won't give a damn for your orders; I'll knock you senseless and carry you out myself if necessary.'

'I will kill you if you do.'

'You're welcome to try; just as long as you pay me first. If he can't be got out, I will get you out. That's what the country needs, and you know it. I wouldn't want you to mistake my action for cowardice – or caring, for that matter. This is a business arrangement; let emotions come into it and we'll like as not be knocked to hell.'

'I have led troops since I was fifteen. I don't need you to tell me that.'

'Well, good,' Cedas allowed. Kerin held back from striking the little fold-out table in his anger, reducing the gesture to a tap of impatience on the drawings he had made earlier. He looked at what he was tapping and picked them up. Cedas gestured at them.

'Might I suggest that…'

'Have these burnt,' Kerin ordered curtly before he could finish, spinning them across the table and into Cedas's satisfyingly clumsy catch before he left.

oOo

Over the next few days those plans were duplicated and destroyed again and again by Cedas, Naylan and Vel; they were the ones who would enter the fortress with Kerin and they needed to commit its layout to memory. Paper was a scarce commodity, so they traced their plans in the dust under

the wagons where no one could overlook their work, raking it
through when they were done. They traced the plans in their
minds too, reciting descriptions of what they would find at
various points in and around the fort; Kerin made them repeat
the lessons until they had the layout off by heart. It was hard
for Renia to hide a smile whenever she passed Cedas doing his
rote learning.

He and Kerin were obliged to spend a lot of time
together, but a grudging respect developed between them –
enough to outweigh the antipathy. They took to exercising
together when they weren't planning Jastur's deliverance.
Kerin was surprised by the rigour of the exercises Cedas put
himself through every day; he did no more than an hour
compared to Kerin's usual two, but in a form so concentrated it
challenged even Kerin's stamina. Vel would join them from
time to time, but the dour rivalry of the other two made him
uneasy. He preferred it when they gave him the chance to
cross sword or knife with either of them. He still struggled
against Kerin but he had learnt enough to recognize his own
strengths and weaknesses; and he was almost a match for
Cedas. That gave him a challenge he could take on with some
hope of success.

Some of their preparations were obscure enough to
make openly – much to the entertainment of the rest of the
Company. Four days from Karn they came upon a meandering
river and Cedas called an early halt to set up camp for the
night. While the Company pitched up he went and found
Kerin, and the two of them strolled to the edge of the ford,
where the traffic had churned the ground into mud. They
spoke for a while, then began to build themselves an
earthwork and discussed it at length. As they walked around it,
Kerin would alter it with a pat of mud added here, a scraping
off there; and the people on the nearest wagons hooted and
called to find out how long Cedas had been entering his
second childhood and making mud pies. Cedas's replies were
good- natured but earthily graphic. Kerin looked amused too,

but he was careful to kick the earthwork down when they were done and trample it back into mud.

Kerin found that, when it came to it, he was curious about the show; he couldn't resist watching that evening's rehearsal. After all, no one would see him who didn't already know he was there. So he sat with Vel, Naylan and an entranced Bighur among the loose circle of watchers. They saw Jesral on the far side of the circle. She waved to them once, but was in conversation with the people she sat with. Renia they could not see, but they thought nothing of it then.

Then the first act started. One of Cedas's rehearsal ploys was to put a new act in at the start of a show when the crowd was an unknown factor, to force new players to learn how to assess and handle a crowd. To be told your act was a 'middle slotter' by him was to imply it was only fit for when the crowd were warmed up and in a good mood.

Kerin recognized Cedas instantly as he walked out. He listened with polite interest as the act unfolded until the hypnotized princess spoke, and Vel started and pulled at his sleeve.

'That's Renia!' he whispered urgently. Kerin had recognized her voice too, though it sounded unnatural and other-worldly. Vel's mind worked fast, and Kerin's was not far behind.

Seeing through a blindfold. A supernatural skill, and one gullible people might think real and not an act. One moment of waking fit such as she had already had, and it would be for Renia exactly as it had been in Mhrydain.

'What the hell is she thinking of?' Vel hissed at Kerin, who hushed him.

'Say nothing now, but as soon as this act is done we

must put a stop to it. Oh, Ren, have you lost your senses?'

'Something wrong?' Naylan enquired. He had not caught the whispered words, but sensed their concern.

'No, just something someone forgot. It will be dealt with,' Kerin replied. He sat, silent and frowning, until the act finished. Then he was up in one movement, stilling Vel who had started to rise too.

'I'd best talk to her alone. She needs to understand this is an order, not a request. I'm not sure how she'll take that.'

He did not put it quite as well as he should have, but Vel waved that off.

'Go ahead. You've got to stop this. But if you make her cry, look after her.'

'I seem to have a talent for making her cry,' Kerin admitted.

'Then you should have got the hang of looking after her by now,' Vel pointed out.

oOo

Cedas was helping Renia up from the litter as Kerin arrived.

'That was good, very good.' Cedas pinched her cheek in a friendly manner and went off to supervise some other part of the rehearsal. Renia gave Kerin an embarrassed smile, aware that close to, the make-up she wore for her part was heavy and garish and did not suit her. She stopped smiling when he took hold of her shoulder, startled by the way his grip hurt her.

'What the hell are you doing?' he demanded.

'What – the act? I have to do something. We can't stay with the Company if we don't perform. I thought Cedas told you earlier.'

'But why that? Why a mind-reading act, of all things?'

'It wasn't my choice! Cedas decided on it. Sun and Moon, Kerin, what do you want me to do?' She was angry now, tired of feeling under pressure when the act was over, and tired of being told she was getting things wrong. She yanked her arm free from his painful grip and abandoned Ilmaenese to pour out her anger in a tumble of Mhrydaineg.

'We thought you were dead. We saw this as the only chance for Jastur, going with the Company. Cedas never wanted to take us in the first place; but no act, no place in the Company, that he definitely wouldn't move on. What did you think? We'd get him to agree to help save Jastur and then say, Oh, no, sorry, I can't do that act. Do you have another one?" I'm just trying to help as best I can, Kerin. I'm trying to rescue a man I've only met in my mind, in a country I know next to nothing about, all the while thinking that the two... that two people I care about are dead. I'm sorry if I'm not doing it the way you would like, but then I haven't had the benefit of your experience, have I?' Tears were close, but they were tears of anger. They served to calm Kerin's rage, at the least.

'This can't continue,' he said. 'It's too dangerous, for you and for what we're trying to do. You understand my meaning? If you were to have a waking fit during a show Heaven knows what you might come out with, and if you did you might as well have gone no further from home than Dorster. Rumours would start, fingers would point – all that would begin again. Melor told me the kind of things that have happened; I fear there are too many of Dailo's type in the world, and others worse still. Don't forget that when fingers point at you, people will start to look at those around you. If you draw attention to yourself, you draw attention to us and what we are doing. That endangers Jastur.'

And she knew full well where Jastur came in Kerin's list of priorities; way above her.

Her head bowed, and the elaborate headdress pulled uncomfortably, so she yanked it off. It made her lose her balance. Kerin steadied her with one hand, and caught the headdress with the other. It was an instinctive action on his part; he took his hand straight off her as soon as she was steady. The anger in her went cold. She could find the words in Ilmaenese now.

'I know that you'd leave me behind if you thought it necessary,' she told him bluntly. 'But I've told you before, I have to be there. Understand that. Understand I know the risks I've been taking. I've done it because, as I see it, we both want the same thing: Jastur out of Karn. Then we can have an end to this. Now you go see Cedas and work out another way to get it, because I'm too tired to think any more. Good night, sir.'

She took the headdress back from him – the temptation to snatch it had evaporated, along with her temper. Fortunately he let her take it without resistance.

oOo

It was misty next morning, a filmy layer that hovered two feet off the ground, so that the wagons seemed to be sunk up to their axles in it.

The tall, dewy grass slapped against Kerin's trousers as he walked through the camp, making him damp to the knees. A few people were about, shaking out mattresses and the like. Jesral was fixing back the shutters, surprisingly quietly since it was plain even from a distance that she was in a mood. She did not bother looking at him as he arrived.

'Renia's packed and ready to go. As requested I'm staying on Atune's wagon, but I'd be obliged if you'd let me know when this supposed row between me and Renia is over. I still regard myself as part of the team, even if you've forgotten that.'

She unhooked the waterskin from the back of the wagon and brushed roughly past him on her way to the stream. He said nothing; her sarcasm made him cross, but she had some reason to be angry. He had discussed his plan for Renia with Naylan and Vel last night, then with Renia herself, and finally Cedas; but when he had invented a non-existent row between Renia and Jesral as the reason for her leaving the show he had indeed forgotten to ask Jesral. That Jesral would be left behind, when in reality she might prefer to join them on Naylan's wagon, had never even crossed his mind. Well, damn it, he told himself, it would make the wagon impossibly crowded with their stuff; she didn't need the alternative as Renia did. He suspected that she wouldn't have taken it if it were offered, not when she had more room in Atune's wagon and the chance to sleep inside in the dry and warm. Renia was going to have to sleep rough under the wagon, as he and Vel did. No use pointing that out; so he took a deep breath instead, and knocked on the wagon door.

Renia called him in. She sat on her bunk, and next to her lay her pack and the two swords, each wrapped in a blanket once again.

Renia bent forward to Atune as the old woman stirred and raised her head to look at them both.

'So, you go then. I thought you would, now your man has come for you.' To his surprise, he saw a tear fall down the old woman's leathery cheek.

'He's not "my man", he's just a friend, but he's worried about things and wants us all together again. I asked Jez to come too, but she wanted to stay with you. She's very fond of you, you know. So am I. I will come back and see you. We're just following the Company.'

'No, no, no. You must go. I understand. I understand better than you think.' She fixed Kerin with a piercing look.

'He's right, and you know it in your heart. You must be more careful of this.'

Renia looked at Kerin in some surprise. He returned it, equally surprised. Plainly, she thought *he* had told Atune. Since he had not, and he doubted that Jesral would have been so foolish, how had the old woman...

Atune gave him a lop-sided smile before speaking to Renia again.

'What you have, girl, is a rare gift, but others have it too. It's a wonderful gift, but it isn't good and it isn't evil, it's whatever you make of it. And you have it in you to make such important use of it. Far more than I have ever done with mine.'

Renia became very still, as if frozen. Kerin started forward a pace and then stopped, staring at the two of them.

'Ah, it doesn't matter that he knows about me, for he knows it is in you already and you trust him. But it may matter that I say *this* when he is listening, for no one can be strong all the time.' Atune reached up and put her claw-like hand against Renia's face. There was some strange quality in that touch; Kerin watched in horrid fascination as Renia caught her breath and pressed her face against Atune's hand. Her expression suggested it was both painful and ecstatic to do so. Atune shook Renia's head a little to reinforce what she was saying.

'What you have is a wonderful gift, but you must hide it, as he asks. You know now how to do that. This is all the help I can give you; the rest is up to you. So many lives depend on you, my dear.' She looked directly at Kerin, who could feel the blood draining out of his face.

She means my life! And Jastur's... and how many more?

But Atune had looked away again now, and back to Renia, who was equally pale.

'You know then what scares me?' Renia asked in a tiny voice. Atune smiled reassuringly.

'Oh, yes, your moment in time. But it may not be what you think. There's probably life to be lived beyond that. There certainly is before it. You want that moment to come so much, and yet you fear it greatly, don't you?'

Tears shone in Renia's eyes now.

'Yes. But I don't understand why.'

'Nor do I, my dear. But trust yourself; if you're meant to be there, there's something for you to do. You'll know what it is when you get there. It's no good being afraid if you can't avoid it. Better to go at it *modig*.'

'*Modig*?' Renia sounded confused. Kerin broke in, hardly recognizing his voice as his own as he told Atune: 'She doesn't know that word.' He found he could not look at the old woman, not wanting to meet those knowing eyes again. In Mhrydaineg he informed Renia: 'Atune means you should be brave.'

'I'll try.' Atune made a little noise of disgust at that.

'"I'll try." What did I just say about a half-hearted attitude? Sir, is she like this all the time?'

'She is,' Kerin had to admit. Atune was pressing Renia's face again.

'What am I going to do with you?' the old woman asked affectionately. Renia's smile was teary.

'I'm sure something will come to mind,' she joked back, and leant down to hug Atune before jumping up to wipe her tears on her sleeve, a little self-conscious. The old woman beamed complacently.

'Ah, well. Get along with you, or the wagons will be rolling before you get your stuff moved. But Renia – don't tell Jesral. She doesn't know about me. Only you two must know.' She sighed. 'I have learnt it is still a thing best kept close; you remember that too. Now, leave your man a little while. I want to talk to him.'

Renia gathered herself and shouldered her pack. Kerin stayed where he was, in slight foreboding, unable to imagine what Atune might want to say to him. Renia's touch on his arm got his attention.

'I have everything else, if you can bring the swords?' He nodded. 'I'll see you soon.'

He turned to watch her go, but that only took so long, and then he had no reason not to meet Atune's eyes. He did so carefully, but she did not look as though she was drawing out his deepest thoughts. She looked more peeved.

'Young man, I don't bite. Come over here.'

He did.

'You are allowed to sit down.'

He did, on the edge of her bunk. He realized he was being uncivil in his confusion.

'I'm sorry. What you two have – I didn't know you shared this. I have no option but to make her leave the Company.'

'You are right, so why be sorry? What, all these tears, you mean? No, you misunderstand. She is a little upset, a little scared, but mostly she cries because she is happy.'

'Happy?'

Atune tutted and moved to touch his face as she had done Renia's. Kerin flinched away, mindful of Renia's reaction. It provoked a cross sigh from the old woman.

'I'm not going to hurt you, I only want to touch you. What a baby!' That stung enough to make him submit to it.

He was not quite sure what he had expected, but all he felt were warm fingertips on his face along the line from temple to jaw and her palm against his cheek. There was some shakiness in her touch, but nothing more.

She made a slight noise of surprise and dropped her hand.

'Nothing at all, not even a smattering; no wonder you didn't realize. That's not what I expected. My, what trust she has in you!' The woman's talk seemed to be in riddles, but he said nothing.

'You see, my dear, to be different is a lonely thing, and she has been lonely for such a long time. What she does frightens people, and she thinks, "Why shouldn't they be

frightened? It's not normal: no one else does what I can do."
But she's just found out that a mad old circus woman she's
fond of can do it too; and there are others as well. Of course,
there aren't *that* many like her and me. I think she realizes that.
But she knows she's not alone any more, that's the difference.'

'Others? But you didn't say… *when* did you tell her
this?' He knew the answer as he asked the question, but she
spelt it out for him.

'Just now, while you were watching. I touched her
mind.'

He had to get up and pace the length of the wagon
while he took that in. When he returned, he sat in the bunk
opposite her and gave her an intense stare.

'But how? How do you do it? How does she?'

'I can only do it through touch. I could explain it all,
but the knowledge is quite useless to you. Renia doesn't know
how she does it, and I haven't told her, not directly. She is not
stupid, but she is naïve; she might put herself at risk if it were
any stronger in her. The trouble is, she has been with me these
many days, looking after me, helping me sit up, lie down,
wash, brush my hair – in short, she has been touching me. I
think she has learnt things; knowledge has… gone across,
without us knowing. I fear she may be able to call up the gift
at her own choosing now, and I say *fear* deliberately, believe
me. She must watch how and when she uses it – you should
discourage her from using it at all, if possible. When I touched
her just now I taught her how to control it, to hide it, which is
all you can ask of her for the time being. When it matters, then
I think she will find her true strength.'

This was barely less of a riddle to him than
everything she had said before, but it was leading Kerin to a
new realization.

'If you know her mind, you know my task. She'll be tempted to use it to help me, won't she?'

Atune shrugged for answer.

'Everyone has their role to play. I know what she's seen events leading to but no one can be certain how things will turn out, least of all those in the middle of them. Don't underestimate what she may have to do – but you try to be there when she does, for she may need you.' Then Atune quoted to him from Ilmaen's constitution, the Book of Crown and Council, that Kerin knew almost by heart: '"Not all bear arms; many fight the battle without them".'

He shook his head, bemused.

'I don't know. I had been assuming that the hard work was mine. Now you're telling tell me all our lives may be in her hands? She's too young for such responsibility.'

'Hah! Listen to the old man. There can only be a few years between you.'

'A few years, yes, but half a lifetime of experience. Only you're telling me it's not the right experience.'

'No one said it was wrong. Ah, you wish you could do what she does, don't you? To take the burden away from her. Well, you can't. You never will be able to. I felt for your mind just now and what is in Renia's is not in yours, not even sleeping, as it is in many minds. You don't have her type of power. But that is a good thing, you know. It gives you immunity from many fears that would stay another man. Thus when you are weak, she can be strong, and when she falters, you can bear her up.'

Kerin smiled wryly at these words. Now the old woman was quoting from the marriage ceremony. And she would keep calling him Renia's man!

'Next you'll tell me I should wed her,' he joked wryly.

'You could choose worse,' she retaliated.

'I'm sure I could, but it's not a choice I have,' he said gravely, marking an end to the discussion.

Atune shrugged once again and changed the subject.

'Well now, you'd best be on your way. You get caught in camp at this time of day, and Cedas will have you in the show before you can say "errand". Besides, Jesral is likely to heat the water for my wash too hot if she's kept much longer, and she'll cook the skin off me. Make sure you let Renia back to do that for me once in a while, or I shall look like a boiled beetroot. And take those damn' swords with you… don't leave them cluttering up my wagon!'

Chapter 19 – ...Is a Dangerous Thing

They were far from any settlements at the end of that day's travel, and it was a night for rehearsal again. Jesral had persuaded them to watch the Company once more. The 'row' between her and Renia was supposedly settled but Renia remained out of the Company, which wasn't going to be a problem for the rest of the players; there were only so many acts that could be fitted into the show and, truth was, they'd sooner a regular player had a slot. This would probably be Renia's first and last chance to enjoy the show properly, with no worries about her own performance.

Behind the stage, Jesral watched Renia and the men join the audience as the openers finished setting up. Renia found some spaces near the end of a bench and held up the lamp to guide Kerin in; Vel tucked himself in on the other side of her, looking like he had every intention of enjoying himself. She waited for Naylan and Bighur to slide on to the bench in front of them before she set the lamp down.

Renia looked to be the one making most of the conversation tonight, chattering to the others as she gestured at the stage. Talking about Jesral: she couldn't hear at this distance but she saw her name several times on Renia's lips. She was probably telling them what to expect from the acts for Jesral had more than one, like most of the performers. Everyone had a stock act that was done for a whole circuit, while the other would change every week or two – as much for the performer's benefit as the public's. Tonight Jesral would rehearse both her stock and her short acts.

The show warmed up with a round song, various

people taking a verse as a solo and everyone joining in the chorus. Then Cedas came on, and Jesral with him. This was her stock act, revived from the old days, and on hearing the opening bars of her accompaniment the Company members whooped and cheered. To those who knew the tune this was Jesral's song, complete and entire.

She wanted to know if the man courting her had enough money to keep her in style, so as she sang Jesral searched through Cedas's pockets to check. He had pockets in some unusual places, and Jesral's search was very thorough but didn't look to be finding much money.

She danced around him teasingly, always managing to find another possible hiding place for his money, while he tried to button down pockets she had already searched. The humour lay in the timing, and they had it spot on still. Jesral felt flushed with triumph but kept focused on the routine. Close to she could see the cold, level look in Cedas's eyes but it did not show to the audience. The act worked even better now than it had in the past. It depended on a degree of interest from her that could quickly turn to indifference, and his past behaviour to her made that easy now. Also she knew from Atune that he had tried to do this act with Nina after Jesral had left, but they had never carried it off. She hoped he caught the knowledge of that in her eyes, as in the song she spurned him and went off to search the audience for funds.

She charmed men in the audience as she sang, getting close enough so that with a little sleight of hand she could apparently produce some unexpected object from each – unless, of course, they had something suitably entertaining on them anyway. Most were transfixed until she had picked their pockets; some sought, always unsuccessfully, to keep her out of them. She got a huge cheer every time she whisked someone's three- day-old noserag out into public view, or tossed aside a stream of withered apple cores from a single pocket; the rest of the crowd teased her victims mercilessly. It was not all cruelty, though. One of the audience 'gave' her a single pink bloom, and at the end of the song he was rewarded with a kiss.

She and Cedas took their bow after the act was over. While helpers tidied the debris away from the circle, Jesral put a dark shawl over her bright skirt and took the ribbons from her hair, ready to deliver her short act. When she took up position again ready for her new introduction, she could not have looked more different.

Hidden in the shadows, Tamli and Eddir accompanied her with a sad, haunting guitar melody while Jesral poured out her heart in song. It was a tale of unrequited, betrayed love, a love that remained strong regardless. Jesral had a light subtle voice but her real skill lay in how she delivered the song. Seen by torchlight she was a small figure, standing straight-backed but so forlorn, her arms wrapped tightly about her as though to restrain the emotions she only dared to unleash in her voice. She sang of a love without hope yet without end. Snuffling could be heard from members of the audience in the quieter stretches of the song. Yet when it was over and the watchers erupted into applause, Jesral stepped forward all smiles for her curtsey, basking in their praise when only moments ago it had seemed her heart was breaking.

She caught Vel's eye as he clapped, mouth half open in amazement and admiration; she held his look, just for a moment. Then she skipped backwards out of the circle of watchers as the musicians played her off with the theme from the first song.

A minute or two later she slid quietly on to the bench next to Vel. He started when he saw who it was. She had the shawl pinned so it was off her shoulders now, which gave her another look entirely: elegant and at her ease. She smiled lightly at Vel.

'She's good, isn't she?' Renia smudged away a tear with one finger. 'I've seen her do that song four times now, and it still makes me want to cry my eyes out.'

'Incredible,' Vel murmured. He was openly staring at her. Jesral affected not to notice this as she shrugged off the praise.

'I have the song to thank for that. My voice isn't that good. They're just easy notes for me to hit,' she averred.

'You have a beautiful voice. Why did you never sing before?' Vel asked, with undisguised admiration in his eyes. She looked wistful.

'It wouldn't have worked so well anywhere else. It's a matter of mood. The atmosphere has to be right, you have to be in harmony, and not just musically, with the players who accompany you.' She gestured to the musicians with a smile. 'It's a combination of things, but mostly it's the people you're with.' She met his gaze then broke eye contact as if suddenly feeling shy. 'Sometimes you're lucky. You can hit that moment and hold it. With the right people.'

Now Vel looked down. Going too fast, she told herself, and changed the mood between them. She leant forward conspiratorially.

'Of course,' she said, low-voiced, 'you have ignored the real skill I showed.' He looked at her – could hardly avoid doing so, when she was so close. She smiled wickedly.

'Shall I get the knot out of this for you?' She dangled a piece of leather lacing before his face, and he grabbed at his hair as he recognized it. She had untied it without him even noticing.

'How did you do that?' She was fiddling with the

knot, trying to undo it.

'Oh, blast, it won't come. I'll have to cut it.' And she opened out the blade of his folding knife, which she had successfully purloined as well. He grabbed her wrist, took back knife and lace as she grinned at him.

'You have criminal tendencies,' he pointed out. The look wasn't disapproving; his grip on her wrist lingered longer than it needed to. She knew she was playing him at the right pace now.

Beyond him, she saw Kerin and Renia with their heads close together. Renia looked anxious. Jesral could only partly hear what she said against the music of the next act.

'... can't tell you here, in the middle of a crowd. We need to...'

Then the music rose and drowned out her voice. If Renia and Kerin were leaving, Jesral could get Vel alone. But she needed something from the wagon if she was going to get this right. She touched his sleeve.

'I have something else of yours. I'll fetch it, if you wait here.'

Cedas watched her as she left, a hard expression on his face. Outwardly she ignored it; inwardly she celebrated. It was just what she had hoped for.

She was away no more than three minutes and in that time Kerin and Renia had gone for their talk as she'd expected. Only Vel had gone too.

Damn. Perhaps they had left together; if so, the most likely way they would go was back towards Naylan's wagon, set on the high ground beyond the rest of the Company's pitches. She hared off in pursuit.

They were indeed together. Jesral nearly ran into them, till she heard Renia's voice. There was a quality to it that Jesral had not noticed before, so she held back and stayed in the shadow of a nearby wagon to listen.

Renia sounded angry. That was interesting; one of the players had said she had seemed to be arguing with Kerin the night all the fuss was kicked up about her act, but that had seemed about as likely as snow in July. Yet here was the evidence in front of Jesral's eyes: and she'd thought the girl wouldn't say boo to a goose.

'…and nothing on our journey hurt you, until you gave away your protection,' Renia was telling Kerin. Vel stood to one side of them with the air of a man planning to stay out of the argument.

'So this is about the Eagle? You're still fretting about that? How very foolish of me not to see. I was concerning myself with more logical worries, like us using rope to get into Karn. Do feel free to check the ropes until you're sure of every inch of them. Did you think Vel and I wouldn't? But that storm was pure coincidence, nothing to do with me giving you the Eagle. I won't take it back.'

'Kerin…'

'No! There's no point in prolonging this argument. We talked this out when I gave it to you, and I won't change my mind now. Please, trust me, and leave things as they are.'

'You can be so stubborn,' Renia declared in exasperation.

'As if you aren't! The difference is, I'm giving the orders. And my order is: keep it. Now I'll say goodnight. I'm off to bed after I've fetched water for the morning. I'm too tired to watch the rest of the show.'

Vel turned to his sister when Kerin had gone, his face thoughtful.

'So you've had this out with him before. Do you really think it's a danger?'

'I don't know. The Eagle, it's so... bound up with him and what I've seen coming. You'll think me silly, but I feel guilty for letting him give it to me.'

'Not if you think it's his protection. But he couldn't take it into Karn, Ren. I wouldn't want to risk going in with him if he had it on him. They'd have the nooses round our necks at once if they found that, and no mistake.'

'I know, I know. You're making sense, Vel. Kerin too. I've probably got it all wrong – but you make sure you check those ropes again, all the same.'

She received a rare display of affection from him then. Vel slid an arm around her shoulders and touched his forehead to hers.

'You worry too much. You know, your predictions are too accurate. The ropes won't be a problem. If you saw nooses, then nooses are what we need to avoid, and Kerin's too clever to allow us to be gallows-bait. I must go now, Jez wanted to see me about something. Are you coming back to the show?'

'No, I'll leave it. I'm tired too.'

If they said any more, Jesral did not hear them as she crept away. What they had already said had turned her cold with misery and fear. They were still keeping secrets from her.

Her fingers slid into her pocket and touched Vel's pressed flower, still carefully wrapped in its cloth. She withdrew her hand again, before the urge to crush her most treasured possession overcame her.

oOo

Two days from Karn, one of the wheels on Atune's wagon started to work loose. It turned out to be the axle pin, repaired on some previous occasion and slipping in its socket after bouncing over the province's poorly maintained roads for so many days. It was the kind of handiwork that Naylan excelled in, which was fortunate as it wasn't the only Company wagon to suffer from the roads. Cedas paid for the first repair, ranted about the state of the roads and Karn's thieving LandMaster fleecing his taxpayers for the full hour and a half it took Naylan to fix the second, and flatly refused to pay for any more after that, so the rest of the Company secretly arranged an extra supper in Atune's wagon one night in return for Naylan's work.

As he ate it he bantered with Atune. He had her measure at once.

'You ever getting up again, old woman?' he asked as Jesral helped her with her meal. Atune scowled and determinedly pulled herself a little further up in bed.

'Soon as you get fit enough to give me a run for my money. Look at you, eating another supper when you've clearly had enough to feed a family for a week already! I don't know what your handsome lad wants with him, Jesral, but he'd better not need him to get through any small gaps,' Atune warned.

'You're not supposed to know about that. Shut up and eat your supper.' Jesral's voice expressed neither amusement nor anger; her thoughts were far away.

''Tis locks, that's my business in this. These past days I've seen lock after lock after lock. Forgot how many I had in my stores – and forgot what little buggers to pick some of them are.' He fell to his supper again.

'So… picking locks, and fixing mighty wagons single-handed,' Atune observed. 'Cedas'll have you out on the circuit as escape artist and strong man if you don't watch it. He's tricksy, that one, knows how to steer you into a corner every time. You ask Jesral.'

'Ummn?' She had not fully registered what Atune had been saying.

'She says Cedas is a sharp little *piru*,' Naylan summarized Atune's comments.

'Well, we knew that already,' Jesral replied, curt without intending rudeness. Naylan shrugged.

'Well, I thank you for the extra supper, ladies. Now I shall try to avoid being trapped into show life by heading home. Jesral, we're taking a night off from the preparations over at my wagon. An evening of gut-rot cider and cards. Room for another punter if you can afford the stakes.'

'Not for me, thanks,' was her reply. He gave up, thanked them for the meal again, and left.

Jesral washed the plates out on the back step, put them away; pottered around doing any number of small, unnecessary jobs. Atune pulled herself up into a sitting position again.

'You threw most of your dinner away. Not like you to be off your food.'

'Just didn't feel very hungry tonight,' Jesral replied.

The conversation lapsed again, until she seemed to run out of things to do and lay down on her bunk. She gazed thoughtfully at her reflection in the foxed mirror that lined the side of the compartment. She gave a little sigh, not meant to be heard, but Atune's ears were sharp.

'You must be bored. You've seen so little of your friends these evenings past. Go on over. Even if you're tired, it'll perk you up a bit.'

'I said before, not tonight.'

'And said the same yesterday, and the day before that. When *are* you going… birch bark month? Girl, you're not the Jesral I knew. What's been eating away at you these last few days?'

Jesral just lay and blinked, considering whether to tell her to mind her own business and go to Hell. From the mirror her own speckled reflection stared back at her; the dim wagon light accentuated the dark shadows under her eyes.

A catch in her breathing – she didn't know herself if it was a sigh or a sob – and Jesral rolled over to look at Atune.

'I'm in out of my depth Atune, and I'm afraid.'

'Oh, girl – you, out of your depth? Didn't think there was a lake deep enough. Jumped in again rather than pushed, I suppose?'

'Why do you always assume that?' Jesral snapped, but calmed herself quickly. 'Worst of all, why do you always have to be right?'

'Does it bear repeating?' Atune prompted her. 'Something? Someone?'

'It's not something I can tell you about. It's Ren's secret.' Jesral stared at the mirror again. 'There's a sort of unspoken promise between us.'

'And promises should always be kept, however they're made. Come here and sit by me,' Atune ordered her. Jesral came and sprawled by the side of the bed, face buried against Atune's blanketed side. The old woman stroked Jesral's hair as if she were two, not twenty. At every stroke it felt like she picked up the fear in the girl, cast it out and replaced it with calm. The process seemed to soothe Atune too; she spoke in a warm, clear voice free from the cracks of age.

'You like her, I like her, and she's an honest soul. If something was going to mean trouble for you, she'd tell you, wouldn't she? I'm guessing you started this escapade before you found out this secret of Renia's, but I think you knew even then this wasn't going to be an easy ride, and that didn't stop you. Does knowing this new thing really change that? You're one of life's survivors. You can deal with anything that's thrown at you, my dear.'

Atune continued the stroking for some minutes, until Jesral chose to raise her head; she seemed solemn, but no longer scared or distracted by worry.

'You always make such sense out of muddle for me. How I wish you hadn't been ill when I left last time! You would have made it all right, I know.'

'Ah, that's time long past wishing; don't let wishes be your master. I'm old, Jesral, and the old fall ill a lot. You've got to start making sense of it for yourself, you know. You can do it. Don't be afraid to follow your instincts.'

'Hmm. That's usually what gets me into trouble in the first place.'

oOo

As they travelled the land changed. Rolling farmland lay far
behind them now and blue hills loomed higher ahead. The
road and its surroundings became craggier still, until in the
early evening two days later Kerin signalled to Cedas to stop.
He was travelling, in rare contradiction of his own rule, on the
Company's front wagon in order to call a halt at the most
suitable place. No one else could do it: the Company had
never included Karn on its circuit before.

       They were on the brow of a hill with a wooded belt of
land to their left. This wood followed the curve of the road
around and halfway down the hill. There the road struck out
over the valley, where it crossed a stone bridge spanning a
river. The bridge looked old, probably pre-Catastrophe and
obviously patched up, but Kerin knew it to be sound. As soon
as it had crossed the bridge the road passed through the first of
the walls that surrounded Karn, the one that protected the
lower town. As it wound on it passed ever higher, meeting
another road that came round the far side of the hill town; the
two roads became one and snaked up through two more walls
into the fortress itself. At the first of these walls the crowded
huddle of town houses came to an abrupt end.

       From here the fortress looked squat and harmless; an
effect of the distance. Kerin knew that inside the town that
double wall seemed to tower over everything, and from the
river, which wound around the base of the cliff on the far side
of the hill to make a virtual island of Karn, the sheer rock face
and fort wall would look unassailable. It was a fortress
intended to convey the might and authority of the Crown; yet
it was almost certainly his prison.

       Cedas stood up on the driver's seat for a moment,
surveying the scene. He nodded curtly.

       'Yes, as I pictured it. Doesn't look much from here,

does it?'

'We are about a mile away. I think that is close enough for tonight. If we stop here now, by the time camp is ready you and Vel will still have the last of the light in which to scout out the riverside. Do you see the fording point I was talking about, just before the river bends?'

'Yes, I have it. We'll make camp fast tonight. I want to do my checks and get back in time to develop my "malady" during supper. The more people see it, the better. We've kept this business close enough to us that they probably don't suspect, and I'd trust most of the camp to say I'd been ill even if they thought otherwise, but no point in forcing a lie on them. They say your enemy offers a pretty sum for information, and money loosens tongues easier than most things...'

Cedas fell quiet as someone approached, but it was only Vel come to take a look. Cedas went off to organize the setting up of camp while Kerin pointed out the major landmarks of Karn to Vel.

His tutoring was interrupted halfway through when a series of sharp cracking sounds echoed across the valley. A pause, and then more of them were heard.

'What's that?' Vel asked.

'Guns. The garrison must be practising.'

'Guns? But I thought they were illegal?'

'They are, for ordinary folk. But we have them for law enforcement and there's the possibility of pitched battle with some of our neighbour countries to allow for. The military use other weapons too. Bows and lances; even siege engines – though they have not been actively used in Ilmaen in my lifetime. Karn was modelled on the forts of pre-

Catastrophe times, when whole armies of men would fight to settle an issue. Barbarous times, when they thought strength alone mattered.'

'That's all very well but if they have guns, shouldn't we have got ourselves at least one? Guns were available in Mhrydain, you know, for a price.'

'Yes, but not over here. They are reserved for Crown troops. The only other people in Ilmaen to have them are professional assassins. Guns are too noticeable – and it is a capital offence to have one if you are not military. Now, if someone saw any of us armed with a gun, where would they think to place us, out of those two categories? Quite. Too dangerous; and unnecessary anyway. The garrison only break them out for practice, emergencies and official visits. Unless we get this wrong, we are unlikely to find ourselves in a situation where having a gun will do us any more good than a decent blade.'

Cedas had rejoined them and caught the tail end of this conversation. He looked at Vel as though he was mad.

'He's not after a gun?' Kerin's acknowledgement made him roll his eyes heavenward in disbelief. 'Does he live in the same world as the rest of us?'

'Not quite,' was Kerin's reply. 'He has been in Mhrydain, after all.'

'Hmm. Ugly weapons anyway. Get issued with bad shot or powder and you're likely to blow yourself up. I could never get on with them in Tor-Milan. Give me a knife any day. And you'd be mad to give up your sword, Vel. The camp's setting up on the other side of the hill, out of sight of Karn. We'll keep the fires low tonight as well.'

He walked off again, shouting orders as he reached

the main body of wagons. Vel cocked his head in puzzlement.

'Was that a…?'

'A compliment? I think it was. Sound advice, too.'

Chapter 20 – Karn

Once camp was made Cedas and Vel were gone. They were back within two hours, while there was still some light left. Cedas was confident of success in entering the fortress. Vel admitted frankly to Kerin that it had seemed impossible to him, but Cedas had partly scaled the cliff to demonstrate it could be done. Now Vel stood again with Kerin on the edge of the camp, watching the light fade from the sky over the town. They could just make out lights twinkling there now, and on one of the fortress towers a bonfire glowed, a reflection of the smaller one down the slope behind them that served the camp. Kerin's eyes stayed fixed on the distant fire. His arms were crossed and there was a thoughtful frown on his face.

'I'm sure Jastur's there, Kerin.'

'Yes. So am I. It's the obvious place to keep him.' Kerin was silent again for a while. After what Atune had told him, he had struggled long and hard against the temptation to have Renia try and see his brother again. This close, and knowing the risk they took in going into Karn, the struggle was renewed. He thought through that strange conversation with the old woman again and all that it implied; the urgency of her warning won out. They would have to go in with no more prescience than before, so he needed to use every other source of information he could find.

'What of the guards on the keep? Could you make out a pattern, a routine, to their patrols?' There should be one. This was Maregh's former province and now under Lemno's control, although rumour happily had the Tekai in Lestar, five hundred miles away. Even so, his influence was such that discipline would be maintained despite his absence.

'We watched them for a while on this side of the river

before we crossed. Two guards. But if they have a pattern it's complex. They're on the move all the time and never pass each other, but where they meet and turn seems to vary randomly. It's the only bit about this I don't like, going in this way.'

'I am not keen myself, but believe me it is the only way. Once we are in the place no one will question it, because they are so strict on the gates. And I know from childhood experience that getting out is a simple process. Jastur and I found escaping into town infinitely more interesting than our tutors and duties in the Fort, and we had many routes. Don't worry, that was nearly ten years ago. No one will know me after all this time, and except for those actively involved in holding him, no one is likely to recognize Jastur.' Kerin stopped, uncertain how much of this he was saying for Vel's benefit and how much for his own. He knew from campaigning those five years in Federin that he would be calm and controlled on the day, but it was always hard to convince himself of that the night before. He turned to face Karn again, but his vision was inward.

The fact that tomorrow would be the first meeting of Renia's fateful trinity, himself, Jastur and Vel, had not escaped any of them. Vel was pragmatic; he told Kerin that he had not come all this way just to sit in the rearguard, and unless he took a trek to the far end of the country, the three of them would have to meet at some time. He was prepared to take his chances in Karn. Kerin was grateful for that but still on edge. He had mastered the urge to ask Renia to try and see more, but he had been watching her; she too had been brooding on the significance of tomorrow. He had noticed her stiffen at that first meeting in Cedas's wagon, when he had named those he wanted to go into Karn with him, and then there was this obsession of hers with the Eagle. Yet since their argument she had said nothing more.

Heaven grant that Jastur was in there. Logic and Renia's conviction pointed to it, but he had to be ready for any eventuality. Kerin had steeled himself for the worst; that Jastur had died here. He had lived with that once before, those few weeks in Mhrydain, before Renia renewed his hope. If all else failed, he would have to live with it again.

He stirred himself, conscious of Vel's patient presence. He must have been wrapped up in his thoughts for some time, as Karn was in complete darkness now.

'We may have to rely on Nina and Jez's performance to get us in,' he said, harking back to the concerns Vel had voiced, 'but that doesn't worry me. The very thought of those two together is distracting.'

Vel was not going to dispute that. To know he was going to miss it came as a blow to him, after hearing the old members of the Company recall it. And bad news made him hungry.

'Want some supper? I think stage one of the plan will soon be under way.'

'I am not hungry, but we had best get something down us. After you.'

Stage one had been evolved to explain why Cedas was not directing the show in town the next day. It would be the first time that such a thing had happened, so it would be remarked upon by the rest of the Company. They had decided that the answer was for sudden illness to befall him and confine him to his bed. If Eddir hung back to drive him and Naylan's wagon stayed to keep an eye out, while the rest of the Company went on with Nina in charge, then each person would be in the place they needed to be; some outside Karn's walls, and Jesral and Nina within to stage their diversion.

Cedas began his subterfuge during supper, underplaying it well. He was quiet and restless, appearing to be in worsening discomfort until Nina, with equal subtlety, persuaded him away to rest. Those around the fire who were paying attention noticed; others who were caught up in conversation did not. That was perfect. Kerin could already imagine them talking to each other next morning: 'I didn't realize he was feeling ill.' 'Oh, yes, you could see it last night at supper, he was all out of sorts then.' He moved away from the fire to settle down under Naylan's wagon, impressed again by the multitude of skills that Cedas possessed.

Renia already lay there on her side, wrapped in a blanket. He thought her asleep, but she turned over at his arrival and gave him one of her sad and worried stares. He stared back without flinching; that look of hers always seemed to be a prelude to some disagreement between them. He was in no mood for it now. She picked up an extra blanket and tossed it over to him.

'It's cold tonight. Make sure you and Vel get some sleep. I'll take the early morning watch,' she said, and lay back down.

Little chance of sleep for any of us tonight, he thought, but he took up the blanket anyway.

oOo

Next morning, looking suitably wan and pinched, Nina called a meeting of the Company and explained the situation. The troupe expressed sympathy and concern and above all determination to put on the show so as not to let Cedas down. Arrangements were made for Eddir to drive Cedas and for Naylan's wagon to stay back with them. At the last minute, Renia decided to travel on Atune's wagon with Jesral and Nina. Nerves had overcome her, and she decided she would be better kept busy helping Atune than fretting beyond the second wall. Besides, Cedas was in no position to object to her breaking his rules. As soon as she was on Atune's wagon, the

Company moved off.

The 'ailing' man let the caravan travel out of sight
before he left his sick bed. He was fully dressed already, in
what had been made up to match Kerin's recollection of the
retainers' dress in Karn. They all wore the same, with a spare
set for Jastur. Each carried a sword, wrapped and strapped to
their backs; Kerin and Vel their own, Naylan and Cedas
weapons from Naylan's wares. Naylan distributed skeleton
keys around his pockets so that they would not jingle together.

Cedas gathered his kit; before he packed his tool roll,
he held up part of it for the others to see. It was a ring attached
to a pin, made of a dull silvery metal.

'To go over how these work… I've about three dozen
of them, and I'll be hammering the pins into the rock on the
way up. That leaves the ring free. As you come up you'll have
the rope round you. When you get to a ring, you hook the rope
in like this…' And he demonstrated the almost invisible catch
in the ring that closed back to secure the rope within. 'If you
do fall off it means you don't go far, and you don't take the
rest of us with you. You will be safe; remember that fact when
you're up there, because it's easy to think otherwise.
Remember also that I may not have enough rings to guarantee
you are in reach of another when you detach from the last; in
that situation you *must* be sure all the other climbers are
attached. The signal to indicate you want to detach is that –'
and he held his hand out with thumb and forefinger making an
O, which he opened wide '– and a clenched fist from the
others tells you they are attached and it's safe to go ahead. A
clenched fist when you're on again, please, in case you're too
exhausted to look up; the poor sod in front of you may be in an
even more uncomfortable position than you are, and desperate
to move.'

Kerin took one of the rings for a closer look,
fascinated by the hidden catch.

'Where did you get these?'

'I picked them up in my soldiering days down south near Tor-Milan Citywild, just over the border.' Kerin took 'picked them up' as a euphemism for 'looted', or even more likely 'stole from army stores'. Cedas continued, 'My captain believed they were pre-Catastrophe, and I've never found out what the metal is. It's very light and doesn't corrode at all. I've been able to use them again and again in acts, they hammer into wood as if it were butter; but I think they were originally made for just this kind of thing, military storming of forts, and not meant for re-use. When we put one in the cliff last night, it was nigh on impossible to get it out again. That's an advantage, frankly; if they're left here it'll point to Tor-Milan military involvement in this mission. Let the authorities go on a wild goose chase there, while we head for the eastern borders.

'Still, I'd appreciate it if the last man up would have a go at getting at least some of them out as he passes.'

Kerin gave him back the ring. He added it to the pile of others and a cloth-muffled mallet in his roll before he fixed that around his middle and manoeuvred it into a comfortable position.

Kerin took up one length of rope, Vel another.

'Are we all ready? Good. Eddir, Bighur, you know where to take the wagons?'

Eddir nodded. 'Know dat town now like back of my hand,' Bighur retorted confidently.

The four men entered the wood that ran beside the road and used it as cover as far as they could. Then they were out in the open the rest of the way down to the ford, but they were fortunate in the lie of the land, which sloped down from the road so steeply they could walk unseen from the town all the way to the bridge. On the side of the river there was a deep stand of trees and shrubs running up to the cliff base to conceal them. It would also serve to mask them from any river traffic until they neared the upper two-thirds of the wall, but the chances of that were so small they could be disregarded. The river was low for early summer but no less cold for that and fording it made them wet to the waist. Still, it was a fine June day; they were dry before Cedas was halfway up the cliff face, laying the rings for the rest of them to hook in to.

He made it look far easier than it was, and Kerin's muscles were screaming when they made it on to the slight ledge where cliff face and fortress wall met. Cedas let them rest a while and Vel, last up, dumped the two rings he had managed to retrieve into Cedas's hands, looking as though he was getting the worst of the bargain – least rest and most work, apart from Cedas. Vel had nearly parted company with the cliff face getting one of the rings free.

Cedas pressed on. He had warned them that this was the tougher section, where the carefully faced blocks of stone gave almost no handholds and there were few cracks to bed the rings into. And indeed, where the first section had taken half an hour the next stretch, although covering no greater distance, took more than an hour.

Within three feet of the top, Cedas stopped and checked the sun's position against the strains of the show music he could hear. Kerin had been able to make out the beat of the tune for the last ten minutes, and Cedas had hammered in time to it to avoid attracting the guards' attention. Now he leant out, showing guts in relying almost exclusively on the ring to hold him while he tried to pick up the tune and fit it to the running order of the show. Kerin glanced quickly down at the others – Naylan would be feeling the strain worst, since he was neither as young nor as light as the rest of them. But above him, Cedas tucked back into the wall and held the flat of his hand out to his side to ensure silence. The guard must be patrolling above him still, so they had no option but to wait.

Since Cedas showed such confidence in the rings, Kerin trusted his weight to his while his hands searched for a better hold. He found it, and looked up. Cedas signalled to him; five fingers, then two. Seven minutes before they could go over the wall. Kerin was appalled at the prospect but acknowledged the information and passed it down to the others.

After four eternal minutes the music changed; this must be Jesral and Nina's piece starting up. He steeled himself to trust the ring again and shook his aching arms out as the act got going.

Then he heard some distant shouting, and a gust of laughter from the crowd watching the show. A nearer voice – one of the guards – calling something back and making some comment to the other guard above Cedas; and this guard said audibly 'They want what?' and moved off. His footfalls faded; his laugh rang out with that of the other guard, on the opposite side of the keep. Cedas signalled Kerin with a tug on the rope, detached himself from the last ring and carefully hauled himself up the remaining three feet. Kerin hurriedly detached himself too, and with Cedas pulling managed to scale the remaining wall without reattaching to the last ring. He scrabbled his way up and fell over the parapet, seeking to prevent his rope from tangling or his wrapped sword from banging against the wall.

The two guards had their backs turned; they leant out over the parapet on the far side of the keep. There was no cover between Kerin's party and the guards. Cedas glanced along their stretch of wall to the nearest of the seemingly distant corner towers, grimaced and shrugged. Kerin had asked him to get as close to one of these as possible, but lack of handholds had forced him further out towards the middle of the wall. No choice now but to get the others over the wall as fast as possible. To do so left them exposed to the guards, but it made no odds: if the men looked over they were done for anyway, so best get on with the job in hand. They both hauled on the line and Naylan followed, purple and almost a dead weight; the long and lanky Vel came last. Once they were untied Kerin beckoned them to follow him to the tower stairs, while Cedas regretfully let the rope fall back over the wall and out of sight. A loss; but a worthwhile one. When it and the Tor-Milan rings were eventually found, the false trail it sent Lemno on would ensure the Company's safety.

Vel took the chance to look at the two guards again as he hurried towards the stairwell. Still they had not turned. Cedas yanked him on to the stairs and pushed the door to.

At the base of the tower stairs they unwrapped the swords and hung them at their waists, like any guard or retainer; the cloth wrappings went out of a narrow window, following the rope down the cliff. Then they split up without comment, each pair knowing their way. Naylan and Vel took one corridor, while Cedas and Kerin went the other way and down another staircase.

In the next corridor a door opened ahead of Cedas and an official looked out. He beckoned them over; there was nothing to do but go.

The man looked them up and down, clearly not recognizing them, but he made no comment on it, instead thrusting a package into Cedas's hands and telling him to take it to the post stables 'with all haste', before disappearing back into the room and shutting the door.

'What now?' asked Cedas, glaring at the packet as if it burned him.

'Best take it, or there may be a hue and cry before we

get Jastur out. You know where it must go, and how to reach the lower guardroom from there?'

'Yes.'

'Then I will meet you there with the others.'

oOo

Atune and Renia sat on the verandah to watch the show. Atune had improved astoundingly in the last few days. She was able to sit and hold her head up if she had a pillow behind it for support, and nagged to be taken outside to see a show after so long. The Company loved it; they might be without Cedas, but the sight of their old leader heartened them, and she waved to them all like an ancient empress receiving tribute.

They set up the show inside Karn's second wall, on the stretch of open ground it enclosed. It was the nearest they could get to the keep. Few were allowed inside the third wall at the top of the stretch of ground, and fewer still into the keep itself, a short distance beyond. Still Jesral and Nina felt it was close enough for their purposes. Quite a crowd had gathered; today would be a rare treat for the townspeople.

Renia had her arms folded on the rail of the verandah, her head resting on them, as she tried to settle herself. The last act had just ended and the musicians launched straight into the next song. Immediately two flashes of colour were in the centre of them: Jesral and Nina, encouraging the crowd to clap along to the music. Copper hair and fair skin, raven and dark; the brightness of their jewel-coloured skirts almost hurt the eyes and the loose white tops they wore bared a lot of shoulder as they danced. The music settled to a lower pitch as the two girls instructed the crowd on the words of the chorus and the steps of the dance, but when the music rose again for the first chorus Renia could see it must be a traditional piece, for the audience threw the words back first time:

O, I'll dance for a rich man, I'll dance for a poor,

I'll dance and I'll dance till I wear out the floor,

I'll dance in the morning, I'll dance in the night,

I'll dance till you manage to get these steps right,

I'll dance till I'm tired and my shoe leather's gone,

But if you're a working man, I'll dance one more song.

Happy that the crowd knew their part, Jesral and Nina now used the next verse to call for any of the town's bakers to make themselves known. Two half-volunteered, half got themselves pushed forward by their friends, and the girls pulled them out to dance the chorus while the crowd sang it, putting in the men's trade in the appropriate line. They received a kiss to make up for the embarrassment and were danced back to their friends. The next verse was a discussion on which trade to choose next, and it turned out to be tailors. A couple who appeared to be father and son came forward, and the father, despite his elderly looks, turned out a lively heel and toe with Jesral.

More discussion, and the two women called for soldiers. They knew from Kerin that none would be off duty in the town; the system at Karn worked in such a way that the garrison would be on six weeks' continuous duty and then transferred elsewhere in the province before being given leave. When no soldiers volunteered, Jesral and Nina enlisted the crowd's help in another verse that harried the men on duty up on the third wall and on the keep. The men on the wall bantered back but were not going to leave their posts, so Nina and Jesral abandoned the verse and tried to talk the men on the keep down with a variety of promises and insults which the crowd would never have risked, but which had soldiers and townspeople alike roaring with laughter. In the end they negotiated the 'release' of a couple of the fort's kitchen scullions as an alternative, and whirled the lads around for a chorus.

They settled back into the pattern of taking traders from the crowd for a verse or two more. Renia finished the destruction of her fingernails as she watched the keep guards go back to their patrol. If anything went wrong it was likely to be now.

Jesral and Nina finished, the next act started, ran through and ended; the guards on the keep continued to patrol normally. Either the rescue party was in, or it had been abandoned. Renia tried to relax and watch the rest of the show. It continued smoothly, barely disturbed by the arrival of a group of men on horses who drew up and dismounted by the stables. One of them, dark-haired, bearded and alert, stayed mounted and wheeled his horse round to stare across the heads in the crowd at the show. It was hard to put an age to him; his hair was black but with streaks of grey, and the beard was showing signs of grey too. Whether they faced him or not, the crowd in his line of sight seemed to move aside as if to avoid blocking his view, even though, from horseback, that view must be unobstructed.

Some of the townsfolk in front of Atune's wagon knew who he was; they nudged each other and murmured together, watching him. Renia leant over and asked one of them, 'Who's that man on the horse?'

'That? That's Lemno.' The man almost spat the words out. Renia sat up and looked at him again in horror and fascination. The man was striking; as Kerin had said, his presence was unmistakable. To see him once would be to know him again anywhere. He could surely have only one reason for being here. He dismounted now and handed the reins to a stable hand, and she caught her breath.

'Renia?' Atune sensed that something was going on now, but Renia didn't dare look away. He still stood there, casting a glance over the players once more; under her breath Renia pleaded, 'Stay and watch, please stay and watch...'

There was no way the others could have had time yet to free Jastur. If they were there and Lemno went in now then they were all done for. There had to be some way to make him stay, some diversion that could be caused!

Lemno turned and began to walk on towards the gate to the third wall. Desperately Renia speeded up her murmured incantation.

And Lemno stopped. He seemed to pause in thought for a moment then swung back to watch the show, exactly as she had wanted.

So why was she suddenly even more frightened than before?

She kept her eyes on him. After a moment of watching the act, he began to look at the crowd. No, through the crowd, as if he was searching for something. Her sensation of panic went up a notch.

Atune reached across and touched her bare arm and Renia felt the panic surge out to her, making the old woman exclaim in alarm. Renia tried to pull away to spare her but Atune held on. At last she let Renia's arm go.

'Inside, now,' she ordered. 'And remember what I taught you.'

Renia stumbled into the wagon, putting too much stress on her ankle and feeling a jolt of pain. It cleared her head a little.

What was it she had to do? Nursery rhymes? Couldn't think of any. List the stars in the constellations? Oh, brain, wake up! Two times table. Two twos are four, three fours… no, three twos are six, four twos are eight...

She calculated on blindly until Atune called out to her.

'You can stop now.'

Renia was breathing as heavily as if she had been running. She felt sick and dizzy, and slumped down on the nearest bunk and rested her head against the frame. With an effort Atune had managed to turn herself around. She looked through the doorway to the grey-faced girl.

'What happened?' Renia asked.

'What you wanted. You asked him to stop, and he heard you.'

'But I was whispering!'

'No, no, dear. He heard your mind; you were sending. Didn't know you were doing it, did you?'

Renia looked at her aghast. 'You mean, he's like us?'

'Almost certainly. And I'd say he was looking for you when I sent you in, and a bit of you half knew that. Good reason to panic. All that reciting business is to shut down the sending he could find and know you by.'

Renia saw the truth of this. The real panic had not started at the thought of Lemno going in, but when he began looking around the crowd. Looking for her.

'What if he finds me?'

'I don't think you could keep him out – when I touch you, I get all you think and feel. And if he got in, he would know everything you know. Everything.' Renia went from grey to white. 'It's all right, he's given up looking. He's gone into the fort now.'

'But the others,' Renia reminded her.

'There's nothing more to be done. But if he comes back this way, I don't want you here. He looked to have other business, couldn't be bothered to hunt you out now. In an hour's time, who knows? So you go back into town, make your way round to Naylan's wagon, get in it and stay in it. No excuses; you're going. See that paper there? Fold it up like a letter. Tell Wosagh down by the green wagon that I'm sending you with a message for Cedas and he's to find me a driver in case those two girls don't get back here.'

Renia helped the old woman to her bunk, shut up the van and limped away from the show.

Chapter 21 – Captive

Kerin arrived at the guardroom first and waited impatiently. It was a busy spot, with guards coming and going either on duty or off. Ironically it was also one of the safest places they could wait. He remembered of old how people tended to hang around here; he knew he'd not look out of place.

It did not stop everyone though. A passing guard sensed the tension Kerin could not hide.

'You after anyone in particular?' he enquired. Kerin couldn't tell if the enquiry was from helpfulness or suspicion. He used the answer he had primed the others with.

'I've been told to wait here for the Provost.'

'The Provost! He doesn't venture down this way often. You been a naughty boy?' The man thought his fidgeting stemmed from youthful inexperience. Kerin forced a nervous smile.

'I don't know. He's never wanted to see me before.' The note of concern he injected into his voice convinced the guard, who gave him a friendly slap on the shoulder.

'Don't you worry. He's not much of a chap, this new one, he's hardly going to take your head off. I'm surprised at the Tekai appointing him; he usually goes for much tougher men. I don't suppose he'll last long though. Only got the one prisoner at the moment and he's a raving madman; as soon as we get a few more, this Provost'll be put off. The damned fool's had the same people guarding this lunatic pretender since they brought him in. That's all right by me so long as I'm not one of them, but damned if I'll be stuck on dungeon duty for months at a time if they get any more in. And it's been

unnaturally quiet here for months now. We're sure to get some
more in soon.'

Vel and Naylan had arrived, approaching cautiously
when they saw Kerin talking to the guard. He looked at them
in surprise.

'What, more new boys?' This despite Naylan's forty-
plus years. 'You here to meet the Provost too? Hell's knives,
he must want to do his guided tour. Good luck with that. I
can't waste any more of my break. Don't let him scare you!'

'Where's Cedas?' Vel asked once the guard had gone
far enough away.

'He was sent on an errand.' There was still no sign of
him, and the guard's words had lent urgent hope to Kerin. He
beckoned the others.

'We'll have to leave him to follow on. I'm not waiting
any longer. He knows the way.'

He led them past the guardroom, down the well-
rehearsed route along stairs and labyrinthine passages until it
felt as though they must be in the heart of the earth. Beyond a
certain point they passed no one, and no natural light entered
the corridors: feeble rushlights gave a faint glow to light their
way, with brighter lamps at intervals.

Finally they paused near the end of a wider corridor.
A stairwell – their escape route – rose halfway along this
passage, and a solid-looking door barred the far end. Beside
this door another stood part open, with lamplight pouring out.
The lower dungeon warders would be there; the last human
obstacle. Kerin looked at the others, and Naylan nodded and
walked up the corridor hurriedly.

He went through the open door; the other two listened

to the conversation that followed.

'Byorin,' burst out Naylan, 'is he here?' They had
chosen a common name to ask about, in the hope that it would
strike a chord.

'Which Byorin?'

'Oh, I don't know his Hed. Medium height, dark-
haired...'

'That describes them both.'

Great. Well, do you know where either of them is? At
least I can eliminate the wrong one.'

'Hed Bergen's gone home on leave. I think
Hedlewen's on second wall duty.'

Naylan did an appropriate amount of cursing and left
the room. As he came up to the others he could not risk
speaking but gave an astonished grin and lifted one finger.
Only one warder! He clattered a little further down the
corridor for effect.

Vel drew out the letter and checked the cosh he had
ready in his jacket. He would have started along the corridor,
but Kerin grabbed him and counted down ninety seconds
before letting him go. Too eager and the warder would
suspect.

Vel followed Naylan's path and disappeared into the
warder's room. Kerin hoped Vel would remember to stand
with the warder between himself and the light before handing
him the letter.

'From the Provost, sir!' his voice echoed. The warder
grunted.

'What does he want?'

Kerin pictured the warder leaning down with the letter towards the light, his back to Vel, and sure enough heard a scuffle and a crash, and saw the light go out. Instantly he and Naylan were off along the corridor, but Vel's voice reached them before they got there.

'Hell and blast, he's broken the lamp! Bring a light, will you?'

They searched both warder and room carefully, but found just one key. Possibly Lemno had taken the rest with him, having no reason to wish the one prisoner free in any way during his absence. They trussed and gagged the warder and tried the key in the heavy door that blocked the passage; it opened. Despite its age and weight, it swung silently.

Confident of the bonds and gag on the warder, they piled him into a cupboard. Vel stayed by the door while Kerin and Naylan continued down the passage until it opened out. There were no lights now but those they carried. The place had a forsaken, disused look – Kerin could not picture a rat living here, let alone any human soul.

They searched the chamber walls for a set of keys to the cells; the hooks were bare. All they could do was peer into each of the cells that materialized from the gloom as they moved on. But they could see nothing, even with the rushlights held to the grille: Kerin could only speak his brother's name at each one.

And in vain. Silence met him at each door. Naylan followed on; Kerin hid the anguish and doubt as he moved on to each cell but he couldn't help looking back, in case the last one did hold his brother and he had failed to catch a weak call, a movement within.

Seven doors. Eight. Nine. Ten. Eleven. If ever he was going to let another man see him cry, it might be now.

'Go away,' a voice from the eleventh cell ordered Kerin as he was about to do so. He was back at the grille in an instant.

'Jastur? It's Kerin.'

'Your humour grows ever more puerile. Go away.'

'It is me! It's Kerin!' He spoke louder and held the rushlight to his face. There was a slight scraping noise in the cell. Fingers appeared at the grille, a face was pressed to it and then it flinched away.

'Wait, wait. Let me get accustomed to the light,' said the voice calmly. Kerin smiled elatedly, recognizing those reasonable tones. He composed himself and peered through the grille. After a moment, the eyes on the other side met his.

'Kerin? He told me you were dead.'

'Wishful thinking. I don't die so easily. I have friends here: we'll get you out. Be patient a little longer.'

oOo

After a lot longer Naylan mopped at his brow.

'This is some lock. I haven't seen one so complicated for a long time. Some foreign make. This isn't going to be a quick job.' Kerin squatted down next to him. 'Make it as fast as you can, Naylan, because we have very little time.'

Jastur leant against the grille.

'There may be more than you think. The guard

changes at eight-hour intervals. They check I am still breathing and leave food and water at every change. By my reckoning, it will be dead here for another three hours at the least.' Kerin took this in and bent again to Naylan.

'How noisy would it be if we forced the lock?'

Naylan left off manipulating the tumblers momentarily, ran his hand over the casing and the outer frame and peered at it.

'I don't think that's going to happen. It's too solidly made.'

He carried on. The two of them hunched around the lock, Kerin directing as much light as he had and Naylan doing the best he could; he laboured delicately and Kerin watched with rapt attention.

They both started up at the sound of running steps in the corridor. Kerin had whipped round with his sword unsheathed before Vel had slewed to a halt in front of them.

'Someone's coming. At least three people, by the footfalls. No way past them. We've got nowhere to go!'

'The cells are all locked. We'll make a stand here,' Kerin ordered instantly. Vel drew his sword: Naylan muttered something and fumbled his out too. 'Remember the training we have done,' Kerin reminded Vel. 'We're not lost yet. If we aren't outnumbered, then we're more than their match in a fight.'

Lights approached and two men entered. They squared up to fight them – but almost immediately lowered their swords. The other men held rifles.

'I told you,' Vel muttered angrily.

'Guns shouldn't be issued,' Kerin countered. 'Not unless…'

A tall, dark but greying man with a neatly trimmed beard had entered behind the gunmen and was staring at them by the glow of his lantern.

'You… still alive? Good God, boy, you have the Devil's own luck.'

Kerin hesitated only a moment. Then he relaxed and, ignoring the astonished looks it brought from Vel and Naylan, sheathed his blade, folded his arms and settled back against the wall with a smile.

'Surprised to see me, Lemno? You're looking well. And I'm fine. I considered washing up dead on some Mhrydaineg beach, but knew you'd miss my company.'

Lemno's outrage only increased. He was used to his gaze annihilating such arrogance but Kerin stared back at him, with every intention of giving offence.

Lemno's glare flicked briefly over Vel and Naylan, and Vel shuddered involuntarily. The bearded face now looked calmly towards Kerin again.

'You've lived a charmed life, young man.' Now Lemno had mastered his anger, his voice was melodious, rich-toned, as striking as the rest of him. 'But this is the day you have pressed your luck too far. Had you any sense, you would have left your brother to his fate and aimed for the Crown yourself. Today I would have aided you in that; I came to put an end to him. Instead I have you both, and this time I shall be sure of an end to you both.'

'What, you and these two?' Kerin looked Lemno's men up and down with a contemptuous smile as though goading some hopeless drunks in a bar brawl. Vel and Naylan were not doing so well though. Vel, whose courage he well knew, looked as if his soul was trying to back out through his spine. No one was better at inflicting mental terror by his mere presence than Lemno; yet once again the man had no such effect on him.

Guns were still levelled at them, though, and despite his confident words Kerin could see no way past those.

Lemno watched him, matching smile for smile.

'Two executioners are here already. The third will be called in a moment. Or shall I… No. I'll not dirty my hands on you again, boy. It would take a better man than you to justify that. You vastly overestimate your worth, like all your family. Hedhakkin!' he called, without looking away. 'Now, what to do with the bodies? One of the deeper oubliettes, I think. We'll have to seal it up, of course. My profound apologies. I know you Reincarnationists can only pass into the next life on a funeral pyre. We'll keep this one for questioning.' He pointed to Vel as the third guard stepped from the corridor to join them. 'You can finish the others. This one first.' He never took his eyes from Kerin. That was a mistake. Confusion then anger spread over his features as a rifle barrel pressed into the side of his neck. He kept quite still; his men lowered their weapons.

'Your other guards are a little tied up at the moment. No, don't turn. You shan't see my face,' Cedas ordered. 'Kerin—' Another rifle flew across the space between them; Kerin caught it deftly and cocked it, covering Lemno while Cedas moved back into the shadows lest Lemno turn.

'I've already seen that the skin you are so fond of is black. Did you manage to overcome my men without them seeing your face, then?'

Cedas laughed. 'They saw me, but if they hadn't the imagination to spot my trap, I don't suppose their powers of description are so great. And Ilmaen is full of black men. You'll be a long time looking.'

'You'll note I chose my helpers for their charm,' Kerin remarked. Lemno met his gaze levelly, even in defeat. Kerin searched him until he found a key, which he tossed to Naylan.

'Get that door open now. If that's not the key, Lemno will find a way to open it or have his guts paint the floor.' And to Cedas: 'The guards: how many and what sort of threat?'

'Two, and not the brains of an ant between them. They're out cold, bound and gagged in the wardroom – oh, and your man in the cupboard was awake and kicking off, so I put him out again.'

'Done!' called Naylan. He started to free the door.

'I'll do that. Watch Lemno.' Kerin passed Naylan the gun and was at the door as it swung open. He caught his brother as he fell through it.

'Jastur! On my life…'

Jastur was a tall man, taller than Kerin. It exaggerated his gauntness, just as his wild black hair and beard exaggerated his pallor, but he braced himself on the doorframe and raised his eyes to the others.

'I will manage. Look to Lemno; he must be dealt with.'

'Be easy,' said Kerin, 'I'll handle him.' Then to Cedas, 'Walk him along the passage, let him get used to freedom.'

Kerin looked into Jastur's cell and cursed to see how tiny it was, and how filthy. He turned to Lemno with a venomous look.

'Long you have wanted what the Hedsarollen were heirs to. Now I'll happily bequeath you something of my brother's. Put them all in here,' he ordered Naylan and Vel as he took Lemno's lantern. 'I would gag you,' he told Lemno, 'but I would sooner think of you shouting yourself hoarse to no avail, and all the while taking in the stench to which you condemned Jastur.'

He slammed the door after the last man and locked it himself. Lemno peered through the grille, but looked past him, to Vel.

'You would have found the wiser, older man's shadow a better shelter than this young buzzard's. And you - you are going to regret not killing me,' he said matter-of-factly, as if pointing out that Kerin had dropped something. Vel said nothing, while Kerin almost smiled, but the hatred he felt was too strong.

'Oh, how I wish I could descend to your level, and do so. When the true order is restored I'll have that chance. Be it by trial or by combat, I'll have that chance. For now, we will be taking every key between here and the next level, so you may be here some time. I trust vermin like you will feel at home in the dark.' He snatched the light from the door.

What Jastur wore amounted to soiled rags; they were cast aside as he dressed himself in retainer's garb in the privacy of a dim corner. Despite the clean clothes he was filthy and stank and looked better suited to a sickbed; Kerin had to prop him up on the other side from Cedas. Jastur had barely any strength in him, and his feet half dragged as they hurried up corridors and stairs, locking every door they could behind them. Kerin sent Vel on ahead to check the route, but they had no hope of avoiding people for ever. They had the guardhouse to pass yet.

'Jastur,' he whispered urgently as they moved swiftly on, 'we have to go past the first-level guardhouse, then down the tunnels and up again to the Corn Lane postern gate. Pretend that you are drunk and we are taking you back to quarters.'

He was so frail it took little to make it convincing. Kerin and Cedas were staggering with exhaustion themselves by the time they reached the guardhouse. By good fortune they passed at a quiet moment and were not noticed. A sharp left and another staircase down and they were in a new set of tunnels, moving further out and under the two inner walls and finally up to ground level again. Ahead of them Vel beckoned, and Naylan hurried past them to the door Vel was pointing out. There Naylan picked a lock that, thankfully, gave him no trouble, and that let them into a small room where he unlocked a second door. The afternoon light streamed in, as sharp and clear as cold water to them, as painful as daggers to Jastur's sensitive eyes.

First out, Vel looked down the lane one way and the other, and then beckoned Kerin out. With huge relief he saw the two wagons were only twenty feet away. To his surprise Renia sat with Bighur at the reins of one. Bighur started it up while Renia clambered through to the back of the wagon as it rolled level with them.

Kerin and Cedas helped the light-blinded Jastur up the back steps and handed him through the open door to Renia. Vel slipped in past them as they jumped down and the door shut as the wagon rolled away. Cedas walked smartly to the back of Eddir's wagon. Kerin waited for Naylan to shut and lock the outhouse door and fling the keys he carried into a midden in a nearby alley, all the while watching Bighur's wagon roll quietly to the junction and turn out of the lane, on its way to the east gate. In an instant he and Naylan were up the steps of Eddir's wagon. They slipped inside, Kerin keeping the door open an inch and his eye to that inch, watching for any sign of pursuit. He could hear Naylan breathing heavily behind him; Cedas was as silent as a cat.

'We should go,' Naylan advised. Kerin could hear how shaken he was, but held up a hand. Naylan knew the plan, and the plan said they would wait. The minutes stretched on and the wagon fell silent until finally Kerin said, 'Let's go.'

Cedas banged on the wagon front and it lurched forward. Naylan let out a long breath.

'Hell! That was close.'

Too bloody close,' Cedas opined. 'How did he come to ride into town the very day of the rescue?'

'It's a knack he has,' Kerin said dismissively, but he had been thinking the same thing.

'A *knack*?' Cedas's glare was baleful. 'You know, something tells me he was right. We should have killed him while we had the chance.'

Naylan said, 'At least it's over.' Kerin shook his head.

'It's not over. That was the easy part.'

oOo

In the other wagon, with the horse plodding along in its unhurried way, it felt like hours had passed.

'Are we out of town yet?' Renia whispered to Vel, who hovered as near the front door as he could without being seen.

'Yes, but the road's busy. We need to keep our voices down a bit longer.'

She turned back to Jastur who lay in one of the bunks trying to muffle his periodic bouts of coughing; he nodded to confirm he had heard. Apart from a hoarse 'Thank you' no word had passed his lips. He looked awful; he smelt worse, it almost made her cough and retch herself. But there was a bearing to this man, a dignity that belied his tramp-like appearance. She remembered the clothes they had set aside for him now and held them up for him to see. He understood her meaning and began unbuttoning the retainer's disguise he wore and sat up to ease the shirt off.

As she helped she realized it wasn't simply dirt on him; he was covered in scabs and wounds. Some of them accounted for the smell as they were clearly infected but he seemed oblivious to them. He helped her to help him as best he could.

'I'm going to wash you,' she told him before she realized her words didn't give him a choice about it, and cast him a guilty look. 'Sir,' she added belatedly. She was startled to see eyes the exact match of Kerin's gazing at her out of such a different face, heavy-browed and squarer-jawed. He said nothing, just lay back to await her ministrations. The stove had been lit, thank goodness, and she thrust the retainer's clothes in to burn up.

He submitted to the wash, though now she was doing it she doubted she was doing much good. The dry scabs she didn't want to disturb, while touching the suppurating ones would just spread the infection. She settled for cleaning up the patches of intact skin between them, and tore up a petticoat to make dressings and bandages for the worst wounds. He bore with it, took the clean shirt and her help in putting it on, all in silence.

'We're well out of town now.'

Vel left the door and came to settle on the other bunk, looking awkward. What did you say to the rightful ruler of a country when he lay in front of you looking like a vagabond?

'Where did my brother go?' the vagabond asked in a thin but measured voice.

'He took the other wagon, said he wanted you and he to leave town separately, sir. We're to meet up later.'

Jastur gave half a laugh, which turned into another coughing fit. 'Now, he follows protocol,' he murmured as he recovered.

'Sir?'

'No matter. May I know to whom I owe my thanks?'

'Sir, I'm Velohim Ty'r Athre, of the Southlands in Mhrydain. This is my sister, Renia. We found your brother after Lemno cast him off the ship you both travelled on. The other helpers are Naylan, he's a tinker; and Cedas, he runs a travelling show.'

'I am honoured to know you. It seems there is a plan?'

Vel and Renia looked at each other, realizing that if there was one, beyond the next hour or so, they didn't know what it was.

'The next steps are down to you and Kerin, sir,' Vel told him.

Jastur glanced between their worried faces and nodded thoughtfully.

'Then I think we may be continuing this acquaintance a little longer, if you are willing. This business is not done yet and it won't be an easy journey. But thanks to you and your companions it is well started.'

Renia closed her eyes, heart sinking. He was right; it was not done yet. The tension of the last few hours was lifting, but that leaden weight in the pit of her stomach hadn't shifted at all. Her vision was not going to be fulfilled today; probably not tomorrow either, or the day after that.

It gave her more time in Kerin's company, at least. Pointless in the long run, she knew, but without that, the fear would be unbearable. If only the two didn't have to go hand in hand: she longed for those first few days, when she had known him without knowing how completely he was going to turn her world upside down.

'It is well started,' Jastur repeated to himself, and lay back exhausted as the wagon rattled on, taking them ever further from Karn.

The story continues...

Restoring the Light

Book 2 of the Ilmaen Quartet

Will be published October 2015

Visit helenbellauthor.com

Acknowledgements

I had a blast writing this, but you wouldn't be reading it now if I hadn't had some help along the way.

Among the many people I need to thank are:

Lynn Curtis for the copyediting and the good advice; Peter O'Connor of Bespoke Bookcovers for the cover design; Simon Appleby and the team at Bookswarm for my author website; Amanda Spice for reading and commenting on one of the many drafts - and asking 'is it published yet?' every year until it was; Mike Dobson and Dave Lewis for checking the maritime and metrological accuracy of Chapter 12 - The Crossing; and last but not least, my family for their patience (and all the cups of tea, even if I didn't remember to drink them).

Helen Bell

48697137R00163

Made in the USA
Charleston, SC
10 November 2015